WHO DONE IT?

Investigation of Murder Most Foul

CONDUCTED BY
JON SCIESZKA
(AND **YOU**, THE READER)

SOHO
TEEN

Copyright © 2013 by Soho Press, Inc.

Published in the United States in 2013 by Soho Teen
an imprint of Soho Press, Inc.
853 Broadway
New York, NY 10003

Library of Congress Cataloging-in-Publication Data

Who done it? : an investigation of murder most foul / conducted
by Jon Scieszka and you, the reader.
p. cm
"A serial act of criminal literature to benefit 826NYC."
ISBN 978-1-61695-152-8 (alk. paper)
eISBN 978-1-61695-153-5

1. Authors—Fiction. 2. Authorship—Fiction. 3. Humorous stories.
I. Scieszka, Jon.
PZ5.W6234 2012
[Fic]—dc23   2012033468

Interior design by Janine Agro, Soho Press, Inc.

Printed in the United States of America

10 9 8 7 6 5 4 3 2 1

Dearest Friend,
You Are Invited To A Gathering!

Where: *The Old Abandoned Pickle Factory*

When: *Eight PM sharp*

Why: *Because if you don't attend, I will*
             have to tell the world everything I
             know about you. (Yes: everything.)

Your Boss/Superior/Editor,

Herman Q. Mildew

INTRODUCTORY INTERROGATION
BY JON SCIESZKA

Ladies and gentlemen . . . and I use those terms loosely because I know you are all writers and illustrators . . . we have a bit of a situation.

You were all invited to this party tonight because of your relationship with Mr. Herman Q. Mildew.

Some of you were not fond of him. Others of you could not stand him. Most of you completely hated his guts.

Mr. Mildew brought you to this abandoned pickle factory because he had something to tell you, something that he thought might make you very mad. And he wanted to see all of you freak out live and in person.

But that is not going to happen.

You see . . . Mr. Herman Q. Mildew is no longer with us.

He shuffled off this mortal coil, took the long walk off the short pier, has gone to glory, gave up the ghost, cashed in, checked out, kicked the bucket, went bye-bye.

He is now a corpse, a cadaver, dearly departed, a stiff.

The problem?

Each and every one of you had a reason to send Mr.

Herman Mildew to the Great Beyond. You are all suspects in his demise. And it is up to me—and the keen reader holding this book—to figure out: Who done it?

As you well know, Herman Mildew was not a nice man.

He was mean, arrogant, loud, large, obnoxious, cruel to small furry animals, delusional, thoughtless, difficult, vulgar, negative, likely to take the last sip of orange juice and then put the empty carton back in the refrigerator, intolerant, sneaky, greedy, fond of toenail clippings and strong cheeses, hugely entertained by the misfortune of others, hateful, quick to anger, unforgiving, mean, gaseous, paranoid, belligerent, unreasonable, demanding, smelly, near-sighted . . . in short: an editor. Perhaps even your editor, or the editor of someone you admire.

Some examples of his sadistic behavior, in no particular order:

- He enrolled Dave Eggers in True Romance's Book-of-the-Month Club.

- He drew mustaches on all of Lauren Oliver's author photos.

- He told Mo Willems what he could do with the Pigeon.

All this is true. So why did you accept this invitation?

Never mind. The more important question is why a quick pat-down of this audience turned up:

- 1 poison-tipped umbrella

- 1 suitcase full of poisonous tree frogs

- 3 throwing stars

- 1 noose, 1 candlestick, and 1 lead pipe

- 2 snakes resembling speckled "friendship" bands

- 1 frozen leg of lamb

What?
Me?
Why do I have a piece of piano wire hanging out of my trench coat?

Why . . . why . . . not because Mr. Mildew once forced me to play "I'm A Little Teapot" on the piano in front of hundreds of booksellers. And I wasn't going to use it to strangle anyone in a most fitting way. I have piano wire because . . . because . . . because I was fixing my piano last time I was wearing this coat. I was just replacing the—

Wait a minute! Our readers and I are running this investigation. We'll ask the questions. And we want answers. We want alibis.

Of course, before you begin, we are bound by law to advise you that you have the right to remain silent.

But who are we kidding?

You are (as mentioned) a bunch of writers and illustrators. You couldn't remain silent if your life depended on it. You would sell your grandmother for an audience.

So tell us your alibi.

Convince us that you did not do in, cut down, rub out, bump off, put away, dispatch, exterminate, eradicate, liquidate, assassinate, fix, drop, croak, or kill the late, unlamented Mr. Herman Mildew.

List of Suspects*

* For the record: Alphabetizing this list was my idea, to speed things up. I am assisting in this investigation only so I can leave the abandoned pickle factory as soon as possible. (It smells much more like "abandon" than "pickles," I can assure you.) Also, there's a special two-hour *Ancient Aliens* on the History Channel at midnight and my TiVo is on the fritz. Point being: I'm not trying to curry favor with Mr. Scieszka, if that is his real name. Okay, full disclosure: I'm a suspect too. But look at some of the other alibis. Not to point fingers, but David Levithan's is in free verse. Gayle Forman's is in "Twitter." The team who wants toddlers to *Go the F**k to Sleep* is in rap-with-illustration, a format heretofore unknown. There's even a Jack Russell terrier, Tillamook Cheddar, who offers her doggy art as proof of her innocence. And what of the suspects who conveniently implicate fellow suspects? (Lauren Myracle and sisters Sheinmel, are your ears burning?) I alphabetized so that you, the reader, can zero in on suspicious people of interest. Yes, I said "people" instead of "writers" or "illustrators." Or even "canines." I am in a generous mood. As long as I make it home by midnight. —Daniel Ehrenhaft

Herman Mildew was definitely the princess who slept on the pea.

Herman Mildew was the Goldilocks to our bears.

We agree; if he is, in fact, dead and he was, in fact, murdered, then it was most certainly someone he knew. It just wasn't us.

Yes, it's true that he used to be our editor.

Yes, it's true that he didn't like our book.

Yes, it's true that we wrote him into the final draft of our book as a villainous, spiteful tree-dwelling gnome.

And, yes, it's true that he fired us from his imprint after he discovered the aforementioned gnome's name, hardly a fire-able offense.

That being said, once we were fired, we were free from him. We were free from his yammering, and free from his pointless line edits. We didn't have to falsely lie in our blogs about how *brilliant and amazing* our editor was to work with (a total lie!) or write a loving acknowledgement in the back of our book like *Thank you, thank you, thank you so much, Mildew, we owe every success of this book to you* (which would have also been a lie!).

Are we guilty of being tacky, naming the villainous gnome after Mildew? Maybe.

Are we guilty of being mean? Absolutely.

But are we guilty of murder? No, not his.

We were mad enough to murder was meant as an expression, not a literal action. We never meant it to be real or even directed at Mildew. Simply put—the reason it was said was that we absolutely drive ourselves insane sometimes. Always talking like this—in the plural first person point of view, simultaneously, like we're the same person, always speaking as *one*. It's enough to make one mad—maybe not

J. R. and Kate Angelella

We were mad enough to murder, but please allow us to explain.

We didn't murder Herman Mildew. You can split us up—in fact, we encourage it—and you can scream and shout and shine a bright light in our eyes to see that we are telling the truth. We have nothing to hide here because we didn't do it. We admit that we said *we were mad enough to murder*, but it's not what you think. We were mad enough to murder, but not mad enough to murder Herman Mildew.

(Is it all right that we use the past tense when we talk about Herman Mildew, or does that make us look guilty too?)

It's true—Herman Mildew was a rat of a man, who nibbled and nibbled and nibbled away at our words, chewing up and spitting out the most beautiful and meaningful parts of our novel. He was never pleased with any draft that we turned in to him on time. He was never happy with our work. He always wanted more, or demanded a whole lot less.

mad like *mad enough to murder*, but more *mad* like *mad like crazy*.

Are we making sense with this yet?

Allow us to be clearer: we were once *mad enough to murder*, but after this falsified murder accusation we are *madder* like *madder* like *incredibly annoyed*, and quickly barreling toward *madness* like *madness at the hands of the late Herman Mildew.*

How is that for clarity?

Mac Barnett

Of course I wanted to murder Herman Mildew. Please understand, I want to murder people all the time, and I never do it. I'm just not the murdering kind. For every person I'm accused of murdering (one: Herman Mildew), there are thousands of people I wanted to murder who are still alive. And so it's just highly unlikely, if not completely impossible, that I killed Mr. H.M. That's just math.

I submit in my defense this list:

PEOPLE I HAVEN'T MURDERED

1. **Mike Dumbroksi.** I went to high school with Mike, and I hadn't heard from him since, until about a week ago, I started getting emails telling me that Mike Dumbroski would like to add me to his professional network on LinkedIn. I do not know what LinkedIn is. I do not understand what Mike Dumbroski's professional network is, or why he would like me to join it. And I cannot figure out

how Mike Dumbroski got in touch with me, since the last time I talked to him, when he asked to copy my homework for Algebra 2/Trig, my email address was BeEfJeRkY@prodigy.net. But somehow I have received seventeen LinkedIn-related emails from Mike in the last twelve days, and yet I have not murdered him.

2. Guy Riding his Bike on the Sidewalk. Yesterday this guy was riding his bike toward me on the sidewalk. It was crowded, and he almost ran into me. He had to squeeze his brakes hard, and the brakes made that awful noise. I darted to my left to get out of his way, and I bumped into an old lady in a purple dress, and she harrumphed at me like it was my fault, when everybody knows that it's illegal to ride bikes on the sidewalk. That guy needed to get in the road. Plus he had a dumb beard. But I still didn't murder him, even though I wanted to.

3. Man with a Funny Accent Who Called My Dog Fat. At first I thought maybe he just meant that my dog was big, but used the wrong word, since he was European. But then he asked me if my dog ate a lot of food. My dog does not eat a lot of food, and he is not fat. But even though I would have been totally justified to murder this man with a funny accent who called my dog fat, I didn't.

4. Inspector 43. I bought a pair of madras boxer shorts two days ago, and when I put them on this morning I discovered that the right leg was significantly tighter than the left. It is important to note that my legs are approximately the same size. Seriously, it feels like I'm wearing a tourniquet right now. This whole disaster is the fault of Inspector 43—I know, because he left a little tag in the bag that said he'd inspected my boxers to ensure they met high standards of quality. And so did I spend today traveling to the factory, demanding to see the badges of all the boxer-short inspectors, and then murdering Inspector 43? No. Instead I stayed home and watched a *Real World/Road Rules Challenge* marathon in my boxers.

5. **My Next-Door Neighbor.** My next-door neighbor has a NO PARKING sign in front of his house, but it's not like the city put it up or anything. He just bought it at a hardware store and glued it to his fence. Or nailed it to his fence—I don't know if he used glue. Regardless, it's legal to park in front of his house. He's not fooling anybody with that sign. But when I parked there the other day, he left a note on my car telling me to park somewhere else. I was so mad! But did I murder him? No. Of course not. I did help send him to jail on unrelated charges, but that is a different story.

Look at that! That's *five* people I have not murdered, right off the top of my head. And there are many, many more. Including, of course, Herman Mildew.

Jennifer Belle

You want to know what the members of the debate team at the Bronx High School of Science mostly did? We discussed how much money it would take to make out with the coach, an enormously fat troll of a man we called Mr. Gunt. We really spent a lot of time on this. Would I for $500,000? I would, but Paolina, a beautiful girl whose mother owned an art gallery wouldn't. $300,000? I was still willing, but others dropped out. At $84,500 I was the only one still able to endure the thought of getting hot and heavy with Mr. Gunt.

Junior year I won Nationals. Winning that debate trophy is the thing I am most proud of in this world. Forget the book awards and the film options. Despite my hatred of Mr. Gunt, or maybe because of it, I went to every meeting and worked as hard as I could. And when I won, I tried to give my trophy to Mr. Gunt as a kind of thank you, but he wouldn't take it. He just said his dog Blanche was a better debater than I was, made me give her the sandwich from my lunch bag, and told me to get out of his classroom.

Herman Mildew reminded me of Mr. Gunt. We had that

love/hate, mostly hate thing. I actually brought the trophy tonight to give it to him. A symbol of respect and a promise to do better for him. You think I was going to bang him over the head with the marble base? Gouge out his eyes with the tip of the eagle's brass wing? No. I was planning to make a peace offering.

When Jessica, Herman Mildew's Assistant Two, called and said he wanted to meet me, I told her I was excited to finally meet the legendary publisher. But she sounded strange, sort of sad and apologetic, like she was turning me on to a new drug. "What does he look like?" I asked. I had quickly done a Google Images search for "Herman Mildew, publisher" but had found Mold & Mildew Contractors in Herman, Nebraska, a lady clown in the UK named Mildew, and a black and white cat named Mildew Herman, and nothing else. It was well known that he refused to have his photograph taken, which most people assumed was because he couldn't stand the hideous sight of himself. But when Jessica later showed me what he made her do to his authors' photos—plant fake mustaches on their faces—I knew it was because he knew the power of Photoshop.

"I'm a huge fan of your work," Jessica said, again apologetically. "I think we went to high school together. You went to Bronx Science, didn't you?"

"Yes!" I said.

"Well then you won't have any trouble recognizing Mr. Mildew. Remember Mr. Gunderson?"

"Of course I do," I said.

"Well, he looks a little like Mr. Gunt, but fatter."

"Mr. Gunt is dead," I said.

"I know, I read about that," she said. "Anyway, I think you'll see the resemblance."

When I sat across from him at the restaurant, he flattered me. He offered me a lot of money if I would leave my editor and come to him. His little ponytail disgusted me but I thought we would be good together. He intrigued me. "If I fall asleep while you're talking to me, it's not that I don't find you attractive. I have narcolepsy," he told me. Then his eyelids drooped and I suddenly felt so strangely alone—like I would do anything to get his attention.

"I had a weird dream," he said, when he had finished his entrée and mine, and a cheese plate for six.

"Do you want to tell me what it was?" I asked, not knowing if he'd had the dream during our lunch or previously.

"I no longer had my beautiful office. My office was a news kiosk on the street. 'So this is the publishing industry now,' I thought. I was so depressed until I saw that all my writers were homeless people lying on the sidewalk beneath me. That was a relief."

When I handed in the book he said I was one day past my deadline so he rejected it and said I had to give back the advance. Money I had long spent on therapy to deal with the things he said to me like, "Belle, sit on my face and I'll guess your weight."

But, I couldn't leave him. I did another book for him and then another.

Of course I'm going to be accused by all the writers here because I am ten times more successful than all of them. It's like a book I once read aloud when I was volunteering at a library, a brilliant children's book, a retelling of the *Three Little Pigs* from the point of view of the wolf. Of course pigs are going to accuse a wolf. Mildew made it no secret what he paid me. I'm probably more hated than he was.

And, as I'm sure Jessica told you, I was also a suspect in

the Mr. Gunt murder, but that doesn't mean I should be a suspect here tonight. Mr. Gunt died at a dinner theater in the small town he retired to. At a show starring Rue McClanahan, one of the Golden Girls, with a prime rib dinner. I had no idea he was a Rue McClanahan fan. I was there on my book tour. The police quickly determined I had nothing to do with it and the fact that I had my Nationals debate trophy on me at the time was simply a coincidence. A good friend of mine is an artist in Minneapolis, which was the next stop on my tour, and he'd asked if he could put the trophy in an art installation. I'd thrown it in my carry-on bag and forgotten to take it out before the theater. Hell, a guy died in my spin class the other day. No one discovered him slumped on his bike until the class had ended and the darkened studio had been lit. People must die in gyms and at dinner theaters and at parties all the time. It's not my fault that I was his favorite writer. You'll find DNA on the trophy all right—blood, sweat, and tears—but sadly, all of it is mine.

Judy Blundell

What? The business card for the YA Mafia? Never saw it before.

Will Whack For Lattes? It's a *joke*. Sure, I've heard the rumors. You can't step into a café in Brooklyn without picking them up. Cranky editors? Elusive agents? Booksellers who banish you just for moving your book to the New and Noteworthy table? Who ya gonna call?

But you'd have to be crazy to have a guy killed just because he hated your similes.

Mildew was my editor, but I never met him. He was just a voice on the phone, telling me that a *really* great book didn't need a marketing campaign, or that digital books were a passing fad, so why bother to negotiate rights?

I have to admit, though, the guy could line-edit. If you didn't mind the belching. And the whistle.

I'd hear it rattle when he put it between his teeth. "That simile is crap," he'd say, and then the next thing I knew my ears would be bleeding. Did I care? Nah. I loved him like a puppy loves kitten-heeled slippers.

Oh—the card for Dabney Dorf, DPM? He's my podia-trist! Sure, Herman gave me the referral. We liked to talk feet, okay? Last time I checked the laws of New York State, that wasn't a crime.

Okay, okay, I did meet him once. At my last appoint-ment, I noticed this hairy guy lurking around the medical waste. He had a huge head balanced on a chicken neck and a mouth the size of an earbud. I couldn't look away. Maybe because he was shaking toenail clippings into his briefcase.

Did you just gag? Yeah. That was my first reaction. But there was something about the way this guy looked—intent, smart, disgusting—that made me look twice. Or maybe it was the whistle around his neck.

"You look as busy as a teenager's thumbs," I said.

His fingers scrabbled at the whistle, but he caught himself in time. "Got the wrong guy, lady."

"Guilty as a nun with *Beauty Queens* stashed in her wimple."

The scream of the whistle shattered the screen of my iPhone. "GOTCHA, HERMIE," I shouted. Temporary deafness doesn't last that long; I'd learned that the hard way. "NOW YOU OWE ME LUNCH."

I asked for Jean-Georges, so he took me to Burger Heaven. I had the grilled cheese. He had the bowl of pick-les. He picked out all the seeds and flicked them across the table. My glasses were speckled with dill seed by the end, but I'd scored a free lunch from Herman Mildew. Not many authors can say that.

"Here's what I want," I said. "A real book tour this time. I'm tired of going to Ho-Ho-Kus."

"I've got contacts in Saskatchewan."

"About time you got serious."

He rubbed the pickle along my wrist and then buried his

nose against my pulse. He must have felt it jump. "They'll slurp you up like ramen in Moose Jaw," he crooned.

We asked for more pickles, but instead, they threw us out. As we hit the street, his briefcase popped open. Papers and toenail clippings spilled onto the sidewalk. My royalty statement for *An Abundance of Hermans* fluttered out and landed on my shoe. I saw the numbers float before my eyes, and like a seagull eyeing a toddler's hot dog, I dived. There it was, a perfect row of six figures.

I grabbed him by his scrawny neck. "You told me that book tanked! I got a royalty check for forty-seven cents!"

"That billion-followers-on-Twitter guy mentioned you on his blog. The next thing I knew, you were outselling that vampire chick. Or was it werewolves? So I held it against unearned royalties on your other books."

"That's illegal!"

He had the nerve to smirk. "Read your contract, sunshine."

"Crook!" Maybe I squeezed a little bit harder. Who wouldn't?

"Remember the book tour," he croaked. "I'll throw in Manitoba!"

Maybe I bruised his windpipe a tad before they separated us. And it's possible that for a second or two I considered calling in the YA Mafia to arrange their signature hit—a little encounter with an exploding Sharpie. But I know about revenge. It's like cereal for dinner. Lucky Charms may go down easy, but then you dream about meatballs.

I was about to get an all-expenses-paid book tour! You know those bathroom products you get in hotels? They're as free as those ads for aftershave that you rub on your neck so that you can smell like cedar and confuse your cat. Here's my point: I didn't kill Herman Mildew. I'm almost out of shampoo.

Liz Braswell

Murder? How *purrfectly* awful.

Murder implies mystery, and I *hate* mysteries. Agatha Hitchcock, red herrings, clues, footprints—*boring*.

Now, comic books on the other hand . . .

Hang on, the cats are demanding their second breakfast. One second.

I have great respect for Herman Mildew. He is brilliant, methodical, ambitious—but very, very evil.

No 2 percent for you today, dear? All right, just a *little* cream though. You haven't been getting out as much as you used to. Don't want to get too fat and too slow, mmm?

It's a little unusual to find someone of Mildew's caliber in a field like publishing. Usually you expect to see his type of villain as a titan of Wall Street or holed up in his own laser-protected compound, issuing directives from a computer screen.

Herman and I first met in person when my own editor disappeared, taken off the series I was working on.

Everyone knows what a monster he is—so I entered his dark office prepared for the worst.

"Why, Miss Braswell. This manuscript is *brilliant*."

All his yellowed teeth shone in the grimace that would have been a smile on anyone else.

I was completely taken aback.

"It's 'Ms.' But . . . really?"

"Why, yes," he said in that oily tone that's been known to make agents put chopsticks through their own ears. "It's really . . . quite . . . *excellent*."

I was stunned. He had never, in the history of his career, said anything nice to anyone.

I'm sorry, let me just get Garfield off you. Your pants will be fine—the threads aren't even torn.

How many? Oh, about six cats at current count. No, I'm not really one of those crazy cat people. I try to get them adopted.

Anyway, something was up. I didn't trust him at all. So yes, I began following him. That's absolutely true. After he left the office every night—usually around nine—I would tail him from above, running across rooftops with the freedom that the night brings. He had no idea I was there, watching from the shadows.

What? He *did* know? That's why I'm a suspect?

Oh, I don't believe that. I'm *very* stealthy.

I only fell through a skylight *once*. And didn't I help the police raid that illegal loft party? OK, not *help* exactly, but I told them about it, right? I couldn't stick around to aid our boys in blue. I had more important fish to fry.

Mildew's routine never changed, like perfectly lubricated—but evil—clockwork. He always traveled from Midtown to the Lower East Side, where he would stop at the Pickle Guys for a kosher half sour.

Dill?

No, no, you have it all wrong. My powers of observation are honed to a nigh-supernaturally sharp edge. It was a half sour. No, I'm telling you . . .

OFF THE COUCH! BAD KITTIES!

Where was I? Oh right. Half sours. And from there I followed him back to his home in the 'burbs, or should I say *lair,* where no doubt he sipped his port and considered more evil plans.

I mean, I *would* have followed him, but it's like forty-five minutes there on Metro-North, and another forty-five minutes back, and I have to give Mr. Scribbles his medicine or he wees all over the carpet the next day.

Then I slipped into my apartment by the side window so no one could see me go in and out—and also I lost the key—and I removed my . . . *working* clothes, and became the ordinary writer you see standing here before you.

Yes, I'm pretty sure all ordinary writers wear sweats and stained tees. Do you like it? I got the absolute last one at Comic Con.

Anyway, then one day Herman altered his routine.

I followed him to the west side, all the way to the river. He stood alone, on a pier, the salty wind blowing his greasy white locks about his face. Then he took out a stack of paper.

My paper.

My manuscript.

He peeled off a page, held it aloft, read a sentence or two aloud and then—

—Lady Grantham, could you kindly wait a moment for me to change the litter box? I'm right in the middle of a story—

—and then he giggled like an insane baby and *CRUMPLED UP THE PAGE AND THREW IT INTO THE HUDSON.*

Again and again and again. Reading my pages and then tossing them into the murky waters below. Muttering and chortling to himself the whole time.

"Said she was *brilliant*. 'Excellent' writing—HA! Best laugh I've had in *years*!"

Was I overwhelmed with epic rage? Did I feel the strength of a thousand strong cats flowing through my blood? Was I suddenly berserk with a tempest of self-righteous indignation?

Certainly. But I would never just *push* Herman into the river. That's so . . . common. If I had descended to the rank of evildoer I would have attacked him in the way that suits me best, with razor-sharp claws. And as you can see, officer, there is no blood under them.

No. They're not press-ons. They're razor-sharp claws. See? I filed them. That would *really* hurt if I scratched you.

I hissed in anger and withdrew back into the loving shadows of the night, where my friends and I apparently belong.

No, my friends are CATS. Not rats. CATS. Shadows and CATS. Haven't you been listening?

And anyway, the night he was supposedly killed I was at the shelter, helping give rabies shots. You can ask Sheila. I was totally there.

Meow.

What? No, I didn't sneeze. I was just. . . .

Oh, never mind.

Libba Bray

I did not kill Herman Q. Mildew. Don't misunderstand me: I had every intention of killing him. Truly I did.

But as anyone who has ever worked with me knows, I have never met a deadline, not once. By the time I figured out whether I should bash in his skull with a pipe (too messy), sing in a pitch that would make his brain melt (interesting, but then there was the question of which song would do the trick and that meant a lot of time spent browsing iTunes), or simply shoot him in the back (you can't go wrong with the classics), the thoroughly despicable Mr. Mildew had already been dead for ages, and his office (or so I've heard) turned into an arcade. (I totally KILLED at Pac-Man, so at least it wasn't a total loss.)

Believe me, no one is more disappointed than I am about this unfortunate turn of events. Please accept my humblest apologies for not getting to Herman Q. Mildew before someone else did. Bummer.

In the good news department, I am now hard at work on a short story about a writer who fails to kill her editor on time. It will be completed in 2025.

Steve Brezenoff

Did I kill Herman Mildew? Not in any real sense.

In what sense *did* I kill him? It's an amusing diversion to pursue this line of questioning, so I'll play along. And I did kill HM, but only in a fantastic sense, and I'm using "fantastic" here as an adjectival form of "fantasy," not in the modern usage that essentially means "quite good."

It would be quite good, though, wouldn't it? Excuse me, I mean it would have *been* quite good. Someone else has, apparently, beaten me to the punch—or gunshot, hanging, stabbing, defenestration, or whatever method was used.

Poison? Poison would be fun, though a bit impersonal. The killer needn't even be in the room. There are other ways of killing with food, and by extension remotely. I once read something about an omelet prepared with chèvre, dill, and crushed glass. Fantastic—and here I do mean "quite good."

I haven't given it much thought.

But I admitted already that I've killed him in the fantastic sense. Here's how that happened; it's no doubt how I'd do it, if I did it, which I didn't. Not really.

HM was fond of the little Szechuan place on Avenue Y. I've been there, speaking of ways to kill with food. If you ever have the choice, I'd recommend having that glass omelet instead. But I'm not here to criticize the man's taste in Chinese food. The point is I'd tell him we should meet in person, as our conversations via email are so impersonal—rather like killing with food. I'd invite him to lunch—let's say earlier today, for the sake of argument—and I'd imply that my agent would be there, because then HM would show up, because my agent is known to frequently pick up the check. He's magnanimous that way. HM, despite well-established industry standards, not so much.

So he'd show, and he'd be early, because he always liked to sit with his back to the corner, where he could face the room and see the door and all the windows and encroaching writers. One member of the wait staff, it's rumored, only took the job to get close to HM.

I'm fairly sure HM started that rumor.

I'd get there a little late. He'd eat dumplings while he waited. He'd drink a second tequila sunrise. He'd be heavy and slow, his judgment compromised, by the time I sat down. He'd be sweating, and I'd be able to smell the garlic ginger dumpling dip oozing from his gigantic pores. He'd gasp for breath and nod at me. My latest manuscript—a beautiful and succinct work, one which breaks genre distinctions and bravely explores untraversed regions of literature—would sit on the decorative plate at my seat. It would be my most important work to date. It would change American letters—at least some of them, like maybe g through r, for example—forever.

"What's this?" I'd say. "My manuscript?"

(I want to point out that I'm still using the conditional

present tense here. The condition in question would be a chrono-dimension in which I'd actually killed HM. That condition has not been met.)

He'd nod. He'd poke at his face with a napkin that had already been through a lot.

"That was quick," I'd say, because HM never takes ages with his notes. He never takes as long as it took me to write the damn thing. That's why my mental health is sound and I have no motive whatsoever to wish the man severe bodily harm.

He'd sip from his third drink and ask after my agent as I flipped through the marked-up pages. They'd be fairly clean, because HM never lets loose with his red pen so that I'd spend hours weeping into the phone to my mother.

"He's not coming," I'd admit.

HM would rise and explain he has a meeting he must rush off to. He'd tell me the notes are self-explanatory, and he'd tell me I could email his assistant Tate with any questions.

I still don't know if Tate is a man or a woman. Is Tate here, by the way? I'd like to meet Tate.

He'd be moving slowly, full of food and drink and ill temper, and I'd drop an IOU on the table and follow him.

I'd stand against the building in the midday shadows and behind a magazine rack, as HM flagged down a cab. And as the speeding car swerved toward the curb, I'd leap from the shadows, knock the editor into the street, and thrill at the sound of screeching brakes—too late—and shattering bone.

It would be over so quickly. He'd lie like a sated, bleeding lump on the hood of the car. I'd slip down the nearby steps to the D train as the cab driver leaned out the window, shouting at the fresh corpse, "Where to?"

That was a bit graphic. The details were sharp and compelling. It rang of truth. But there is one problem: I've never even met Herman Mildew. Not in person, anyway. But we're friends on Facebook. Now excuse me; I want to be the first person to write something snappy and touching on his timeline.

Elise Broach

L ook, I'm not going to lie to you.

I worshipped Hermie. That's right, I called him Hermie. It was the name between us . . . you know the way a nickname can capture everything about a relationship—the specialness, the intimacy, the sense of a magical circle being drawn, with the two of you enclosed and protected, utterly separate from the rest of the world? That was how it was with us.

To be fair, he insisted that I call him "Mr. Mildew" in public. And in private, too, come to think of it. But I understood . . . that gruff, ungainly exterior masked an essential shyness, and it was one of the things I adored about him. And yeah, okay, maybe he said something about "professionalism," and "respecting boundaries." Something about "I don't like you that way." Something about a restraining order. Whatever. He was always Hermie in my mind.

You don't believe me. I can tell. You don't think anyone could feel close to this tyrant, this monster, this despicable shell of a human being, Mr. Herman Q. Mildew. Well, anyone except that Sara Shepard, apparently. Who IS she, anyway? Are we really supposed to believe they hooked up? One word: delusional. And I can tell you I certainly never saw her follow him home from work, or skulk around his favorite cheese shop, or sneak into his house during those quiet hours between midnight and dawn, when the city finally catches its breath; the hours of lovers the world over. That was my time with Hermie . . . though of course we couldn't be together physically, because of the restraining order.

How did I know it was love? I can see how you might ask that. Aren't these the fundamental questions that haunt us all in life's journey: *Is this love? Is it real? Will it last?*

The only way I can think to answer that is to tell you one small story about Hermie that will prove the depth of our bond. Because that bond is my alibi, and my final, pure defense against the insanity of this accusation. Okay, okay, I know—there's not a "witness." There's no "proof." There's nobody to "vouch" for me. I am not one to get bogged down in technicalities, or the legal mumbo-jumbo you all like to spout during a murder investigation.

Here's the story: Many years ago, in the early stages of our relationship, I gave Hermie my nine-hundred-page young adult novel about a beaver who saves his pond from imminent environmental devastation caused by the toxic effluvium from an old pickle factory. It had everything: enough pages to be taken seriously, a spunky main character with an important environmental lesson to teach readers, a thorough and near-academic discussion of the effects of toxic run-off on ponds and streams, and the fearless use of profanity, because I will not be stifled in my art.

I met Hermie at his door as he was coming home from work one day, and thrust the manuscript into his arms. Each time I tried to give him my manuscript—my opus, my life's work—he kept shoving it away. He could be really playful like that. Finally, when he jammed his key into the front door and rushed into the house, I heaved the manuscript in after him, right before the door slammed shut. Now listen. A few minutes later, the manuscript came flying back out again! Pages scattered all over the concrete steps. And I admit, my heart plummeted through my chest like a television set pushed off the roof of a building, crashing down on an unsuspecting passerby.

But just before he slammed the door shut again, Hermie said two things to me that changed my life forever. What Hermie said was this: "Are you crazy? Who would read this thing?" And then he unleashed such a stream of profanity that I realized, though mere seconds had passed, he actually HAD READ my manuscript! Or at least part of it.

And in those two spare sentences, he gave me more profound advice than any editor I've ever worked with; really, than any human being I've ever known. Because I realized that what Hermie was saying was this:

1. You have to be crazy for your art. Burn all the bridges, throw out the script, and start from the whirling dervish center of your own madness. Therein lies your genius.

2. Think of your AUDIENCE. Because the moment of communion with the reader is like a love affair. A crazy, inexplicable love affair.

What did you say? Oh, that? In my pocket? Yes, that's right . . . it's rat poison. I'm surprised you recognized it—good for you! You really know your stuff. Excuse me? No, no, don't be silly. There are lots of rats at the old pickle factory—the place is overrun with them.

Look, I'm not going to lie to you.

Peter Brown

You need to understand, it's tough being an author and illustrator. I spend 99 percent of my time writing and drawing in my studio. Alone. Isolation can do funny things to a person. I'm told that I've developed the personality of a newt. That my breath smells like rancid truffle butter. And that my clammy skin, pained expression, and hunched posture lead people to think I have chronic diarrhea. But I don't have chronic diarrhea. I've just become seriously awkward. Seriously.

So then one night I found myself at Herman Mildew's pickle factory party. The place was packed with the biggest names in publishing. I was really hoping to make some new friends, but as usual, my social awkwardness got the best of me. After an hour, the only conversation I'd had was to ask a pregnant woman when she was due. Turns out she wasn't pregnant. She was a guy.

My blunders got worse from there. I accidentally guided a blind man into the women's room. I sneezed my bubble gum into a literary agent's mouth. I elbowed an old lady right in the boob. And I mistook another guy for a pregnant woman. I could go on. . . .

One thing was clear: it would take a miracle for me to make any friends that night. And a miracle happened. I walked into the restroom to do my business and found Herman Mildew dead on the floor. I don't know what killed him. But however he died, I was not going to let that golden opportunity slip away. I mean, Herman was the most hated man in ALL publishing, everyone knows that, and he was already dead . . . what's wrong with using his death to my advantage?

I hid Herman's body as best I could, walked back to the party, and grabbed a microphone.

"Excuse me, can I have everyone's attention?" my voice boomed from the speakers. "Thank you. I'd just like to apologize to anyone I may have offended tonight. I don't get out much. But I think you'll all forgive me when you hear this fantastic news. I KILLED HERMAN MILDEW!"

The party was silent. For a moment I feared my little white lie had backfired.

"That jerk is gone forever!" I squeaked. "It's true!"

And then it started. One person began to clap. Then another. And another. More and more people began clapping and hooting until the room was bursting with applause! The music fired up and the party was ON! Everyone thanked me! Everyone loved me! Everyone wanted to be my friend!

So I lied about killing Herman Mildew. It was worth it. That was the single greatest night of my life.

Jen Calonita

"I wouldn't even feed these pages to that rat you call a dog!" Herman Mildew bellowed.

He was standing in the hallway outside his corner office, holding my latest manuscript high above his head. He crumpled the pages into a tight ball. He'd only had them for five minutes so I have no clue what set him off. I didn't have time to ask because a second later, to my shock and horror, he made his displeasure even more evident by kicking Captain Jack Sparrow, my ten-pound Chihuahua.

That was the day I wished the man who signed me to my first book deal dead.

Okay, maybe it wasn't the *first* time I wished him dead, but it was certainly the moment I knew I meant it because no one—and I mean no one—kicks my dog and gets away with it. Jack is the sweetest Chihuahua in the world (well, when he isn't peeing on my luggage because he knows I'm headed out of town). I only brought him in to Herman's office that day to introduce him to my latest junior editor who has a Chihuahua-obsession like I do.

Did I mention how much I like my junior editors even though none of them have made it past the five-month mark with Herman? The juniors don't bark at me for manuscripts three weeks *before* they're due or threaten to kill my latest contract. They send pleasant emails asking about my kids (Herman doesn't even remember I have them) before inquiring about where my long overdue acknowledgements are. They put thoughtful edit notes in pretty pink note bubbles in my manuscript document and say things like "please" or "it would be great if." Herman just writes RUBBISH in big, murderous red script across every page, leaving me to figure out exactly what he hated (did I mention he still doesn't edit on a computer yet? When he edits my work, I have to write all my notes by hand). Thankfully, Herman's usually too wrapped up in his famous celebrity lunches—where he's tried to sign everyone from "Tommy" Cruise to the "Biebs" Justin Bieber to a book deal. That means I rarely have to deal with the oaf. And that's just how I like it, which is why when I got that invite to his party, I thought about faking every disease in the book to avoid going. But there is no avoiding Herman. Especially when he has more dirt on the young adult community than the FBI has on the Mafia.

I was only there five painstaking minutes when I ran into him. He was up to his elbows in ribs and was using his Armani silk shirt as a napkin, but he turned to me with a wicked smile and said, "Did you try these yet? I had them brought in from Thailand. They are 100 percent pure Chihuahua meat." His stare turned deadly. "Bring that rat of yours in again and I'll make him my next meal too."

The fork I was holding came dangerously close to stabbing him in the throat, but I'm a lady and ladies don't do such things. They just dream about them. So I left the party.

Ask Elizabeth Eulberg, if you don't believe me. I was sobbing to her about the bounty on Jack Sparrow's head in the bathroom. Then I pulled myself together and headed straight to the gym to take a late-night spin class because our gym, um, has those sorts of things. Doesn't every gym offer spin at ten at night? Mine does, and I spent the next hour whipping my legs into a frenzy to work out my aggression toward that Mildew of a man. Did I picture my bike running over his head the entire time? Maybe, but that doesn't prove anything, does it? That's just pure and simple spinning motivation.

Patrick Carman

When I was a boy my family lived at the foot of a mountain that was home to a Sasquatch. It was widely understood among the gang of kids who lived on our dirt road that if our parents were stupid enough to take up residence within a thousand miles of a ten-foot-tall-monkey-man with magical powers, they were also going to be useless when it came time to protect us in the middle of the night when it knocked down the front door, picked us up by our feet, and dragged us up the mountain so it could rip our arms off. It was for this reason that we never, *ever*, invoked the name of the Sasquatch to blame him for things that had gone terribly wrong in our lives.

Only sometimes we did.

Joey Turnbuckle, a snot-nosed kid who collected mud under his fingernails so he could eat it for lunch, spilled a gallon of paint on his living room rug when he was seven years old. When his mother found him sloshing around on the carpet like a seal, Joey's paint covered face went wide with terror.

"The Sasquatch did it!"

Later we all agreed it was the paint fumes. Joey wasn't in his right mind. But that didn't change the fact that he'd called down the wrath of the Sasquatch.

The next day, Joey Turnbuckle's dog was gone.

The doghouse was lodged in the branches of a nearby tree, about fifteen feet up. A large family of squirrels had taken up residence and stared down at me and Joey, chirping like little maniacs.

"He's a big one," I said, looking down at my tennis shoe, which was sitting inside of a footprint the size of a large watermelon.

"And tall," Joey added.

When Joey's dad came outside and stood next to us, Joey pointed up to the doghouse.

"The Sasquatch did it."

From this incident we learned some important pieces of information. If the Sasquatch really *did* do it, then you could say so and it would leave you alone. You could even joke about crazy things the Sasquatch may have done, like pushing a giant tree over on top of your house (this actually happened, different story). As long as it sounded cool, the Sasquatch seemed fine taking responsibility. But no card-carrying Big Foot wants to take credit for spilling paint in your living room. It's beneath him. The number one rule at the foot of a mountain: don't *ever* blame a Sasquatch for stupid crap you did yourself. The incident with Joey Turnbuckle was the first time any of us understood how serious this rule really was.

The consequences got a lot worse.

My uncle Clyde said it when my aunt found a red sock combined with a load of whites, which had turned her favorite sun dress a blotchy shade of pink.

"The Sasquatch did it!"

Three days later, uncle Clyde's head fell off. I'm not making this up.

My big brother said it only once in my entire childhood when my mom caught him smoking on the side of the house.

"The Sasquatch did it!"

This was an egregious use of the Sasquatch name, mostly because it didn't make any sense.

"The Sasquatch did *what*?" my mom asked. She didn't understand what my brother meant, but then again she was so stupid, she made us live in a town cursed by a known Sasquatch. I guess the apple doesn't fall far from the tree, because my brother was even more stupid. Who blames a Sasquatch when you get caught smoking?

Legend has it my brother looked at the cigarette in his hand, flicked it into the grass, and began crying like a three-year-old. My mom enfolded him in her arms and told him she wouldn't tell my dad. But my big brother wasn't crying about getting caught smoking a dumb cigarette. He was crying because he knew he'd blamed it on the one creature you don't blame things on. No Sasquatch likes to be made a fool of, especially when it's being blamed for something.

That night our house burned to the ground. We found a marshmallow roasting stick in the back 40 the next morning, stuck in the dirt between two footprints.

"Nice going, bro," I said.

He lit a cigarette and stared off into the woods. "Could have been worse. At least my head didn't fall off."

He had a point.

You'd think this would have been enough to run my marble-headed parents out of town for good, but they were even more stupid than I thought, and that's saying something.

We moved in with my widowed aunt, four doors down, who was still mourning the loss of uncle Clyde. Her house smelled like burnt coffee and bleach, and she had a weird hang-up with lampshades that led to my one and only face-to-face encounter with a Sasquatch.

It started out innocently enough. My mom had taken me and my brother down to the crummy general store about a million miles away on foot and given me two quarters to spend as I liked. I wanted a BB gun so I could shoot squirrels, rabbits, and the occasional Big Foot, but fifty cents wasn't going to get me the BBs, let alone the weapon. So I bought a squirt gun instead. And a Tootsie Roll.

The trouble began in the garage on a cold January morning. There was a stark white light bulb over my head, burning bright like a little sun as I sat on the concrete step leading back into the house. I don't know what made me shoot water at that light bulb, and I sure as heck didn't know it was going to be so much fun. If it had been boring I would have stopped, but that's the trouble with trouble. We rarely see it coming when we're having such a good time. The first few seconds were the best (also true about most kinds of trouble). I squeezed the plastic trigger on the squirt gun, shooting a laser-perfect shot of water at a light bulb that had been left on all night long and into the morning. It hissed gloriously, steam pouring off its sides like billowing smoke. So of course I kept on shooting, who wouldn't? On the fifth shot the light bulb exploded with a fabulous *pop!* showering the floor with thousands of tiny pieces of glass. I went directly into the house, where my aunt's compulsion to remove all lamp shades sent me on a mad tear through every room, blowing up light bulbs like a G.I. Joe sharpshooter. The carnage was magnificent, a true joy, until I flopped down on the plastic covered sofa and realized what I'd done. The gun was in my hand. I'd laid waste to every light bulb in the house. I'd blown them all up and had a hell of a good time doing it.

If only I'd had time to think, I'm nearly sure I wouldn't have lost my head. But my aunt walked in carrying a paper bag of groceries under each arm. Her head stuck out over the tops, as if it had been removed from the rest of her body. It was unnerving, the way it turned back and forth, surveying the scene. She saw the blown out bulbs and the gun in my hand and before I knew what had happened it was too late.

"The Sasquatch did it!" I screamed.

My aunt dropped the grocery bags and let the contents pour out all over the tile floor. She marched over to the couch, ripped the squirt gun from my hand, opened the patio door, and threw it outside. I didn't stay long enough to see whether the jars of peanut butter and mayo had broken open. I was already down the hall and into my room with the door shut behind me.

I wasn't afraid of my aunt or what she would say to my parents when they got home.

I was afraid of what was coming down the mountain.

On a good day, the mountain cast its black shadow over my room by three o'clock in the afternoon, but in the dead of winter, I only saw the sun until a quarter past one. It was on exactly that kind of day that I found myself trying to extract tiny pieces of glass from a thick layer of shag carpet. It was 2:30 P.M. and the sun had already long been hidden. While I cleaned up the mess, I wondered what kind of awful doom the Sasquatch had planned for me as he lumbered down the canyon, his hairy knuckles dragging in the dirt as he went. Would he use his mastery of ancient-mountain-magic to make all my fingers fall off? Or maybe I'd turn to stone in my sleep. I hoped he'd go easy on me and take the decoy I'd long since set up for just such a predicament. My cat, Snuggles, who I deeply distrusted and took no enjoyment in, was a creature for whom I faked total adoration. Maybe, in the end, I could trick a Sasquatch into ridding me of a cat who liked to cough up fur balls on my pillow.

At dinner, I pushed crunchy green bean casserole back and forth on my plate. It was my last meal, a thoroughly depressing plate of slop, and I sat there wishing for two all-beef patties, special sauce, lettuce, cheese, pickles, onions— all on a sesame seed bun. And some fries. I went directly to my room post-casserole, hungry and afraid, hoping against all hope that the Sasquatch would go easy on me.

I lured Snuggles into my room an hour later, said my goodnights to everyone in the house, and did what any kid in my situation would have done: I got into the closet with my baseball bat and shut the door. The middle of the door was made of slats, so I could see out as Snuggles jumped on my bed, coughed up something wet and hairy, and settled in on my pillow.

An hour passed.

I heard my parents and my aunt go to their rooms for the night. My brother took the couch, which he loved, because he stayed up late and watched *Benny Hill* reruns at eleven thirty. Sometimes they showed naked ladies on that show. It was a big deal.

By midnight I was slumped over in the corner of my closet wishing I could trade places with my cat. And that's when I heard the sound of the Sasquatch getting closer. Sasquatches are denser than normal creatures. A lot of people don't know that, but it's true. If it were like a human or an ape, a ten-foot Sasquatch might weigh, at the outside, a thousand pounds.

And that would be a really fat one. But a ten-foot Sasquatch weighs roughly the same as a '67 Ford pickup truck loaded with boulders. That's why you can hear them coming. When they walk, it's like a series of little earthquakes.

Boom.

Boom.

Boom.

I took a deep breath, held the bat like I was ready for a home run swing, and peeked through the slats.

Snuggles jumped off the bed and started meowing at the window.

Yes! I thought. *What a decoy! No Sasquatch can resist a snuggly companion he can cook for breakfast!*

The window fogged white in the moonlight as the Sasquatch breathed heavily. He leaned closer and I saw his eyes, glowing and fierce, darting around the room in search of the bad kid who had blamed him for shooting out light bulbs.

Come on, I thought, gripping the bat so hard my knuckles turned white. *Take the cat.*

Instead, he reached one wooly hand up and slid the window open. I'd left it unlocked for two reasons: one, he'd be way too big to crawl through anyway; and two, if he were going to reach down and grab a cat, he'd need to get his long arm inside my room.

My heart was pounding like an Indian war drum as the Sasquatch hand entered the room. He was holding something, and as the giant hand moved, I realized it was a gun. It struck me as a little bit unusual that he'd shoot me dead, but then I remembered that Sasquatches are smarter then they look. He was going to murder me in my own room and make it look like my aunt or my headless uncle had done it out of spite.

The gun turned on the cat, and for a split second I felt

sorry for it. Then the Sasquatch started firing, and I realized one more thing about Sasquatches that most people don't know: they have a sense of humor. It was squirting Snuggles with my squirt gun, a relentless barrage of water that drove my cat under the bed, but only after it darted back and forth helplessly for a good five seconds. It was hilarious.

The Sasquatch laughed, low and slow just like you'd expect, then he turned the gun in my direction and sprayed the slats until all the water ran out. I was drenched in liquid shrapnel by the time he was done, but I was alive and so was Snuggles. The Sasquatch dropped the empty weapon on my floor and slid the window shut, then started the long walk back up the mountain.

I checked for all my limbs and found I was still in one piece. No terrible mountain magic! The cat came out from under the bed and I gleefully picked it up and threw it out the window.

It had been a very, very close call, and I knew one thing for certain: he'd let me off easy. If I ever invoked his name again for something I'd done, I was a goner for sure.

I say all that to tell you this:

I haven't got an alibi. I have no idea where I was on the night Mildew was snuffed out. I might have been golfing. If I was on one of his legendary deadlines, I was probably watching a movie or playing pinball. I honestly don't remember. But then again, I don't need an alibi, because you know what I'm about to say and the terrible weight of each and every word.

I could not have killed Mildew.

The Sasquatch did it!

Susane Colasanti

Seriously with this?

I can't believe after everything we've been through you'd even think for one nanosecond that I'd be capable of killing Herman Mildew. True, it was his fault I was evicted and ended up sleeping on the street. But that summer was unusually cool and dry for New York City. I was enjoying all the refreshing outdoor time. And when you get evicted from your rent-controlled, three-bedroom, 2,320 square-foot apartment in the West Village that was only $435 a month, really, it's a gift. Do you have any idea how long it took to clean that place?

You're probably wondering why I got evicted. Herman Mildew made a promise he didn't keep. He told me that if I wrote a teen novel featuring vampires, death, and magic, he'd turn it into the next mega bestseller. He was going to make my big New York dreams come true. But he gave me a deadline. An insane deadline. I had two months to hand in a polished six-hundred-page manuscript. My memories of chugging crazy quantities of Red Bull, throwing screaming tantrums, and blasting Led Zeppelin at three in the morning are blurry. Let's just say the neighbors weren't having it. Next thing I knew, my time was up, the manuscript was only half done, and I was out on the street.

But it was all good. This is New York, where anything is possible and dreams come true. As any Manhattan real estate broker will tell you, you have to make sacrifices for location. So I was feeling groovy about my new digs in an abandoned cheese warehouse under the Fifty-ninth Street Bridge. First off, free rent, so yay. Plus I had access to the bathroom at the YMCA across the street. The handiest first-floor squatter, Bartholomew, even hooked me up with some bootleg electricity and a mini fridge. The mini fridge didn't have a freezer, but freezers are *so* overrated. I mean, ice? Really?

I was reading the gigantic bestseller *Rabbit Stew* by the light of a cactus lamp I found in the dumpster when Herman Mildew burst in, all skipping a jump rope, his watermelon-shaped head bobbing. His jump rope was purple and sparkly. Like, what, did he steal it from an eight-year-old girl or something? Even more annoying than his rope jumping was his interest in knitting. You could totally tell he knitted the bright green poncho he was wearing himself. It was all scraggly. The hem was crooked. It looked awful.

I was like, "It's not easy being green, Hermie."

"Where's my manuscript?" he demanded. He'd kindly extended my deadline.

"In a safe place. Let's go get it."

Hot gossip around the warehouse was that the staff of *Late Night with David Letterman* used to party there back in the day. Somehow, that ninety-ton hydraulic press Dave used to crush watermelons in ended up on the roof. You could totally imagine a certain someone's watermelon-shaped head being crushed the same way. But, you know, only if he deserved it.

We went up to the roof. There was no manuscript. There was only a ninety-ton hydraulic press.

Memories of my previous life rushed in. My big New York dreams I wanted so desperately to come true. Friends who took showers. My massive apartment. Heat. Ice. But of course I just wanted to show him the view. It completely takes your breath away.

I did not direct HM toward the booby trap Bartholomew rigged. I did not crush him like he crushed my dreams. And I certainly did not toss his mangled body off the roof.

I mean, *seriously?*

Elizabeth Craft

Note: The following is writer/procrastinator Elizabeth Craft's interior monologue as she waits her turn to be interrogated in the case of the dead Mr. Mildew:

Ohgodohgodohgod. They think I did it. They found that Mr. Mildew death threat I posted on the Internet. As I sit here in this pickle factory like a caged animal, they have people searching my apartment. People who have no doubt already found my secret stash of Justin Bieber and Zac Efron photos. I know a forty-year-old woman hoarding pictures of teen idols is creepy . . . but is it illegal? Why oh why didn't I spend my online time researching such legal matters instead of perusing Mindy Kaling's blog? (Sidenote to self: purchase Mindy-recommended L'Or Celeste Starry Loose Powder if I ever get out of this pickle factory.)

And what about my candy collection? I swore to my nutritionist that I would stop eating sugar, wheat, dairy, meat, and anything that might contain mercury. But a woman can't exist on black beans alone. I need those Nerds. And the Starbursts are practically medicinal. HELL-O hypogly-cemia! As for the empty In-N-Out bags stuffed underneath my bed, I'm down to one Double-Double a week. Plus an order of fries. That's not so bad. Is it? Is it? Who am I kid-ding. . . ? It's terrible. From now on, I promise I'll only eat healthy fast food. Like Subway. I'm talking the six-inch oven-roasted chicken sandwiches, not the meatball subs I've been know to consume in the past . . . SHIT!

If they found my Justin and Zac pics, and my candy col-lection, they probably also took a look at what I have saved on DVR. Which includes Keeping Up with the Kardashians and Kourtney and Kim Take New York and Finding Sarah. It doesn't matter that I've never actually watched the show about the Duchess of York. It's there. Waiting. And I don't delete it. Will it be a mitigating factor that those shows are clearly treadmill viewing only. . . ? No. They don't care. They're out for blood.

Oh lord. I just had a horrible thought. If they're look-ing on my computer for that Mr. Mildew death threat, then they're obviously going to check the emails in my Save folder. It's not fair! Those emails were never sent for a reason. They are the ravings of a madwoman after too many Nerds. Ohgodohgodohgod. They're gonna nail me for the email I wrote to my grade school gym teacher. Although . . . I will maintain in any court of law that it is her fault I not only detest but fear team sports. It's because of her I have a mental block against knowing exactly where the halfback is supposed to stand during a field hockey game. Even hearing the words "wind sprint" sends a chill down my spine.

Damn these detectives for turning over every metaphoric rock in my world. I should be allowed to hide my shame *with dignity. Death threat against Mr. Mildew aside, I'm not hurting any—*

Here, Elizabeth Craft's interior monologue is interrupted by an approaching investigator:

Investigator: Ms. Craft?

Elizabeth: *(tremulous)* Yes?

Investigator: There's been a mistake. Your name shouldn't have been on the list. You're free to go.

Elizabeth: *(big sigh of relief)* Thank you, sir. Not that I was worried. Not at all. I'm an open book. Yep. No secrets here—

Investigator: Ms. Craft?

Elizabeth: *(perky)* Yes, sir?

Investigator: The Justin and Zac photos are pathetic.

And with that insight, writer/procrastinator Elizabeth Craft went off to write yet another un-sendable email to her grade school gym teacher.

Melissa de la Cruz

Darlings,

Why would I ever want to harm such a dear man? I, for one, am a close personal friend to my editors, yes! And dear Herman was one of my very best friends. Why, we went to Cannes together, and to Rio, for my latest book. We had to do some very important research concerning cocktails and cabana boys. The last time I saw Herman we were kiss-kissing at a fashion show. He looked a bit pale and chubby in his last-season suit, but no matter. I allowed the paparazzi to take our photograph nonetheless.

Of course, I should add that Herman always did pay my advances with discount coupons to department stores, and that when I was forced to use them, I would be told that the coupons were not only expired, they were fake. There were other . . . shall we say . . . minor irritations. . . . He would insist that I stop sending my latest novels on ivory stationery with pink ink. He claimed he was allergic to the perfume the pages were soaked with!

When I came to New York for our annual editor-and-writer lunch, I was decked out for the usual three-martini tête-à-tête at Michael's, only to discover we would be dining alfresco in front of Gray's Papaya. I did not realize papaya juice had such a frozen consistency, or that it tasted a bit like cough medicine. Although the hot dogs, I must admit, were divine. (The Pigeon was right about that one.)

So where was I the night Herman went missing? And why was my hair in disarray and my clothes splattered with dark red spots? It is simply the latest fashion, my dear. Deshabille is very "in" right now, and yes, red UNDER the fingernails is *trés trés* chic as well. My hair? It looks as if it has been pulled in many different directions? And the black eye? As if I was in a fight and pummeling a very short round editor for a long time until he finally collapsed in a heart attack? But no, *mes chères*. This again is just the latest trend. "Fright wig" is very in right now, and a fake black eye will be gracing the red carpets and the fashion pages very soon.

No, I don't know where he is or what happened to dear Herman Mildew. I do hope he's all right and that he has lost a bit of weight. He's been looking a bit puffy, poor man. Perhaps he should do a cleanse. Now please excuse me, I need to lie down a bit. My eye is starting to throb—no no, it's just an allergy to makeup.

Thank you & ciao!

Julia DeVillers
with illustrative help from
Paige Pooler

I did not kill Herman Mildew. I mean, psssht—I write cheerful fiction. Most of my book covers are bubble-gum pink, lavender, sparkly with glitter foil. Ah-bviously it was someone else here in this pickle factory. Someone like. . . .

Lemony Snicket? Squee! Lemony Snicket is here!!! And ooh! There's Mo Willems!!! Fangurl squee!

Wait! No squee-ing. This is a serious situation. Just like the time, not so long ago, that Herman called me into his office to discuss another *serious situation*. . . .

"Julia," Herman said. "It's time for you to write something different for us. Something edgier, something darker. Less 'tween-y.'"

"Omg!!! I totes can do that!" I said. Then I had a troublesome thought. "Is there a concern about my book sales?"

"I don't care about your book sales. I care about me. I can't take it anymore!" He pointed a gnarled finger at his wall. "Look at your section of my bookshelf!"

"I know, yay!" I perked up.

"That's not what I meant! All that pink and purple. . . ."

Herman shuddered. His office décor was early medieval torture chamber, so I thought my books added a welcome touch of whimsy. "Your sparkly reader mail alone is enough to kill me!"

"They're written in glitter gel pens," I pointed out. "Doesn't that just melt your heart?"

"Heart?! You mean that thing your readers dot their *i*'s with?" he grumbled. "And what's with the exclamation points? Why do they have to put three, four, seventeen exclamation points after a sentence?"

"They're showing enthusiasm and love!!!" I was getting offended. "My readers are intelligent *and* sparkly tweens."

"What the hell is a *tween* anyway?" he shouted. "And while we're on that topic, what's that high-pitched spastic squealing noise they make when they see you at book signings? It makes my ears bleed. I need a break, DeVillers!"

"Okay, okay!" I threw up my hands. "What should I write?"

"Edgy," Herman snarled. "Push the limits. Blood. Gore. Brutal death. Swear words."

He spun his chair around, pointedly facing the stuffed taxidermy heads of picture-book animals hanging on the wall behind him. Elephant and Piggie, giant pangolins of Madagascar and hey, wait a second—that new one wasn't an animal. It looked an awful lot like E. Lockhart. Gulp.

"Edgy. OR ELSE," Herman hissed. "Do I make myself clear, Julia?"

"Clear as the lip gloss my character wears when she has her first kiss with a hottie," I stammered. "K-thx-bye!"

I raced home, changed into my pajama jeans and opened my hot pink laptop. My screensaver of Boo (the cutest puppy in the world!!!) appeared. Okay. Edgy. I can do this. I Boo'lieve in myself.

I stared at the page. I kept staring for weeks. At first, I didn't panic when Herman emailed to ask how the manuscript was going.

It's going ☺ ! <3! xoxo!!! Jules.

But it wasn't going ☺. It was going ☹ and :o. Panic set in. I ignored Herman's emails. His calls. His texts. And I kept hearing Herman's voice, like a thousand fluffy bunnies tap dancing on my skull: "Edgy! Or else."

Finally, Herman gave me an ultimatum. I had one more day. If I didn't turn in my manuscript, I would have to give back my advance and he'd cut my bookmark and postcard budget in half!

Herman Mildew had pushed me over the edge. The edge of edgy. I checked my pink Domo clock and yes, there was time to run a few errands.

Shopping List:

- Perfume

- Nail file (v. v. sharp)

- Shoes (spiky stiletto heels)

- Outfit (all black, because I'm edgy)

After shopping therapy, I was in the perfect mood to stop by and say hi to my beloved editor who often worked late and alone. Anyway, that visit's not really important.

What IS important is that after I came home, I sat down at my computer and the story began to flow as if it were, well, nonfiction. An *edgy* story about a kick-ass murderer who's really a heroine, because the victim deserved it. Now,

I don't want to give away too much before the ARCs go out but . . . just as Herman had so brilliantly suggested, there was:

- Violence: the victim was blinded by a blast of perfume

- Swearing: from the victim

- Brutal death: as he was stomped through the heart with stilettos

- Gore: and disemboweled with a metal file

It was a killer manuscript.

I had my agent submit it widely, because I didn't expect to hear back from Herman. Since he's so busy with his other authors, of course. Authors like. . . .

Dave Eggers! OMG! Dave freaking Eggers just walked into the pickle factory! I totally have to get a picture with him for my mug shot! I mean my Facebook page! Squee!!!!

Oops, sorry, Dave! I didn't mean to step on your foot. I know, my stilettos are very sharp.

Larry Doyle

This looks bad, I know.

All this blood.

On me.

But I assure you, this is not Herman Mildew's blood;

or if it is, he placed it there voluntarily;

or if not, it was stolen from him by a person or persons unknown and then planted on me as the most likely suspect, based on:

certain unauthorized tweets made to my account @killmildew;

that Facebook status update ("it's stabbin' time!"), posted at 3 A.M. when I was fast asleep with all my knives safely under lock and key, having taken an extra half an Ambien, fearing a long night of bitter drinking would bring out the demon dreams, the terrible memories of the murder of my first book, page after page run red with illiterate scribbles and derisive Xs, the protagonist Cassius sex-changed to Cassie, the title diminished from *The Sorrow Clouds* to *Love Nerds*, my proposed cover, a piquant detail from Van Gogh's *Starry Night* jettisoned in favor of a girl wearing pink socks, my lovely, brutal coming-of-age tale debauched by some bastard whose name I can't recall at the moment, and then remaindered before its time;

and, should you obtain a search warrant, some items in my apartment that could be easily misunderstood, including:

maps and schematics I found on the street and brought in because they might be important to whoever dropped them there;

a voodoo doll that could be any older obese bald guy with glasses, the pins fairly obviously placed where anybody might go about stabbing someone and how many times;

tear-stained copies of my first book, with the title and imprint gouged out by an unidentified sharp instrument;

on my computer, an exchange of emails, the tone of which could be misconstrued, which is a real problem with email as you know;

and some search terms on Google, including:

"discount stabbing knives;"

"juiciest artery;"

"music to kill by;"

and "faking insanity,"

which taken together might lead you to a conclusion other than the correct one, which is it's all research for a new book I'm writing that I'm not prepared to talk about just yet;

or, if none of that is flying, there are any number of alternate theories that could raise the shadow of a doubt for any jury, including:

that animal-rights activists, upset by Mildew's new coffee table book *Veni in Furs,* featuring models petting the very animals they were wearing, went to see Mildew and, becoming enraged to find him wearing baby chinchilla finger warmers, slit his throat with his conflict-diamond-encrusted narwhale-ivory letter opener, drained his blood into an elephant-foot wastebasket, and then threw it on me, for some reason;

or that I was on my way to make peace with Mildew, having recently become a secret Buddhist, when I slipped and fell into this puddle of blood, rolling around to get my bearings, and then I picked up this knife to keep any small children from finding it;

or that whatever happened happened but I was insane at the time, though I'm better now;

or, actually, it's coming back to me now, wow, and I'm going to go with my first alibi, which is that it's not Herman Mildew's blood at all, and I should probably get to the hospital.

Sarah Beth Durst

Last time I talked to Herman, it was a very productive conversation. I value his artistic input. He has . . . or *had* . . . such a keen intellect and a firm grasp on the current market.

Me: I had an idea for my next novel. A mermaid discovers she's—

Herman: Hate mermaids. Remind me of sushi. Next.

Me: Okay, I had another idea. It's about a shapeshifter who—

Herman: Hate shapeshifters. Too indecisive. Can't abide indecisive people. Next.

Me: How do you feel about witches who—

Herman: Can't stand witches. Pointy hats revolt me.

Me: How about zombies?

Herman: Too gooey.

Me: Angels?

Herman: Too glowy.

Me: Vampires?

Herman: Too sparkly. Also, too thinly disguised metaphors for sexual angst.

Me: Phoenixes? Gryphons? Aliens?

Herman: I want you to write about frogs.

Me: Um, frogs? You mean, like, a spin on the Frog Prince? I suppose. . . .

Herman: Just frogs. Red frogs. Purple frogs. Yellow frogs with green polka dots. Did you know that the largest frog in the world is called the goliath frog? Weighs as much as a housecat. You write about him.

Me: You want a book about a goliath frog?

Herman: And toss in a love triangle.

So you can see that I had zero incentive to murder Herman Mildew, since he had practically promised to buy my next novel about a vampire zombie frog with ninja training who is in a love triangle with a beautiful girl with a hedgehog head and her best friend, a sheep.

He'd requested another meeting to discuss changes to my synopsis, and as everyone knows, Herman prefers to act out the stories as he discusses him. So that's why I packed the suitcase full of frogs.

I swear the frogs were plastic when I packed them.

In retrospect, I should not have put in the vial of dragon's blood, but I thought it would make a nice gift. It must have shattered in the suitcase when I fainted after hearing the horrible news about Herman's death. And you know what happens when dragon's blood touches plastic.

Or maybe you don't know, since there is a government conspiracy to suppress the truth. It is a fact that when dragon's blood is applied to plastic, the plastic takes on lifelike properties. That's what was behind the Barbie Massacre of '98.

Herman collected dragon's blood. He kept it in a liquor cabinet in his office, and in between meetings, he used to sprinkle it on toy soldiers and instruct them to destroy unpublished manuscripts. Sometimes it was G.I. Joes. Sometimes those green army guys. Once, he said he used My Pretty Ponys, but they left tiny plastic poop pellets all over his desk.

So really, I know he would have loved the gift of dragon's blood. I certainly did not intend to sprinkle it on the plastic poison frogs and release them where he'd find them. Why would I? As you can clearly see, I had no motive. He always loved all my ideas.

Dave Eggers

I did not kill Mildew, but I tried. Repeatedly. So my alibi is really just a list of failed attempts.

I started trying to kill Mildew back in the mid-1970s.

As you know, Mildew is a gluttonous man, so back in '78 I thought I'd send him giant sausages every day, hoping that he would eat each one and have a heart attack by the end of the month. It didn't happen. These were huge sausages, at least four feet each, but he ate all thirty-one and asked for more. Now the man is six hundred pounds and covered in boils. And he still eats a giant sausage every day.

He thanks me for it.

In 1979, someone had just made a disco version of all the songs from *Star Wars*. I bought the record and sent it to Mildew, hoping it would melt his brain. It didn't. He hums the theme, the disco version, every time I see him.

He thanks me for that, too.

In 1980, I intercepted a shipment—long story—of a particularly smelly type of banana called a durian. At first I thought I would send the durians to him, hoping he'd eat them all and choke—or suffocate from the smell. But I'd learned from the sausage experience, so instead I figured I'd just drop them all on his house. So I rented a cargo plane, loaded it with the durians, and dropped them from about 4,200 feet. They crushed his house, sure, but he survived. He was in his basement, eating sausages. That's where he eats them.

Turns out he wanted to renovate his house, and the durians flattening it gave him the push and insurance money he needed to get the job done. He invites me over to his new place all the time. *I want to thank you!* he says.

Since then, I've tried a few dozen different ways of doing him in. I sent an infestation of hermit crabs into his house. I'd heard they were aggressive around fat men, but this was not true. They were tame, even friendly. So I sent in those kinds of frogs that give you hallucinations if you lick them. Mildew, though, who licks or eats anything he can reach, didn't lick them. He *named* them.

Now he thanks me for introducing him to the crabs and the frogs. *They're some of my best friends,* he says.

A few years ago I met a monkey who seemed like it could be trained to kill a guy like Mildew. So the monkey and I went through six weeks of intense Mildew-killing training. I taught the monkey how to kill Mildew with a wiffle-ball bat, a handsaw, and a pair of pliers. Lots of stuff like that. Finally I felt like the monkey was trained well and ready to go. I sent the monkey into Mildew's house—his new house—and what happens? Three months later they were married. Turns out the monkey was a girl, and Mildew really had a thing for lady monkeys.

He thanks me for that, too. *You introduced me to my wife!* he says. *Come over and let me thank you with dinner! You can visit the frogs and crabs, too!*

Since then, I've tried offing Mildew with schemes involving the usual tools—ball-bearings, duct tape, okapis, groups of Canadian teenagers. None of these things have worked. The sinkhole did not work. The locusts did not work. The bundt cake filled with C-4 did not work. Sending him the collected wisdom of Rick Santorum did not work. Mildew is a hard man to kill.

So when I heard Mildew was dead, it was bittersweet. I was glad he was dead, but sad that I had not been the one to do it. I'm probably alone among your suspects in that I'm not going to bother with an alibi. I wish I'd done it, but I did not.

Daniel Ehrenhaft

To begin, I offer your own ludicrous accusations as rebuttal. These are your words, not mine:

- Concerning the discovery of a poorly crafted "voodoo puppet" (Mr. Ehrenhaft's words) on his person;

- Furthermore bearing the vague likeness of Herman Mildew, a generous term given the artistic quality;

- In addition smothered in Mr. Ehrenhaft's fingerprints;

- Finally pierced with a plastic spork emblazoned with the brand moniker Chilly's Cold Chili! It's NOT Gazpacho!™

Second things first: before this incident, have I ever claimed to be a puppet maker, puppet owner, or puppeteer?

No. Well. Sort of. Sure, you may have overheard some synonym of "puppet" that I've tossed around once or twice. But in answer to any question regarding puppet-related crimes or puppet-related conspiracy, I offer an emphatic *not yes*.

Let's get to the more important issue: "voodoo." We can clear that up right away. I don't recall ever mentioning in casual conversation, "Oh, I also handcraft beautiful dolls in a variety of materials to be used in evil occult practices, among them, voodoo." If you can find someone who can remember I said that, I'd laugh. I'd give a hardy-har-har (a particularly disdainful form of laugh) if you can find someone who could claim that I'd ever threatened, "Raid my fridge again, and you'll meet your demise at the hands of a wondrous figurine imbued with your soul, you Terrible Hot Sauce of All Things Awful. Because I never forget anything."

Do you have such a witness? If so, please bring him forward. Good luck to you.

Besides, only a very angry person would accuse a guest of raiding his refrigerator. My fridge is a bountiful treasure chest of chilled soups, up for grabs to anyone I invite over. Not that I don't stock other food. Like sour cream, for instance. And frozen cheese. And those yummy little croutons. (Best served ice-cold! ☺) Granted, I never technically "invited" Mr. Mildew to my home in the first place. The point is: I am a very happy person, unlike this poor murder victim you're hounding me about. So why would I freak out if he devoured the last of my delicious cold chili on a day so hot that all my wax effigies melted? Happy people don't do that.

Back to this supposed "evidence" against me. It may interest you to know that countless credible websites offer incontrovertible proof that aliens reproduce fingerprints, retinal scans, DNA, scrumptious frozen crudité, sporks, and Eternal Bliss—among other incriminating flotsam and jet-sam—at a moment's notice. Still, like typical members of the mainstream law enforcement community, you deny what's staring you in the face. (A face I'm happy to reproduce in your choice of stunning three-dimensional formats, by the way, once these charges blow over.) Ever been to Roswell, New Mexico? Of course you haven't.

I rest my case. You're not thinking logically.

In fact, I'm feeling so generous right now that I'll leave you with a gift. If you do ever visit Roswell, there's a great chili stand near the crash site. Stick that chili in the freezer for twelve hours, and *then* eat it. When you're stuck in the hot desert, discovering the truth about aliens and lamenting a jerk who's better off dead, you'll thank me.

Elizabeth Eulberg

First off, let me explain my reaction upon hearing of Mr. Mildew's demise because it has been blown out of proportion. I take issue with the allegation that I was caught "dancing on his grave." There are many reasons why this isn't fair: (1) He hasn't even been buried yet, hence there's no grave to be danced on; (2) I wasn't aware that it is a crime to dance on a table; and (3) Since I'm under oath (like that would've ever stopped Ol' Milly), I can verify that this was not the first time I have danced on a table. So this really isn't unusual behavior for me. Ask around.

Okay so yeah, I wasn't *devastated* when I heard that Mr. Grumpy Mildew had passed. I mean, have you ever met him? I doubt there's a single person on this planet who has ever received even a kind word from him. He certainly hasn't done me any favors. Just off the top of my head: he refused to learn my name for the first year we worked together and would only call me "You there," and his response upon reading my first book was, "No wonder you don't have a boyfriend." And then there was the cheese incident. I'm still upset about it, but figure you'll hear about it from somebody so it may as well be me.

Please note, this is a very touchy subject and a time in my life that I'd prefer to forget. But alas, the truth must be known. It was three months ago. I went into the community refrigerator in the kitchen to get a snack. I opened the door in anticipation of having my favorite cheddar cheese, which my parents shipped to me from Wisconsin. When I opened the box it . . . it was replaced with one of Milly's gross, smelly French cheeses and a note that simply said, "Get some taste." Let me tell you something, you do not mess with a Wisconsin girl's cheese. You. Do. *Not*.

But alas, you aren't asking me about that. (And last time I checked *stealing* was a crime.)

Yes, I was nearly fifteen minutes late to the pickle factory. Anybody who knows me knows that I'm nothing if not punctual. That's a word I've heard people use to describe me, along with dependable, honest, non-murderous, lactose-tolerant, embarrassment-prone, sometimes in the wrong place at the wrong time. . . .

But it wasn't my fault I wasn't there on time. I was meeting David Levithan, but *he* was late. I was waiting for him at our normal meeting place and after a few minutes I started texting and calling him, but nothing. Finally he came running over to me, out of breath (and a little out of sorts). I didn't really think anything of it at the time (you know how guys can be). But now. . . .

So yeah, there are like ten minutes that I was alone and don't have an alibi (save the random people walking past probably wondering what a young, *innocent* girl like myself was doing all alone in such a seedy part of town).

But if I may just bring up a really good question: where

was David? A person can get into a lot of trouble in ten minutes. Not like *I* would know anything about trouble. I'm not throwing him under the bus or anything, I'm just asking a simple question. I knew they didn't really get along. I once had to listen to them get in a long argument over the use of "who" or "whom" and honestly, I zoned out because isn't that what a copyeditor is for? Is there anybody out there who really cares? (Or is it whom. . . .)

All I know is I was where I was supposed to be. I did nothing wrong . . . except maybe choose an inappropriate time to bust out my sweet dance moves.

Helen
Fitzgerald

Give me a time and a date and I'll tell you what I was
doing.

It's called hyperthymesia, my condition. I remember every
minute of every day of my life. Well, since I was three. I can
recount where I was, who I was with, and what I was doing,
down to the last second.

At 10:25 A.M. on Tuesday, July 5, 2010, for example, I
was having lunch at Del Rio's on Bridge Street with Herman Mildew. I ordered the garganelli. Herman, he had three
cheese platters and two bottles of their best champagne. He
spent four hours and seventeen minutes with me because my
debut novel was gonna make me bigger than J.K. Rowling.
That's why I paid the check.

You can forgive a man anything when he's handing
you your dream. Sweaty armpits? Just endearing evidence
of a hardworking and passionate man. Fart concerto? He
must've been allergic to the cheese, poor man. Ah, the egg-y
smell of success.

At 12:56 P.M. on Saturday, May 28, 2011, I was at my

writing desk pressing F5 to refresh my browser. A delivery van was parked across the road. It was 76 degrees. F5 . . . F5 . . . F5 . . . Herman hadn't responded to my emails. Probably busy trying to turn things round. I'd give him a few more weeks. F5.

His lousy assistant told me not to go to Famous McFabulous's (not the author's real name) book launch on November 12, 2011, and then hung up, rude cow. But I snuck in behind that bitter, twisted, failed author from the *New York Times* who wrote in his YA fiction round-up: "The only good thing about Fitzgerald's debut is that it's mercifully short." From my hiding place in the Self-Help section, I heard Herman introduce this new writer twerp as "The next J.K. Rowling." The first print run was 300,000, he said, at 7:05 P.M. Well whoopee! Mine was the same.

Sometimes at night I wonder what they did with the other 298,423.

So go on, I dare you, ask me. Any minute of any day and I'll tell you what I was doing—and it *wasn't* killing Herman Mildew.

What have you got on me? Disappointment? I don't *do* disappointment. Anyway, that wouldn't make me a killer.

So what if you found a receipt for blue cheese in my shoulder bag? I like it, especially the Roquefort from Dino's. Got it there 3:55 P.M. Friday, as it says on the ticket.

The lighter . . . I bought that on 21 September 2010, and one pink candle, for the birthday cake I baked for my forty-fifth.

Oh I *always* carry a can of gasoline. So would you if you ran out on the Forth Bridge like I did at 9:35 A.M. Monday, January 2, 1987. It was minus twenty. My nose hairs froze. Never again.

Is it empty? Oh dear.

What?! You think I ignited his post-Stilton farts? Set him on fire? Ha! That's funny. Might use that in Book Three.

So what you're implying is I sent him the cheese, assuming he'd eat it.

I'd have had to get him alone after he'd stuffed it in his fat gob, broken into his house or something, through the wee high-up window in the laundry that he always forgets to lock, or some such.

This is hilarious. Let me describe what you're suggesting, set the scene. I'm good at it. It's what I do. . . . So, *then*, I'd have had to sneak up on him while he was bending down— maybe because he noticed his pet rat had died, from drinking drain-cleaner at 10:37 A.M.-ish, or whatever—and put the lighter under his bum.

Ha!

That wouldn't kill him, anyway. Burn his bottom hairs maybe.

Right, unless I poured gasoline round the room first. And *then* lit his bellowing bottom eruption, just as he was sobbing, "No Bobby, NO!"

Bobby! What kind of person has a rat for a pet!

Why not just pour the gas over him and light it, forget the natural passing of wind, which afflicts all of us mortals? Unless the killer felt compelled to be poetic, I suppose. Herman's demise was sparked by his own grotesqueness! At least that's what the killer might have thought, but how should I know?

Then, what . . . I ran from the blaze, out the side door, to the getaway vehicle in the lane?

Really, you're cracking me up. Such good material. You should be a writer. I can give you some pointers if you want.

I've just finished Book Two. My new agent's sending it out to the Big Sixty next week. She's works in telesales by day. Hungry, though, and knows the book world, boy oh boy. Says it's gonna be big.

Says I'm the next J.K. Rowling.

Gayle Forman

BREAKING _NEWS

Renowned editor Herman Q. Mildew is dead. Foul play is suspected.

Editrixxie
RT @BREAKING_NEWS: "Renowned editor Herman Q. Mildew is dead. Foul play is suspected." Did you see this @gayleforman?

gayleforman
@Editrixxie I did not see this, but now that I do, I'm going to go celebrate. This calls for ice cream cake.

Editrixxie
@gayleforman Ice cream cake?

gayleforman
@Editrixxie Yes. In honor of Herman. He was lactose intolerant and prone to frozen brain.

Editrixxie

@gayleforman Phew, thought it was because you are glad he's dead.

gayleforman

@Editrixxie Not glad. Overjoyed. I'll dance on his grave. Do a polka, a pogo, a . . . you fill in the blank, you're my editor.

BrokkenRecord

@gayleforman @Editrixxie: A pachanga. A paso doble. A pole dance.

gayleforman

@BrokkenRecord @Editrixxie: I appreciate the alliteration but I'd NEVER pole dance on Herman's grave. Wouldn't give him the satisfaction. And Eww!

AuthorsLTD

Maybe @gayleforman should cease with snide remarks about the murder of Herman Q. Mildew in light of her likely role.

gayleforman

WTF? RT @AuthorsLTD "Maybe gayleforman should cease w snide remarks about the murder of HQM in light of her role." My ROLE?

BrokkenRecord

@gayleforman Well, you did publicly threaten to kill him when he put that vampire on your book jacket.

gayleforman

It was a middle-grade coming-of-age book about chess

geniuses, @BrokkenRecord! It was craven to put vampires on it, right, @Editrixxie?

Editrixxie
@gayleforman @BrokkenRecord I would never do that.

gayleforman
@Editrixxie @BrokkenRecord And that's why I left Papyrus Publishers and Herman and am refusing to publicize Pawns of the Night. #WorstTitleEver

Editrixxie
@gayleforman I promise I will never foist a terrible title/ cover on you to sell books.

gayleforman
Mwah, @Editrixxie. And besides, @BrokkenRecord: That tweet was like a year ago: Who pays attention to that shit?

AuthorsLTD
RT @gayleforman: "If I ever see Herman Q. Mildew again, I will put an ice pick through his beady little eyes."

lvngmybooks
RT@ AuthorsLTD RT @gayleforman: "If I ever see Herman Q. Mildew again, I will put an ice pick through his beady little eyes."

yaReadathon
RT@ AuthorsLTD RT @gayleforman: "If I ever see Herman Q. Mildew again, I will put an ice pick through his beady little eyes."

13StoryBooks

RT@ AuthorsLTD RT @gayleforman: "If I ever see Herman Q. Mildew again, I will put an ice pick through his beady little eyes."

ramsbookramble

RT@ AuthorsLTD RT @gayleforman: "If I ever see Herman Q. Mildew again, I will put an ice pick through his beady little eyes."

woven_36

RT@ AuthorsLTD RT @gayleforman: "If I ever see Herman Q. Mildew again, I will put an ice pick through his beady little eyes."

nicole_seaLegg

RT@ AuthorsLTD RT @gayleforman: "If I ever see Herman Q. Mildew again, I will put an ice pick through his beady little eyes."

ValiceAlliance

RT@ AuthorsLTD RT @gayleforman: "If I ever see Herman Q. Mildew again, I will put an ice pick through his beady little eyes."

gayleforman

Oh, no, that Authors Limited bitch did not just retweet that all over the place, @Editrixxie, @BrokkenRecord.

Editrixxie

@gayleforman @BrokkenRecord Oh, yes she did. How did she even find that? Don't old tweets go somewhere to die?

BrokkenRecord
@Editrixxie @gayleforman They live in yr profile. You also blogged that you want to drink his blood in a Slurpee cup.
http://www.gayleforman.com/?p=3020

gayleforman
@BrokkenRecord Christ, take that down, Paul!!!!!!! It's embarrassing. The Breaking Dawn reference is so obvious!

BrokkenRecord
@gayleforman Sorry. ;(. It's done.

Fangirlywhirly
I am soliciting books or manuscript critiques to auction off to raise money for the @gayleforman defense fund. Please donate now!

Wwwriterbabes
Support @gayleforman's murder defense. Choose your #twibbon here.

gayleforman
@BrokkenRecord @Editrixxie: HFS! I'm DMing you NOW!

Direct Message BrokkenRecord

gayleforman
OK, this is starting to freak me out. I didn't kill Herman w/ an ice pick! I don't even know what an ice pick is! What do you use it for?

gayleforman
I have always had ice cube trays. I hate Twitter. Can't we just go back to the old-fashioned days of email, please?

Direct Message Editrixxie

gayleforman
Do I need a lawyer?

BrokkenRecord
Um, @gayleforman, @Editrixxie #gayleformanicepickkiller is totally trending right now.

gayleforman
@BrokkenRecord, @Editrixxie: BUT I DIDN'T KILL ANYONE.

gayleforman
Attention, Twitter: I DID NOT KILL HERMAN Q. MILDEW.

gayleforman
@BrokkenRecord @Editrixxie: Wait, I'm trending . . .?

PapyrusBooks
Check out #gayleformanicepickkiller's new thriller about chess, middle school, murder and intrigue. Pawns of the Night!

Direct Message Editrixxie

gayleforman
What is going on? Why is my old publisher, Papyrus, also publicizing me as a murderer?

Editrixxie
Your Amazon #s for Pawns just shot up, that's why . . . hang on.

gayleforman
Also, in Pawns, no one gets murdered. Someone's gerbil dies, but that hardly counts.

Editrixxie
I've got sales here and they want to repackage Summer Stage as a murder mystery.

Editrixxie
Shoot a cover w a Slurpee cup with blood on the cover. Image is already iconic. Futz with title. Creep it out.

gayleforman
But it's a book about girls at a performing arts summer camp! This is just the kind of crap Herman pulled! You promised.

Editrixxie
I know. It's sales. Don't threaten to kill me. Actually, on second thought . . .

gayleforman
Not funny, Trix!

Editrixxie
THIS is funny: Yr Amazon numbers for Pawns are under one hundred and pre-sales for Summer Stage are in the mid-one hundreds.

gayleforman
!!!!WTF???

Editrixxie
You SURE you didn't kill Herman?

gayleforman
I gotta go. My Twitter feed is out of control.

Fanygirlywhirly
We have raised over $5,000 for the @gayleforman defense fund because we believe she's innocent. #gayleformanice-pickkiller

Wwwrtiergirls
Show yr support for @gayleforman with a Twibbon. #gayleformanicepickkiller

IndianaStateWomensPrison
@gayleforman We support you. Can't let the bastards take advantage. Also, can u send books to our library, please? #gayleformanicepickkiller

WallStreetJournal
@gayleforman We're doing an article about HQ Mildew & depravity in publishing. Plz DM us your email to set up interview & photo shoot.

gayleforman
@WSJ Sure. I just did. #gayelformanicepickkiller

END

Aimee Friedman

I was on my way to kill him, but I got waylaid.

Let me back up a few paces. Herman Q. Mildew (he once sneeringly told me the Q stood for Quixote, as in Don, but I remain doubtful) wasn't always my editor. I was unceremoniously thrust under his stewardship after my longtime editor, the warm and lovely Amelia B. Merriweather, was fired (by Herman) for putting one-too-many smiley faces in the margins of a manuscript. Needless to say, I was predisposed to hate him.

By way of introduction, Herman offered to treat me to lunch (spoiler: I ended up paying). Before we met, he emailed to ask me if I had aversions to any type of food. I was surprised by his thoughtfulness; Amelia, who never spoke ill of anyone, had on occasion blurted out how "emotionally constipated" her boss Herman was (she would then turn cherry red, apologize, and hand me a cupcake).

Just one, I wrote from my perch at my kitchen table, which doubled as my writing desk. *I can't stand cheese. Parmesan, pecorino, pepper jack, blue, Roquefort, Stilton, and Taleggio, too—please, none of these.*

Little did I know that Herman Mildew lived for cheese—the stinkier, the better. And little did I know that the restaurant he selected—a trendy little Soho spot slyly called Curds & Way—had nothing else on the menu but macaroni and cheese in a million different varieties, but none, alas, without cheese. While Herman dug greedily into his reeking plate of mac n' Limburger, I tried in vain to hold my breath and sip my water at the same time.

"I took the liberty," Herman told me, chewing with his mouth wide open, "of going through Amelia's files on you and reading your previous novels. And I have to say, I found your books—" he took a breath, like an actor about to launch into a monologue—"facile, boring, inconsequential, silly, with the purplest of prose and the flattest of characters, and oh, yes." He stabbed his fork into a macaroni elbow with finality. "The covers are hideous."

I sat there, slack jawed, almost too stunned to feel the tears in my eyes. I wondered how we looked to the rest of the restaurant: a vile little man in a natty suit and a hat, twirling his expensive glass of wine, while across from him slumped a hungry young woman wearing a (wasted) fancy new dress and a stricken expression. Before I could begin to recover and defend myself, he launched a fresh attack.

"And your latest proposal?" he guffawed. "A *cookbook* for young adults? Pray tell, what does someone with your obviously *limited* palate—" he gestured to a string of Limburger hanging off his bottom lip—"know about cooking?"

I ground my teeth together, my shock and humiliation giving way to anger. "My dislike of cheese notwithstanding, I am quite the foodie," I spat. "I make a mean lamb stew, an unforgettable coq au vin, and even an impressive veggie burger. If you'd give me a chance to prove—"

"Fine," Herman snarled, tossing his fork down and sending a glob of cheese onto my pretty plaid dress. "In a month's time, I'm hosting a potluck dinner party at my home. I was going to invite only literary luminaries, intellectuals, and the brightest minds of the generation, but I suppose *you* can come, too." He looked down his crooked nose at me. "Make me one of your so-called 'impressive' dishes, and I'll see if I can be persuaded to let you scribble a cookbook."

And with that, he was gone, leaving me with the hefty bill and a lingering sense of rage, despair, and doom.

For the next month, Herman continued to belittle me. When I called to inquire about the sales of my most recent novel (my agent had come down with a rare but severe case of avian flu and was incommunicado), Herman let out a braying laugh and said I was responsible for the U.S. economic downturn. Sometimes, for no reason at all, he'd send me a video of a goat defecating, and the subject heading would be "Your career." He signed me up for Cheese of the Week club, and I began receiving nausea-inducing packages every Monday. Most evenings, he'd call me and ramble on about himself for hours (this was when he shared his questionable middle name, and also that he had planted hidden video cameras in the homes of all his authors) while tossing in random insults and threats ("I'd bury you alive if I had the resources!") just to make sure I was listening.

The worst part was, I had no one to turn to. My fiancé, Boris, had recently left me for the world's most famous supermodel/unicyclist. My parents had moved to the wilds of Alaska in a misguided attempt to live out their senior years adventurously. My cat, Madame Bovary, had died after eating one of my ineffective mousetraps. I tried to reach out to other authors who were suffering at the hands of Herman

Mildew, but they were each too numb with self-hatred and paranoia to respond. Usually, cooking calmed my nerves when writing didn't, but each time I turned on the stove, my hands would tremble and my spirit would sag, and I'd have to order in a cheese-less pizza.

I have always been the over-sensitive, mildly unstable sort—I suppose all writers and artists have that tendency. That shouldn't excuse me from ultimately succumbing to the call of crime, but one has to understand, by the day of Herman Mildew's dinner party, I had hit rock bottom.

I arose that morning planning to make my delicious lamb stew—the dish that would show my evil editor that I was in fact capable of authoring a wonderful cookbook. I stood in my kitchen, armed with the ingredients: golden potatoes in a heap on the counter, bright orange carrots in a cheerful bundle, a bouquet of bay leaves, an array of spices, and a leg of lamb waiting in the freezer. But I felt more frozen than that lamb—my inspiration was sapped and my will was broken.

Then, suddenly, a dark, slithery idea took hold. *No*, I thought, *that would be so wrong*. But also, somehow, all too right. Before I could second guess myself, I threw on my black woolen poncho, black hat, and sunglasses, and crept out of my apartment.

Glancing left and right, I stole across the street and down the block to the shady little hardware store on the corner. They already knew me there due to my mouse problems, so the man behind the counter barely raised an eyebrow when I requested a sack of rat poison. I slid my money toward him, then snuck out of the store, hiding the purchase against my chest.

Back at my apartment, I got to work with the kind of frenzied intensity I usually reserved for past-deadline writing or a midnight game of Angry Birds. I tied a bandana around my mouth and nose so I wouldn't have to smell the Cheese of the Week cheeses as I took them out to cook. I'd stashed them all in my fridge, hoping I could use them someday for the mousetraps. Instead, I put them to better use: I made a big, bubbling pot of cheese fondue especially for Mr. Herman Quixote Mildew. I added salt, pepper, and finally, the contents of the sack of rat poison. I felt a twinge of remorse, but then the feelings of humiliation came rushing back at me and I stirred the concoction heartily. I turned the heat off the stove, plopped a lid on the pot, and prepared to go.

Now the trick was to ensure that Herman, and *only* Herman ate the fondue—I didn't want to kill off any innocent literary luminaries. My plan was to get him alone in his kitchen before the party commenced and ask him—in a humble, plaintive tone—if he'd do me the honor of tasting my contribution. He'd surely scoff and make some remark about my meager talents, but no doubt he'd dunk a square of toast into the melted cheese and pop the poisoned treat into his mouth. Then, hopefully he'd expire within minutes, I'd escape with the offending dish, and the dinner party would be cancelled when the butler found his body.

But what if Herman were somehow immune to rat poison? It seemed likely, given how toxic his internal organs must have been. So at the last minute, I grabbed the heavy, frozen leg of lamb from my freezer. I stashed it inside my nifty cooler/tote bag. That way, if the poison didn't get my editor, I'd brain him over the head with the lamb.

Food had been my introduction to Herman, and food would bring about his demise.

With the cooler/tote on my shoulder and the pot of deadly fondue in my gloved hands, I tiptoed out onto the street.

Night had fallen, and the city was blanketed in soft, treacherous darkness. My heart was pounding and my palms were clammy as I took back alleys and empty avenues toward Herman's luxurious town house. Dressed in head-to-toe black, I hoped I was invisible as a ghost. Once, a taxicab sped by, but I ducked behind The Old Abandoned Pickle Factory until it had passed. Then I went on my furtive way again.

I was a block away from my destination when I heard footsteps behind me. *Herman!* I thought and felt a knife-slice of fear in my belly. I remembered his offhand remark about putting hidden cameras in his authors' apartments: could it be that he had seen what I had done to the fondue? My teeth chattering, I changed direction and swerved into another alley. I tried to walk as fast as my high heels would allow. The weight of the heavy, hot pot made my arms ache.

Almost immediately, the sound of determined footsteps echoed once again, coming closer and quicker. I was being chased. I began to run, my breath coming in sharp huffs and the fondue pot threatening to slip from my grip.

Before I could reach the end of the alley, someone tackled me from behind. I fell to my knees, the pot of fondue landing on the pavement with a clang. I whirled around to confront my attacker and reached into my bag for the leg of lamb. . . .

"Amelia?" I gasped as a sliver of moonlight revealed the face of my beloved former editor. She sat behind me, also out of breath, her halo of golden curls disheveled.

"I had to stop you," she said mournfully. "I know what you were going to do. I was worried when I heard Herman took you on as an author, and so I've been stalking—er, observing you—just hanging around outside your building to make sure you were okay."

"I'm not okay," I whispered, my lower lip trembling. A coldness settled in my stomach. Had I really been on my way to commit such a heinous act?

Amelia nodded sagely. "I saw you buy that rat poison today. And I knew Herman's dinner party was tonight: he'd been boasting about it on Twitter. I put two and two together, and decided to catch up to you before you made a horrible mistake."

As I sat in the dank alleyway, the realization of what I'd been about to do sunk in. *Me, a murderer?* It didn't make any sense. I wasn't a cold-blooded killer. I was a writer and an amateur chef. Herman Mildew had driven me to the brink of madness, but that didn't mean I had to tumble over the edge. I could have been nabbed by the police to spend the rest of my days in prison—or worse, tortured by my own guilty conscience. I blinked at Amelia, who was watching me with a mix of terror and hopefulness.

"You're right," I finally sobbed, embracing her. "I don't know what I was thinking. Madame Bovary died, and Boris left, and you were fired, and Herman took me to a cheese-only restaurant. . . ."

"I understand," Amelia said soothingly, stroking my hair.

"Thank you," I added, pulling back to gaze at her soberly. "You saved my life."

"And Herman's," she said ruefully. "Though, trust me, I'd bet you're far from being the only author who'd love to write his gruesome ending."

Amelia helped me to my feet and we dumped the poisonous fondue pot into the nearest garbage can. She walked me back to my apartment, where she promptly put me to bed, cleaned my kitchen, and fixed me a batch of her famous cupcakes. As I shivered under my blankets, I managed to croak out that since she was out of a job, maybe the two of us could collaborate on the cookbook together, and look for a different publisher. Amelia said that was a good idea.

Days passed, and I felt myself recovering. Though Herman continued to bombard me with mocking emails and demanded to know why I hadn't come to his party, I felt immune to his wickedness. I had gazed into the maw of my own darkness, and now knew I could never attempt something so heartless. With Amelia's assistance, I began cooking and writing again. In fact, I hardly gave much thought to Herman at all—until the invitation arrived.

Herman wanted me at The Old Abandoned Pickle Factory? This seemed like the kind of gathering I *couldn't* avoid; Herman's threat to reveal my secrets to the world made me wonder all over again if he had in fact spied on me, and seen my attempt to poison him. I figured I had to show up, if only to face that fear.

So here I am, you see, meaning no ill will toward the man of the hour. And it is just by accident that I have a frozen leg of lamb on my person—after the trauma of that night in the alley, I forgot to remove it from my handy cooler/tote bag. I certainly never brought it along with the intention to *harm* Herman. . . .

And the bag of rat poison someone may have seen me purchasing again this morning? Well, that was for my rodent problem at home, of course. It's very difficult to catch mice without the help of Madame Bovary, after all.

```
Margaux Froley
```

Why didn't I even *attend* Mr. Mildew's party at The Old Abandoned Pickle Factory?

You'd have to know a little more about Mr. Mildew before I could answer that question.

It was no surprise that Mr. Mildew would call all his writers and illustrators to meet him there. He loved that place. We all know that Herman loved pickles more than, well, more than he loved pickles. He could eat pickles until every jar within a five-mile radius was empty. And that was just to give the jars still pickling new pickles time to catch up with his appetite. Plus, he rarely traveled outside his five-mile radius because he knew the best pickles were from The Old Abandoned Pickle Factory.

But it wasn't always The Old Abandoned Pickle Factory. No, that place has more meaning than that. For Mr. Mildew, The Old Abandoned Pickle Factory was his throne, his seat of triumph, his sovereign land, his tour de force, his encore presentation, his "a very special episode" of Herman Mildew, his master stroke. I should know, you see, because he bought The Old Abandoned Pickle Factory from my father, Augustus Old.

Father told me that he built that factory before I was born. Back then it was just The Old Pickle Factory. Herman used to be our neighbor, you see. He watched the factory go up, plank by plank, pickle by pickle, from his bathroom window. It was clear from the minute Father noticed Herman sitting on his front porch next door, eating a jar of pickles for dinner (as he was known to do) and staring across the street, that Herman had his eye on The Old Pickle Factory.

Father was quickly coronated The Pickle King. He loved that factory almost as much as he loved me. With just the two of us in the house when I was growing up (Mother ran away with the Sauerkraut Kraut when I was a toddler), Father and I were particularly close. When I wanted a pony, I just had to ask politely ("I want a pony! Now!"), and there was a pony waiting outside for me the next day. When I wanted to go ice skating in July ("I want my own ice skating rink! Now!"), my father managed to build me a personal rink inside the factory. When I wanted to go to a Swiss boarding school, he sent me. When I didn't like Switzerland (too much skiing) and instead thought I'd give Australia a go, he footed the bill ("I want to go to Australia! Now!"). And when I wanted to be a Great American Author (we'd of course hire a ghost writer so I didn't have to do any of that ghastly writing, and then put my name on the cover and take a glamorous photo for the book jacket), Father called Mr. Mildew.

But Mildew drove a hard bargain. Money wouldn't do. Fame didn't tempt him. No, not Herman. He claimed to be above fame.

So when Father called, Mr. Mildew calmly said he would make me the next Great American Author, but only if Father gave him the pickle factory. The shiny, clean, successful, Old Pickle Factory. Father didn't have a choice between my hopes and dreams ("I want to be a famous book author! Now!) and Mr. Mildew's offer. He handed the keys to the factory over to Mr. Mildew, and my ghostwriter got started on my Great American Novel.

Mr. Mildew took over the factory and immediately it stopped selling pickles. Instead, he built himself a grand pickle tasting room with butlers (butlers!) holding trays of different scented, and spiced, and pickled, and canned, and jarred, and frozen, and burnt, and fried, and battered, and boiled, pickles! So many pickles! And all were pickled for the sole purpose of being eaten by Mr. Herman Mildew.

Soon Mr. Mildew couldn't keep up with his butler payments; there were so many butlers, you see. And the factory became neglected with Mr. Mildew spending all his time eating the pickles instead of hiring anyone to make more pickles. Mr. Mildew didn't love the factory like Father did. He didn't love every plank of wood, every nail, every empty jar and brine mixture. It didn't surprise anyone when Mr. Mildew stopped making pickles completely and only used the factory for his swanky book parties, which all his writers felt obligated to attend.

It didn't take long for Father to slip into a deep depression, which turned into a deep flu, then a deep bout of pneumonia, and then a deep coma. Just before he died, Father opened his eyes and squeezed my hand. "I want you to get the pickle factory back from Mildew. Now!"

Never had I had more purpose in my life. Never had I had more rage at the vicious, vile, vain, verboten, vitriolic, vociferous, vexing, violent villain, Mr. Herman Mildew.

Another word appeared while I was flipping through the V section of my thesaurus: victim. Yes, *victim*.

Not that I did anything about it, mind you. How Mr. Mildew died of course had nothing to do with me. Yes, he invited me to that party, and yes, it piqued a certain murderous vein in me, that he would dare to have a party in the factory while my father was buried on the edge of our property so he could gaze at his beloved factory even in the afterlife. But, the mere idea that Mr. Mildew was found in a vat of pepper-spiced brine, floating and green like the horrible pickle he was, is just wretched. What? Oh, you didn't release the information about how he was killed? How did I know that?

Well, you can see The Old Pickle Factory from my house. And did you notice it started making pickles again?

Claudia Gabel

Today was the first time I set foot in my editor's cluttered, swiss-cheese-smelling office. I'd heard he was a hard man to work for, but I didn't expect to see this. The executive assistant was sobbing at her desk as she typed on her computer. The editor-in-chief was locked inside a conference room, surrounded by manuscripts and drinking straight from an economy-sized Maalox bottle. The managing editor was scribbling like mad on a dry erase board and repeatedly muttering this sentence to herself: "I am not a dimwitted moron! I am NOT a dimwitted moron!"

I almost turned around and walked right out the door. Looking back, that would have been the smart, sensible thing to do. But at that moment in time, the two bounced rent checks in my wallet outranked smart and sensible decisions, so I accepted Mr. Mildew's offer of temping as his filing clerk until my next advance check came in, which my best guess was the year 2019. My next novel was an 874-page epic, Homeresque poem/romance for teens set on a planet named Sexagon, and though Mildew thought it was my most brilliant piece of work thus far, it was also far from being finished.

Filing seemed like an easy job, and I was prepared for it to be pretty boring and mundane. Given how unstable everyone seemed to be at Mildew Central, I was actually happy to learn that I would be working inside a window-less, dusty room for eight hours a day with barely any human contact at all. I thought I was just going to put invoices in manila folders and sort P&L reports until my fingers bled.

I had no idea then that being cast down to the Mildew archives would rock my world.

I was on my fifth hour of sifting through production esti-mates when I stumbled across it: a memo dated nine months ago from Mildew to his staff. He was notifying them that he was canceling my "horrid, absurd joke of a book." My heart felt like it was being tied up with barbed wire. Nine months?! Horrid, absurd joke?! This couldn't be real. The day before, he told me how proud he was of *Worm Hole: A Love Story.* He told me it was my ticket to stardom!

I kicked over a box of papers and watched them fall into a messy pile on the floor before storming out of the room and going to confront his people with this atrocity. When I got there, his editor-in-chief was dancing with the managing editor on top of Mildew's desk as loud music erupted from the executive assistant's computer speakers. They were all holding glasses of champagne and doing the macarena and cheering like they'd just won the lotto.

"I want to speak to Mr. Mildew—NOW!" I screamed over the sweet Latin-inspired groove.

"Sorry, you can't!" replied his editor-in-chief, giddily.

"Why not? This is urgent!" I demanded.

"He's dead!" his assistant said, laughing along with her two cohorts.

The only thing I'm guilty of, dear readers, is not being sad when I heard the news. Oh, and teaching his staff how to do the macarena properly after finishing my own glass of champagne.

But that's it. Now if you don't mind, I'd like to get back to my horrid, absurd joke of a book.

Michelle Gagnon

Honestly, I don't even know why I'm here. I mean, I barely knew Mildew. Hey, that rhymes. Get it? Knew, Mildew?

No, I'm not nervous. Why, do I seem nervous? In case you're wondering, I'm not the kind of person who makes bad jokes when I'm stressed. I make them all the time, no matter what kind of mood I'm in. Ask anyone who knows me, they'll back me up on that. That was actually one of my better jokes. Can I borrow your notebook? I want to write it down so I can remember it for later.

Fine, keep your little notebook. I'll write it on my hand. I've already got my grocery list there anyway, a little more ink won't hurt. Anyway, I was going to the pickle factory for a completely different reason that night. No, I won't tell you why, it's personal. What do you mean, I have to tell you? Last I checked this was America, muchacho, and where I decide to go at 8 P.M. on a Tuesday is really none of your. . . .

Oh, really? So it's going to be like that, is it? No, I don't want to call my lawyer. Actually, I kind of do, but he's not taking my calls anymore. Long story, but it basically involved a llama and a terrarium. We've all been there, right?

Fine. Yeah, I was at the pickle place. But like I said, it had nothing to do with Mildew, or any of those other people. I was there on a completely unrelated errand, so you can imagine my shock when the doors creaked open and I was confronted with that hideous crowd of misfits. I mean, there I was, just trying to collect some special vinegar to add to my custom facial cream. That's right, I make my own cream. You know why? Because no one, and I mean no one, has yet to match the hydrating, pore-shrinking, anti-aging benefits of what I concoct on my own. You have no idea how incredibly beneficial the appropriate combination of pickle juice, vinegar, and tomato paste can be for your skin. Guess my age. No, don't check your precious little notebook, that's cheating. Just guess. What? Forty-two? Now you're just messing with me. No way do I look a day over thirty, and you know it. Wipe that smirk off your face.

All right, where was I . . . right, the pickle place. Well, I saw a bunch of miscreants lurking there, and knew right away that getting involved would be a mistake. I mean they looked like they were a couple of flaming torches and pitchforks away from storming a castle. So I turned to leave, only to discover that the way was blocked by a shadowy figure in a long trench coat.

I panicked. Ahead was an angry mob, and behind me was a guy who could have doubled as Hagrid in those *Harry Potter* flicks. Spotting a steel ladder to my left, I raced up it. I'm not in the kind of shape I used to be in, back when I won the JV trophy for hurtling—no, that's not a misspelling, it's "hurles" with a "t." Just like hurdling, but instead of jumping over metal you run while throwing things. It is too a real sport. What, you prefer curling? I swear, a couple thousand more signatures on my petition, and you'll be cheering for the world's top hurtlers in the next Olympics. Which reminds me, if you wouldn't mind signing right here. . . .

Later, then. I can give you a demonstration if you like. Of course I know it's unnecessary, and I'm not limbered up anyway, but if you've never experienced hurtling, you really don't know what you're missing.

You're kind of pushy, anyone ever tell you that? One track mind, too. Not me, my brain is constantly in motion, I've got at least a dozen things hurtling around in there at any given moment.

All right, fine. I won't use the word hurtling anymore. Although I can't exactly promise something like that, what if it just comes up naturally in the course of our conversation? You'd be surprised by how appropriate that term is for a slew of different things.

Sheesh, you're sensitive. You should take something for that headache, rubbing your temples doesn't really help. You know what would? A good, strong dose of pickle juice mixed with castor oil. I swear by it. Keeps the constitution regular.

Right, Tuesday night. Hey, I want to get out of here just as badly as you do. Maybe even more—I've got a salisbury steak dinner at home with my name on it. And I mean that literally, because if I don't mark things my squatter eats them. Not just food, either. I caught him downing my anti-aging cream by the spoonful just the other day.

Anyway, I reached the top of the ladder and found myself on a narrow catwalk suspended above the crowd, with a perfect view of the scene below. I searched frantically for an escape route, but it must have been bottling week at the plant, and the far end was blocked by stacks of boxes filled with what I'm guessing were jars. They smelled pretty awful, though, come to think of it, and some sort of vile fluid was seeping out the sides . . . no, it definitely was not vinegar, if there's one smell I know well, it's that. Whatever was in there had nothing to do with pickling. Or hurtling.

Sorry. Couldn't resist.

I had just about resigned myself to hunkering down for the night when a scream split the air. I looked down and saw the crowd scatter, dividing around a spreading pool of red. You know that story about the Red Sea parting? Like that, but without the guy with the long beard. Although maybe there was a guy with a beard, now that I think about it. Or a lady who hadn't been waxed in a while. Kind of tough to tell from that height.

Before I could process what I was seeing, something razor sharp zinged right past my forehead, taking a chunk of my hair with it and nicking my ear. See? Not that side— and no, I don't go to Supercuts, I paid forty whole dollars for this look, thank you very much. And now it's ruined, thanks to some Jackie Chan wannabe with a set of throwing stars.

I did what any sane, rational human being would do. I scrambled over the boxes, getting covered with some sort of nasty crud in the process. Came out of there smelling worse than Lindsay Lohan after a week of volunteering in the morgue, and the whole time these things were zooming through the air around me. I was lucky to escape with my life. Just past the boxes was a door to the outside. I slammed through it, setting off the emergency alarm, and scrambled down a fire escape, praying the whole time that none of those lethal weapons had pierced my vintage acid-washed denims. Fifty dollars on eBay, in case you're interested. But don't bid against me, my username is "picklejuicebeauty."

I think it's safe to say that no one has ever suffered so much for a jar of homemade face cream.

Anyway, that's all I saw. Can I go now? I'm doing a home facial tonight and don't want to miss the beginning of that new *Housewives* show. I hear it's going to be hurtling. As in, awesome. See? Like I said, it fits virtually any situation.

Adam Gidwitz

I did not kill Herman Mildew.

The alley was not dark. There was no unmarked steel door under the buzzing, phosphorescent lamp. I did not have to strain my eyes to read the scrawled note I held, nor was the handwriting scratchy and spidery, skittering across the page in ferocious bursts. In the flickering light, I did not read the words:

My Dearest Adam,

Your manuscript has raised a few questions that I would love to discuss with you. Might it be convenient to meet somewhere? Perhaps the Central Gowanus Sausage Processing Plant? Shall we say two? In the morning? There is a door in the alley off 3rd Street. Would you be kind enough to go in? Up the stairs to level two? Overlooking the grinding vat? Yes? Lovely.

Your devoted editor, HM

I did not examine the steel door, certainly did not reach for the handle, did not find it unlocked—and would never, ever, have leaned against it and pushed. The door did not screech and scrape against the pavement, nor did its eerie echo ricochet down the empty alley. I certainly would never have even considered poking my head into the darkness of the Central Gowanus Sausage Processing Plant and, after having cursed his devilish name for the millionth time, made my way into the whirring darkness.

As everyone knows, Herman Mildew is one of the most universally respected, best-beloved editors in the business of making books for young people. A single smile from him in a crowded restaurant will make a man's reputation. Well, hypothetically. If Herman Mildew has ever smiled, I don't believe it has been reported. His authors are devoted to him. One may even say slavishly devoted to him. Which is probably accounted for by the contracts he writes for them, which are modeled—quite explicitly—on 18th century writs of human bondage. There are few editors with so keen an eye and such exacting standards.

And you accuse me of killing a legend like Herman Mildew?

The interior of the processing plant was not all hulking, shadowy machines. The grinding did not cause the concrete floor to shake, nor did the sounds of gristle getting caught in blades make my heart stutter. I did not scan the gloom for stairs, did not turn and climb them with tight knees and white lips and dilated pupils. My position was not made obvious by my clanking footsteps to whoever awaited me on the second floor, overlooking the enormous sausage grinder. I was not afraid.

I did not nearly jump out of my skin when, huddled by the railing, I glimpsed a bent, sinister, shadowy form.

I did not say, "Mildew?"

The bent shape did not approach. It was not carrying an accordion file exactly the size of my manuscript. And when it stepped into a square of moonlight that shone through a skylight in the roof, it definitely, absolutely, without any doubt whatsoever, did NOT possess the leering evil face of Herman Mildew.

"Hello, Adam," the man who was not there and certainly was not Herman Mildew did not say.

My face did not contort as if I had just eaten a fistful of rancid meat.

Herman Mildew did not continue toward me, with his free arm outstretched. I did not freeze, did not panic, did not *not* know what was happening. As he did not put his arm around my neck, I did not stiffen. Nor did I hear with an acute awareness animal meat being processed in the black void below.

He did not pull my head down to his goblin-like level, did not raise my manuscript until it was just below my nose, and did not ferociously say, "Sniff."

"What?" I did not reply.

"I said sniff, Adam."

I did not sniff.

"Do you smell that?" he did not ask me.

"I don't know, Herman."

"Sniff, dammit!" he did not growl. I did not sniff. "Do you smell it now?"

"Yes, Herman."

"Do you know what that is, Adam?"

"No, Herman."

"That is the stench of failure. It makes me sick. It is wafting, of course, from the detritus you call a manuscript." He did not bring his pock-marked, cratered, goblin-like face right up to mine, did not grin wickedly, and did not hiss, "You are over, Gidwitz."

None of the following happened:

I felt a force like a tidal wave build and rise through my heart, my chest, my shoulders, my face. I flung my arms against the bent form of the editor who was intent on ruining my livelihood, my future, my very life. He stumbled back, and I grabbed him by the collar and ran at him, pushing him before me until he was up against the railing, and the giant vat of a meat grinder hummed hungrily below him. My face was inches, centimeters, millimeters from his. His nostrils were flared, his breath smelled of pickled haddock. I held him there. And then Herman Mildew did what Herman Mildew does. What makes him Herman Mildew. He said, "Congratulations, Adam. This is the first time you've ever created suspense."

I could have thrown him over the railing. But I didn't. Because none of the above ever happened.

And then I did not pick up my manuscript, did not slip down the stairs, past the mechanical behemoths, did not listen once more for the sickening sound of a blade caught on gristle (was it the gristle of Herman Mildew? No. No, it was not.) and did not push out of the door and into the alley. I certainly did not go straight to a twenty-four-hour copy and package shop. I would never have used a public computer to look up the address of a rival publishing company. And I am sick at the disgusting insinuation that I would immediately post my manuscript to that rival publisher—with a note that I was now free from all contractual obligations and was wondering if they were interested in a love story between a dog and a dinosaur.

Indeed, as this written testimony makes redundantly clear: I could not have, would never have, and could not even *imagine* killing Herman Mildew.

Anna Godbersen

Of course I hated Herman Mildew. Everybody did.

But, you know, there are those of us who were with him in the old days, when the Story Factory was young and brash, when everybody wanted to work for him. Nobody ever seemed to need sleep back then, and there were parties every night, and in the wild-eyed mornings we would go for a coffee (no one had heard of a cardamom squash flower latté in those days; we would have laughed you off the planet if you showed up with one of those things), and then go to the movies, and afterward debate 'art' and 'life' and the 'meaning of it all' in rugged cafés.

Those of us who were around in that era can remember Mildew as he was—a gorgeous tyrant. A sublime bully. The Muhammad Ali of publishing. He looked like Warren Beatty, he really did, and I mean *Shampoo*-era Warren Beatty. In those days nobody had time to eat. It was before Mildew discovered cheese. It was before the XXXXL pants, before his ninth marriage crumbled like an aged bleu over a dusky whole wheat cracker.

Don't get me wrong. We hated him then, too. He was always dissatisfied, always demanding more. It was a bad day when the endings came out wrong, when somebody screwed up and the boy didn't get the girl. It was happy endings, or heads would roll. On those days, he used to storm through the typing pool with his shirt off—and you know he always had a thing going with at least two of the secretaries. That was part of his legend; he used to play them off each other! There were catfights. I broke some up, and I won't lie to you—this is all on the level—I pulled some hair in my time. And those were the days when a girl had her hair blown out three times a week!

Oh, he was terrible to the women. But he was worse to the men. He used to throw manuscripts at their heads. "Your story is an abyss!" he would yell, so that everyone could hear it, in all the cubicles, in every corner of the Story Factory. This one time we're moving around the story blocks in the story lab, and the big shot writer of the moment is overseeing all this very pompously (I'm taking notes; women weren't thought of as writers in those days), and Mildew stands up. And he takes his piece of chalk. And very slowly he draws a straight line all the way across the board. "That," he says, as he tosses his chalk on the ground for somebody else to pick up (probably me), "That's your story."

But despite all that, he cared, he really did. Like when Agnes, one of the secretaries, came in with her son Alsop. He had these messed up teeth—and we made pennies then, we really did—and Mildew sees this kid, this gangly buck-toothed kid, and his mother, all she wants is for him to have a fair shot like everybody else. And Mildew has tears in his eyes. *Tears.* And pretty soon the rumor went around; he'd paid for his own dentist to do the whole job. And you know what? Alsop ended up an Abercrombie model. That kid still sends me a Christmas card every year, of himself in jeans, and I tell you, he only gets better looking with time. That was Mildew's great gift, his fatal flaw, even when he was smashing up the office furniture: all he wanted was to be adored.

Most of us got out eventually. It just became too crazy. Some became mathematicians, some became carpenter's wives. Me, I fell in love with an artichoke farmer and then I went on the road with his brother, who was in this punk rock band. Then I found God. Then pagan dance. Then Jah. Then yoga. And—

Would you re-light my cigarette, doll? Thanks.

Anyway. The place I ended up for years and years was this little ashram in Texas. And I spent twenty-seven hours standing on my head, and I saw colors that aren't recognized by the "traditional" rainbow, and I bonded with the medicine woman I was four lifetimes ago, and I realized, you know what? There's no such thing as a happy ending. Or a sad one, either. Life is just life, and every wonder is an end in itself, and nothing matters, not really. So after that I got very depressed. And in my depression I kept seeing Mildew. Mildew! MILDEW.

Then, one day, I received an invitation from the mighty man himself.

I looked at his name engraved on that ivory cardstock, and I thought, *If I do one thing right on this earth, I'm going to get through to Mildew.* I'm going to tell him: *I remember that beautiful, lithe spirit of yours.* I'll ask: *What happened to you, Mildew?* And, *How did you get so corrupt?* And then maybe, if he's receptive, if his eyes water the way I remember them watering during some particularly cornball movie, if

I see a flicker of emotion behind those big blues, maybe I'll finally confess, *I love you, Herman. For you. Not because of all the ways you were great, but for all the ways you weren't.* And then, if it's going really well, maybe I'll show him my manuscript. The one I had in the drawer all those years at the Story Factory when he thought I was just a typist whose affections were ripe for the toying. The manuscript about how it felt to be me as a girl, the one with the ending everybody always says makes no sense at all.

So it's true. I was there that awful night. Two days I rode the bus, and I walked the rest of the way from the Greyhound station in the rain. I sat in the Story Factory's sleek black lobby, where I waited for him to finish work. I had my manuscript in my purse and—sure, under that, a revolver I bought off a trucker at a rest stop. Because people react differently when confronted with the truth. Sometimes violently. A girl has to protect herself in this day and age. And— ha, ha, ha!—I don't know why I'm laughing. Everybody reacts differently, you know, to death and loss. Anyway, I waited and waited.

You can ask the doorman—we must have had about twenty cigarette breaks together, just like in the old days. I was there, but I wasn't there to kill him. I still think maybe I was the one who could have saved him. I waited, like I've always waited for Herman. But he never did show up.

John Green

From: John Green

Date: OMITTED DUE TO PENDING LITIGATION

Subject: Herman Q. Mildew

To: OMITTED DUE TO PENDING LITIGATION

There are so many reasons I couldn't have killed Mildew that I hardly even feel inclined to defend myself against the accusation. I don't live in New York; I harbored no ill will toward Mildew; and I do not have the physical constitution for violence, especially murderous violence. Who's making the accusation, anyway? Scieszka? Now, there's a murderer. I'm not accusing anyone of anything, of course, but I will note that Scieszka is bald, and that a 2004 study by Harvard University found that men with male pattern baldness are seven times more likely to kill literary editors than men with full and plush heads of hair. So allow me to submit to evidence Exhibit A, my majestic puff of hair. You can't deny my puff. It wasn't me.

Adele Griffin
and Lisa Brown

HOW COULD WE?

MURDERERS, YOU CALL US? WE BEG TO DIFFER.

◇◇◇◇◇◇◇◇◇◇◇◇◇◇◇

Yes, Lisa loves a crime. Yes, Adele loves a little blame–but only from the comfort of our suite at the Ritz. Why, here we are now. And with us, some Reasonable Doubt.

"We didn't, we couldn't, we'd **NEVER** *kill Mildew because..."*

1· Lisa saves her strychnine for family reunions.

2· The shih-tzu's dinner does not require homicide, merely gentle dismemberment.

3· Cute-wise, a pickled corpse's got nothing on a stuffed rat.

4· Adele is running out of places to stick editors.

5· We'll have plenty to eat once the monkey gets fat.

6· Adele's new jacket is lovely, but restrictive.

7· Our new window treatments preclude wandering.

8· Mrs. Mildew is way worse, & luckily we forgot where we put her.

9· Lisa's been preoccupied with sticking pins in all who call death to the picture book.

10· Besides, this case is solved. Stop pointing your fingers: the real killer's locked in our closet.

"Almost time for lights out, Mr. Willems."

Lev Grossman

That, sirrah? No, sirrah. That is not a sword. No.

Well, yes. That is a hilt, projecting up over my right shoulder. I would be a fool to deny it. It is indeed a hilt. Actually it's very awkward when I try to sit down.

Don't touch it! Don't. It is not for the likes of you, or, just for example, the likes of Herman Mildew, to touch.

Here. I will touch it for you.

Yes, I will pull up on the hilt. You'll see that it is attached to a blade, razor sharp, wrought of steel storm-cloud-grey, forged and tempered in the wine-dark blood of emperors. Well, one emperor. You can get a surprising amount of wine-dark blood out of one emperor, if you try, especially if he drank a lot of wine beforehand.

To be clear: *you* can't. But then you are not a *New York Times* bestselling fantasy novelist, like me. You're probably not a *New York Times* bestselling novelist *of any kind*. Once you are inducted into that elite society, let me tell you, the ancient secrets of efficiently ex-sanguinating emperors are secrets to you no longer.

There: it has come free of its scabbard. Hear how it sings faintly in the air. That is a song of bloodlust, a song such as you will not hear on Spotify, or indeed on any other online music service. For I told you the truth. This is not a sword.

This is a Sword of Legend.

You see what I did there.

Could I have slain Herman Mildew with this sword? Undoubtedly. It would have been no problem. I'm like, what, a twentieth-level paladin compared with him. Next to me he's like, I don't know, a kobold or something. An unarmored kobold who's like really fat and old. A kobold that's in a coma practically. I could have killed him that easily.

But I didn't.

When did I last see him? I saw him just yesterday, in that degraded hell pit that he called an office. Though it was a little hard to see him, because I'd brought the manuscript of my new book with me—a manuscript of such surpassing beauty that the very pages shone like the sun, and one must look away from them, or have one's eyes seared from their very sockets.

You wouldn't be seeing much after that, I can tell you. Not without any eyes.

But actually it was mostly hard to see him because my manuscript, a fantasy epic called "The Trilliad Lays of the Omni-Conch," took up most of the office. It's about 35 million words at this point. A lean 35 million words, mind you—seriously it reads like a 30-million-word book, easy.

I feel like the book shows a lot of artistic growth on my part, as a writer. It's far more epic than my last book, *Lonely Windsurfs the Badger-Lord*. Just for starters, there's way fewer badgers this time.

But would you believe it? Herman Mildew—that cur, that

wretch, that wretch-cur—told me it was too long. He told me to cut it down.

I told him that I'd already cut it. He told me to cut it more. I asked him do you cut rainbows? Do you cut panda bears and space-unicorns?

He said yes. Sometimes. When they're too long and boring.

I told him that to tell him the truth, I thought the book was already pretty lean. He told me it wasn't lean, in fact it was fat. I told him *he* was fat.

Then, yes, sure, I guess you could say it got a little ugly.

I told him I could not cut this book even if I possessed the Sword of Legend. He pointed out that I did in fact possess the Sword of Legend. I said OK, right, point taken, but I would never use the Sword of Legend for such a profane and frankly misguided purpose as this.

He said fine.

Herman opened his desk drawer and took out a sword of his own. I knew it for what it was. It was the Other Sword of Legend. He prepared to cut my book with it.

At this point I drew my own sword—the first, original Sword of Legend—and the fight was begun. In a trice he had donned the Black Mail of Otherwhere, which I guess he had in a different drawer. It was a big desk. I then conjured and hurled the Fire Spear of Nannerl Grimbrain. He parried with the Four-Times-Accursed Blackmace. It went on like that for a while. I winded the Horn of Babylon. He countered with some Forbidden Kung-Fu—he was actually pretty spry for a fat dude. And so on.

And then he made his mistake. Because I was wearing my favorite cologne, which is Cerruti 1881 pour Homme, which as I'm sure you've noticed features notes of sandalwood, bergamot, patchouli, and ylang-ylang. And everybody knows that the Thornwood Shield of the Underbramble has only one fatal weakness, and that weakness is ylang-ylang. I could have cloven straight through that shield with the Sword of Legend—straight into Herman Mildew's fat face, and bathed my blade in a blood that is even more powerful than the wine-dark blood of emperors, and that is the martini-pale blood of editors.

But I didn't.

Look, I'll show you, sirrah. If I had killed Herman Mildew, the Sword of Legend would bear the Crimson Aura of the Editorslayer. And look—see there? It totally doesn't. It's more of a mauve aura.

That's just some ranch dressing from lunch.

Janet Gurtler

First of all I want to point out that I actually had to shower and put on clothes, clean clothes at that, to venture out into the real world for this meeting. If that's what we're calling a get-together at an abandoned pickle factory these days. Is it because there's never a dill moment in pickle factories? Of course I'd relish an opportunity, any opportunity to have a conversation with a real live person.

You think I came here to kill someone? No. There's another reason.

Look at me, not the pieces of grass in my hair or the mud on my boots—I tripped in the bushes on the way in, but if you overlook that, I'm clean. I smell fresh. Seriously, I put on deodorant. How could anyone who committed murder smell pleasant? Like lavender shampoo. Or maybe Dove soap.

I get that Herman was thought vile by most, but honestly I considered Herman a friend. Don't look at me like that. Good old Herman. I mean, if you overlook the way he constantly criticized everything, the relentless berating and name calling weren't really so bad. Maybe he was even my best friend. I don't have a lot of people to talk to. I mean real ones. So just because every time I talked to Herman, I *might* have cried and locked myself in my closet to punch my favorite pillow (the one I clutch like a baby every night when I'm sleeping), that doesn't mean I wanted him dead. Even though I'm being treated for a skin condition brought on by a stress disorder my doctor believes could be cured if my self-esteem improved. No.

How could I kill Herman? He called me. All the time. All day long, even when I was working. Over and over. It didn't always interfere with my creative process. Not every single time. Herman told me I was special and that's why he didn't believe in emailing or even texting me. No, he thought it was super fun to have a phone phobia. He told me he was trying to help by forcing me to talk on the phone. All the time. And if I didn't answer, he'd just keep calling and calling until I did. Hilarious, right?

So what that he didn't stop talking and sometimes I realized I'd stopped listening to him and that I'd made myself a pot of coffee, drank most of it and had a full meal while he still jabbered on? Even though I caught myself saying things under my breath, with increasing urgency, like *just STOP TALKING! Shut the heck up!* At some point he'd pause and demand to know if I agreed. I appreciate a man who speaks his mind. Like all of it. Every single thought he ever had even if it's not politically correct. Or nice.

Anyhow, I didn't kill him. Trust me. The only reason I came here was to make sure Herman didn't tell people what he knows about me. Especially that one thing. Yes. That one. Because if that gets out not only will I have to change my name, I'll have to cut my hair short, dye it, and move to Canada. Wait. Too late. I already live in Canada. Some-where else cold then. Siberia?

Damn Herman and his satanic ways.

But no. I mean. Good friend. He was a good friend. I would never hurt Herman. Not badly.

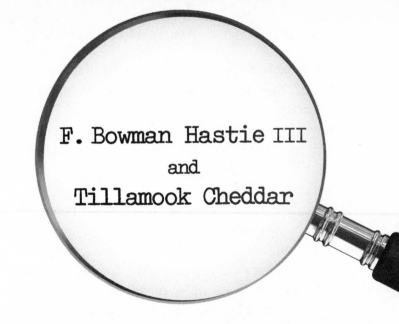

F. Bowman Hastie III
and
Tillamook Cheddar

Note: I must warn you that the following address to Herman Mildew and/or his so-called interrogators is full of vitriol (look it up!) and a few other sophisticated words. If you encounter a word you don't understand, please use the context of the sentence to figure it out, and then confirm the word's definition in the dictionary. Thank you.

Sincerely,
FBHIII

Dear Mr. Mildew:

First of all, I don't believe you are dead.

You've always been mealy mouthed at best, and at worst a liar.

So why should I accept the spurious announcement of your demise, especially when it is intrinsically linked to (yet another unpaid) writing assignment? Honestly, the fact that the solicitation of an alibi for your purported murder comes with no promise of payment—and that this anthology is intended to benefit such a worthy and reputable organization—as 826NYC—are chief among my reasons for accepting the assignment.

Knowing at the outset that neither my accomplished dog nor I will be compensated for our efforts, I am spared the dread that you will once again bilk me of payment for services rendered.

Due to your imposed limitations on word count, I will refrain from recounting the numerous shady book deals into which you (and your ilk) have lured me over the years, whereby you led me on, led me astray, and/or flat-out flimflammed me. Not to mention, all the instances in which you so heavy-handedly "improved" my prose. For a more lengthy discussion of our acrimonious professional relationship, I refer our young readers to my forthcoming blog: I-Should-Have-Killed-Mildew.com.

Second, you are well aware of my hostile feelings toward all editors, and especially toward you, Mr. Mildew.

Please bear in mind while you are "editing" this alibi that any suggested revisions will be met with extreme malice. If you change as little as one comma or semi-colon within this document, I promise that I will hunt you down and make absolute certain that you are indeed dead. If you are not really dead yet, and if you so much as mark one of my words herein, then mark *these words*, Mr. Mildew: I will kill you. And if you happen to be already deceased when I find you, then I will flog your corpse like a dead horse.

There. Now that I've dispensed with my preamble, please let me take this opportunity to profess my innocence: I. DIDN'T. DO. IT. (And remember: leave my punctuation alone; any editorial noodling will result in grievous bodily harm to the editor.)

Now, onto the defense of my innocent dog, Tillamook Cheddar. Mr. Mildew, you cannot be serious. How could you possibly presume that my dog Tillie, the world's preeminent canine artist, had anything whatsoever to do with your death? Why would you drag my dog's good name through the dirt, unless you intended to leverage her good name to sell more books? While I myself am relatively unknown, Tillie is far more famous than the vast majority of the other contributors to this anthology. She has nothing whatsoever to gain from lying, telling the truth, or contributing artwork to this collection. You, on the other hand, hope to boost book sales, and make a name for yourself as a deceased crime fiction editor, all on the backs of the most successful living animal painter, a handful of notable writers and illustrators, and a slew of nobodies. Having said all that, I've decided to play along with your dead man's ruse.

I asked Tillie, point blank: "Did you do it? Did you kill Herman Mildew?" She barked twice. I had no idea what this meant, but I continued my interrogation: "Do you know who did it?" Again, she barked twice. Still clueless, I decided to set up the materials for her to make a painting. Since she had barked twice two times, I decided to have her make two paintings.

After thirteen years of living and working with Tillie, I have a shamefully limited understanding of what her barking means. When she barks her head off, it usually means that she is in the middle of making a painting, or someone is at the door, or both. When she only barks once or twice it usually means (a) she's hungry and/or wants a bite of whatever I'm eating, (b) she needs to "go outside," or (c) she wants to make a painting. Since she had recently been outside and we had both just eaten lunch, I opted for option (c). Realizing that the editors of this anthology wanted to include at least one of Tillie's paintings in this book, I figured this was our best course of action.

Having spent a total of about ten minutes writing my own "alibi" for this anthology, I gave Tillie five minutes to work on each of these paintings. I welcome the editors/interrogators to include one or both of the paintings Tillie made that day. Just as with Tillie's barking, after all these years I am still at a loss when it comes to interpreting her paintings. Perhaps our young readers will shed some light on their significance to this purported "murder?"

Innocently yours,
F. Bowman Hastie III (& Tillamook Cheddar)

Exhibit #1 (Tentatively "Alibi"): Abstract representation of how neither I nor my manager, FBH III could have murdered Mildew; we were sharing a plate of bacon at the time.

Exhibit #2 (Tentatively "Mashed Investigator"): Expression-ist representation of the sort of mess I might make of a silly person who wastes an important artist's valuable time.

Geoff Herbach

Yes, I wanted him dead. Herman Mildew. I hate his face. I hate his fat ears. I hate the white monkey tuft he calls his hair. I hate his dirty hands and his fish belly fingers that wiggle when he talks.

Yes. Dead. Good.

Love is what? Love is desire. I am in love with Mildew's death. Love! My desire is to pop a serrated grapefruit spoon into Mildew's eyeball. My desire is to drop his eyeball into my soup. Butter. Vermont cream. Parmesan? Yes, please. Pepper! Will Mildew feel this pain?

No more . . . no more. Oh, walnuts.

He is dead but not from me. I am sorry.

I wanted this.

Here's a story: It was a beautiful morning. I did my stretches in my favorite pocket park. Seven floors up Mildew stood at his office window. The sun warmed my tight hammies. The park's pavement radiated into my chest. I loosened. I breathed. I thought, *You'll be fine, little dumpling.*

But then a cawing. "Caw!" I turned from the ground. Monkey-tuft hair, sun lit at a window.

"You!" came a cry. Then came the laughter.

"Me?" I asked.

"Keep your day job, Herbach, you rambling putz!"

"Who are you?" I cried.

"Mildew! Your nightmare. Your words are turds!"

Herman Mildew had my book, *Ricky's Big Day*. I wrote it on an IBM typewriter over a period of fourteen years. One. Copy. Only.

Mildew said he'd take it. I thought that meant publish it. Instead, Mildew tossed it from the window above. It exploded on the pavement next to me. Confetti took to the air. One scrap settled on the ground in front of my burning eyes. The only sentence I have left? "Ricky loves tacos."

Yes, I am in love with Mildew's death. But I did not do it. I wanted to.

And, so, yes, I was in the Mildew mansion. And, yes, I crept, a ghost, through the upstairs hall as a party bubbled below. I brandished my grapefruit spoon and also a bowl of warm soup. I found Mildew alone, drinking tea, slumped on a leather chair. I entered the room and pointed my spoon at his awful face.

"Ah. Herbach." He nodded.

"It's go time," I said.

"Come for your revenge?" he whispered.

"Don't blink," I said. The grapefruit spoon sparkled in the lamplight.

"Do it. Put me out of my misery," he said. "But know, it is I who should be carving you with that . . . is that a spoon?"

"Yes. Spoon," I whispered.

"My wife cannot forget your lips," he said. "So kill me."

I stood straight. "These lips?" I shuddered, smacking. "Your wife?"

"You kissed her at a Lemony Snicket reading in 2006. She says you smell like a pumpkin." A tear spilled from his left eye.

I dropped the spoon and dumped the soup into my sandals. "I do smell like a pumpkin!" I cried.

He nodded. He winked.

I ran. I crashed through the party below. I threw myself into the bushes in the yard.

Only later did I wake in those bushes and think, *I've never been to a Lemony Snicket reading. He lied. He lied. He dies!*

And now I find out he's already dead? Why not by me? I want to eat Mildew's eyeball in my soup.

Joanna Hershon

I didn't even know the guy. I mean, yes, I'd *met* him. But only once. He came snooping around my farm last spring, asking all kinds of questions about raw milk cheese, like why it tastes so much better than the pasteurized kind. He claimed to be looking for someone to write a book about cheese and he'd heard I was both a writer and cheese maker and he was *just so passionate about my cheese*. I should have known something was suspect; have you ever known a grown American man to weep while scarfing down Taleggio? Say what you will about this man, he did love cheese, and I let my guard down. I answered all his questions. And there were a lot of them. He was so informed! I told him I'd work on a proposal.

Just so we're clear, I didn't always live such a bucolic life. I grew up on the Lower East Side and I had a single mother who was never home. I dropped out of high school and I worked as a pedicurist uptown, which I didn't mind (I have this weird thing about toenails, which was how I ended up in beauty school instead of, y'know, bartending or waitressing like a normal person who wants to be a writer), but I went through my cash like you wouldn't believe. The city is so freakin' expensive—don't get me started—I don't know how you people live here.

ANYWAY. Where was I? Right—my hardscrabble upbringing, my thing about toenails—look, this is crazy, of course I didn't murder him!

Seriously—look in my bag.

Yes, I realize it looks like a frozen leg of lamb. Because it *is* a frozen leg of lamb.

For Herman, of course.

Because, on his trip to my farm, he mentioned he wanted to start eating meat without hormones, okay? It's for Herman. From me. Why would I bring a hormone-free frozen leg of lamb for someone I planned on murdering?

Have you not figured it out by now?

He's my father.

Yes, seriously.

Well I'll definitely take that as a compliment.

But it's true. He's the father who abandoned me before I was even born, the father I've tried to imagine my whole life, who I've written books about—albeit obliquely—and who I've fantasized about meeting for as long as I can remember fantasizing. I guess he was finally curious enough to find a way to meet me. He didn't tell me who he was. Not even after I signed a book contract with him. Didn't have the stomach for that, I guess. Imagine finding out *that* guy is your father? Herman *Mildew*? When I told my mother about the fellow who came around asking me to write a book about cheese, she actually fainted. When she came to, she told me the truth about Herman and her. And Herman and me. She also mentioned he was lousy in bed.

Embarrassing? Utterly. In every way. But I'm completely innocent, I swear. Or almost completely. I did feed him some raw cheese that was definitely not FDA approved. And it made him really happy. At least I have that.

Mandy Hubbard

(Regarding her absence on the esteemed guest list, and the presence of a certain item in the pocket of her blue jeans. Which is easily explained. And totally not suspicious.)

You ever hear of a red herring? It's this thing authors use. According to Wikipedia (and let's be honest, that's all any author worth her salt uses for research), it's "a figurative expression in which a clue or piece of information is or is intended to be misleading, or distracting from the actual question." In a mystery novel, a red herring is a suspect, planted in the middle of things, and so clearly guilty that the reader would never suspect the *real* killer.

I'm the red herring, which means I'm most definitely not guilty. You can't be a red herring and be the actual killer. But see, I'm the only one here who's not actually on the guest list. I swear to you, that's just some kind of a technical difficulty. I heard that Lauren Myracle was in charge of typing up the guest list because Herman was too lazy to do it himself, but she passed the buck to Jon

Scieszka, who probably couldn't read Herman's handwriting anyway.

Because here's the thing: I don't hate Herman. He hates me. I could care less about him.

It all goes back to this conference we were both at, this swanky affair in Manhattan where he was regaling a table full of would-be writers with a bunch of bizarre stories. He's an editor, you know, so he could have been talking about varieties of buttered toast, and they would have hung onto every word. But did he talk about toast? No. He was telling tall tales, boasting about the silliest things, and no one was the wiser. As I walked up, Herman was spinning a tale about his week at a dude ranch, where he went cow tipping.

And therein lies the problem. Because a girl like me, a girl who grew up on a dairy farm and once was tripped by her own cow and fell face first into a mud puddle, I know cow tipping's just not possible. A guy like Herman, what with his office facing the Statue of Liberty and his MetroCard and shiny black shoes; he didn't know what I knew.

And so, in front of scores of admirers, I called his bluff. I asked him how he tipped the cow. And he told me it was sleeping, and he snuck up on it. And I asked him, right then and there, if he knew the difference between a horse and a cow. Because see, he was thinking of a horse. Cows sleep lying down. When everyone realized what I had shown— that Herman was a big, fat, sniveling liar—they walked away, and Herman spent the rest of the night glaring at me from across the room.

So see, what I'm saying is I don't hate Herman. He hates me. Just because I had a Swiss Army Knife in my pocket doesn't mean I was going to use it on him. Like I said, I grew up on a dairy farm. I showed cows at the County Fair. Girls like me, well, we carry Swiss Army Knives everywhere we go.

Like I said, Lauren was in charge of typing up the guest list. Maybe *she's* the one who turned me into a red herring, to take the heat off her. You ask me, you should be looking a little closer at *her.*

Emily Jenkins

The history of pickles in North America is a fascinating one. I will tell you about it at some length. Yes, I will! When all this unpleasantness is over.

It is well known among my Facebook friends and Twitter followers that I am an amateur cook of some enthusiasm. I have tried my hand at pickling myself. Yes! Carrots, cauliflower, green beans. I have pickled them at home. I have boiled Mason jars and pulled them out of bubbling water with tongs. I have given holiday gifts of homemade pickles, tied with shiny green ribbons.

Something less commonly known about me is that I have written a book entitled *Pickles and You: Insights from the Heart*. It's not a history of pickles in North America. I told you I would get to that another time. It is about the way pickles make us *feel*. It is a how-to guide for understanding the deeper meaning of pickles in your life.

I know that's not the kind of book I usually write. I write amusing novels for young people, full of cute toys and invisible friends. Yes! But I think my Facebook friends and Twitter followers are ready for my pickles. I think they are primed, in fact, for me to release upon them my full understanding. There is a whole chapter on pickle juice.

The manuscript of *Pickles and You* is nearly completed. Mr. Mildew and I had lunch about it last week. We ate pickled onions and stinky cheese on rye toast at an eatery on the Lower East Side. Ask the waiter if you don't believe me. Mr. Mildew paid with a credit card. That's evidence!

I imagine you did not realize the party venue, the factory in which Mr. Mildew planned his big announcement, was a producer not of cucumber pickles—that common pickle that non-pickle-eaters think of as pickles—but of *specialty* pickles. Specialty pickles! It's true.

Sadly, these pickles are now lost to the ravages of time. I have only read about them in my favorite publication, the magazine *Pickle History*. (Do you know that magazine? It is indispensable.)

Anyway, *Pickle History* describes the beetroot pickles of the now-abandoned factory in which Mr. Mildew's murder occurred as "flavored with a dash of cardamom, a touch of sesame oil, and large doses of piquant mystery." It likewise describes the apricot pickles as "orange globes of fire."

Yet the factory closed down, some four years ago. I have done an extensive search for remaining evidence of its products, all to no avail. It seems anyone who owned a bottle of these pickles has eaten them up.

At the time of Mr. Mildew's demise, I was in my apartment kitchen with four bottles of rice vinegar, some unusual chili peppers, a large box of apricots, and enormous quantities of salt. I was trying to recreate the orange globes of fire to create a climactic ending for *Pickles and You*.

Mr. Mildew had informed me that the book lacked

drama. In fact, he dared to suggest I publish it under a pen name. A pen name. The very idea. Do you think I am the sort of author to use a pen name?

However, none of that means Mildew didn't have faith in my project. No! That man could eat more pickled onions than anyone I've ever met.

My neighbor, Mrs. Emerson, knocked on my door and complained about the smell from the rice vinegar and the cooking apricots. You could ask her all about it if she hadn't died the next morning. Very sad, very sad.

But some other neighbors complained as well. I have no doubt you can ask around and find someone who will confirm my alibi.

Maureen Johnson

INTERVIEW WITH SUSPECT / TIME: 21:50

NOTES: *Suspect was observed attempting to wheel a fourteen-foot cannon out the back door of the Old Abandoned Pickle Factory when apprehended.*

You guys. This . . . is not how it looks. I know how it looks, okay? I know exactly how it *looks*, and I want to tell you that how it looks and what it is are two *very different things*.

First of all . . . okay, *first of all*, this cannon has been in my family for four hundred years. My family were pirates. I come from a very long line of pirates. Perhaps the longest line of pirates ever assembled into a line. And to a pirate, a cannon is like . . . well, you know how cowboys have horses? Well, pirates have cannons. It's the same thing. I mean, you can't ride a cannon, but it's mostly the same thing. And unlike horses, cannons don't die. The family cannon gets passed down. And while I've never been in the pirate trade, it doesn't mean I can't respect my family tradition of taking our cannon with us wherever we go.

His name is Mr. Hinkles, by the way, and I'd appreciate it if you don't touch him.

(Noise on recording indicates that a copy of How to Fire a Cannon *was found on the suspect's person.)*

Oh that. Look, people send me things. When you have a cannon, people give you a lot of cannon-related gifts. When I was a kid, I had to make my own cannon for my Barbie, because they don't make a Barbie Cannon. I made it out of a toilet paper tube and a can. It looked awesome.

(Noise on recording indicates that a cannonball was found in the suspect's purse.)

Mr. Hinkles has to *eat.* That's his *dinner.* What are you, a monster? No, I don't think you need to question me further, as a matter of fact. Look. . . .

(Suspect began to sing.)

Oh, I'm a pirate look at me
I float around on the great big sea
Got my cannon I bring for fun
It's a decoration and not a gun . . .
Oh, a jolly, jolly pirate, been to France!
Now I do my pirate dance!

(Suspect began doing what can only be described as a crude soft-shoe with loose jazz hands, then broke off running. Was apprehended two minutes later while hiding, very poorly, behind a small, potted plant. Released shortly thereafter due to lack of evidence that suspect had any idea how the cannon actually worked.)

Lindsey Kelk

I didn't kill Herman Mildew. But you know what? When you find the guy who did do it, give me a call so I can come down here and shake him by the hand. Herman Q. Mildew was an odious, selfish, cowardly excuse for a man, a destroyer of dreams, a breaker of hearts. He has been dead to me for years. Let me tell you a story. . . .

It was so many summers ago. I was a naïve, young writer, romping through New York City and searching for my next big love story. I just didn't expect to star in it myself. I was sitting in the quiet café where I worked, tapping away on my laptop when I should have been working, looking longingly out of the dirty window and waiting for my muse. But instead of being struck by inspiration, I was bashed in the head by a moldy muffin. I turned to seek the origin of the blueberry-studded missile and that's when I saw him. Tall, handsome, cheekbones you could slice bread with. He told me his name was Herman and I knew it was love. We spent our days in the café, talking about the future, when I would be a successful writer and he would be my glorious publisher, and after hours, we danced on the streets of the Lower East Side, raced each other across the Brooklyn Bridge, and kissed on Soho street corners. Those were the most wonderful weeks of my life.

Then, one day, my laptop was stolen while I was handing out an apple bran muffin. I was mad but not so much. I could buy a new computer; only my one true love was irreplaceable. But Herman, my Herman, had already moved on to another passion. The next day, I arrived at the café to find him missing. The manager told me he just hadn't shown up for his shift and sent me outside to talk to "the others." I should have known. "The others" were a gaggle of young, literary-minded ladies, all with a yen for my Herman and a missing laptop. I ran away, unable to face the facts. A few months later, sad and heartbroken, I was browsing in a bookstore when I saw it. The first novel from Herman Q. Mildew press. There was a photo but it didn't look like him; he was bent and cruel and mean. But inside, the words were familiar, every single syllable taken from my stolen laptop.

From that day on, I couldn't write another word. I ended up dividing my time between my apartment and a place called the Brooklyn Superhero Supply Company. Ask them; they'll tell you where I was when he was killed.

I never heard from Mildew again. Not until I got the invitation to the party at the Pickle Factory and I had half a mind not to show. I also had half a mind to turn up with a semi-automatic or a rusty breadknife and make him regret stealing my work and breaking my heart. But it looks like someone got there before me. Good for them, I say. Good for them.

Jo Knowles

Where have I been the past few hours? I can explain. Believe me. But first, let me tell you that I am truly heartbroken to hear of Mr. Mildew's demise. He was so kind to invite me to this party. He even called me his "favorite Vermonter" on the invitation. It's our little joke, you see, because even though I live in Vermont, the people born here are the only ones allowed to claim the "er" status.

Mr. Mildew knew all this because he visited me recently during fair season. He came all the way from New York. He said he loved our cheese—the stinkier the better—and cows. The cow part was a bit odd. "Do you know they have the most wonderful toenails?" he asked me on our way to a local fair. I did not. "I'm fond of toenails," he added wistfully. I started to explain that cows have hooves not toenails, but he turned to stare out the window at the fall foliage, silently cutting me off. Well, I try not to judge. Cows are sweet, gentle souls. I think their best quality is their big, beautiful eyes. But I suppose their hooves are perfectly admirable as well.

Mr. Mildew was very particular about being sure to visit

me during fair season. He fancied himself a cheese judge on the fair circuit. Unfortunately, he had trouble convincing the local committees to let a non-Vermonter on board. You know, I think we bonded over that, being treated as outsiders and all. I think the two of us are true Vermonters at heart. I mean *were*. Poor Mr. Mildew!

After he was refused as a stinky cheese judge, I admit things got a little strange. That's when Mr. Mildew shifted his focus to hooves. He said that care of cow hooves was taken very seriously by the young 4-H members who showed their cows at the fairs. He said that one of his lifelong dreams was to become a hoof trimmer. And then he whispered, "Toenails, big beautiful toenails. . . ." under his breath.

You can imagine how disappointed Mr. Mildew was when every kid he approached with his hoof trimmer turned him away. I don't think it helped that Mr. Mildew wore a paisley scarf that covered his face. All you could see were the dark shades of his sunglasses through one opening in the scarf. He never took either off, even at night. You know, I realize I don't even know what Mr. Mildew looked like! How sad.

Anyway, at this point, Mr. Mildew seemed extremely discouraged. I tried to suggest that the fairs had lots of other things to offer too—fried dough, candy apples, fresh cider, maple sugar candy. But he waved me away. I think he was crying.

But I suppose you're not here to listen to all that. You want to know why I was late to the party, right? Late enough to make me a prime suspect? There's a simple explanation. Like I said, when Mr. Mildew invited me to the party, I was very honored. Especially after my state had treated him so . . . unkindly. So, I went to the country store near my house and ordered five pounds of their stinkiest cheese. And then, well, I suppose they'll find out eventually, I snuck over to my neighbor's dairy farm and . . . yes. I collected some hoof shavings—*toenails*—for Mr. Mildew. Obviously, no one wanted to sit anywhere near me on the train from White River Junction. I wrapped the cheese in thirty-nine layers of plastic wrap but the stink still escaped. Eventually, several people complained to the conductor. And that's why I'm late! I got kicked off the train in White Plains. I had to take seventeen different taxis to get here because none of the drivers lasted more than a few minutes. I offered them bribes and everything! But no one wanted signed copies of my books. I suppose the stench won out. You don't want a copy, do you? I suppose not. Paper is so good at absorbing odors. Don't ask me what I'm going to do with all these stinky cheese books.

Anyway, I'm sure if you called the taxi service they'll vouch for me. But don't give them my number, all right? I'm afraid they might charge me to replace all their pine tree air fresheners.

Gordon Korman

First of all, I don't like pickles, so the smell of this place turns my stomach. Seriously, the air is so thick with brine that my back teeth are floating in the stuff. It kind of reminds me of the way I feel when I think of Herman Mildew. Yes, I'm speaking ill of the deceased. I always spoke ill of him when he was alive. Why should I change now?

It has been said that an editor's job is to separate the wheat from the chaff. Herman Mildew took this one step further. He separated the wheat from the chaff, and then published the chaff. He notoriously asked an author to cut seventy pages from a manuscript only later to reject it because it was "too thin." Another writer he compelled to change "hard" to "difficult" and back to "hard" again so many times that the poor man abandoned his career, shaved his head, and joined a monastery. Herman Mildew could wreak more havoc and destruction with a blue pencil than most people could with a flamethrower.

I'm not surprised somebody killed him. I'm just saying it couldn't have been me.

I don't dispute my doorman's statement that I left my
building at six thirty last night and didn't return until after
ten. Tuesday is my weekly appointment with Dr. Balthazar. If you'd bothered to listen to a renowned genius, and
not a slack-jawed troglodyte who opens doors for a living,
I'm sure Dr. B. would have described in glowing terms the
progress we've been making on my various personality dis-
orders. Emile Balthazar, PhD (University of Trinidad and
Tobago, College of Herbology and Acupuncture)—New
York's "Albert Schweitzer of the Isolation Tank"—has con-
nected my anger management problem to a number of key
factors throughout my life: my parents' withholding of my
pacifier at the impressionable age of seven; my fear of two
of the four Teletubbies; my inability to distinguish subcon-
scious memories of the birth canal from conscious ones of
the Panama Canal; and, most recently, my unmanaged anger
at a certain chaff-publishing editor, who (although I didn't
kill him) more than deserved his fate.

In Dr. B's miraculous sensory-deprivation tank, suspended
in viscous liquid heated to exactly ninety-eight-point-six
degrees, all that mental ballast falls away, and I'm free.
Here, Balthazar argues in his memoir *I Am Not a Quack*,
a patient is removed entirely from the physical world, and
his psyche can be observed in the absence of any outside
influence or interference. Thanks to revolutionary synaptic
sensors developed by Dr. B himself, I now understand that
much of my recent frantic brain activity has been taking the
form of revenge fantasies starring Herman Mildew. It's certainly nothing cruel or sadistic. Mostly, I order pizzas to be
delivered to his apartment, or remove his name from the
National Do Not Call Registry. Some of the dreams involve
dog poop or itching powder, others simply a length of piano

wire. One features handcuffs, fire ants, and maple syrup. And let's not forget that oldie but goodie: a dart gun and a seed of uranium-235. . . .

Wait. That sounds bad, doesn't it? I mean bad, as in prejudicial to a jury? They're just *fantasies*, after all. I'd never act on them. And even if I wanted to, I was shut in an isolation tank. Trust me, no one would voluntarily pass up the womb-like comfort of warm viscous liquid for anything as trivial as committing murder. That would be like getting out of bed to go to the bathroom on a cold morning when the furnace is on the fritz.

Besides, you'll have to subpoena Dr. Balthazar's notebook to find any evidence against me. That's protected under physician-patient privilege.

Isn't it?

David Levithan

herman mildew ate
the plums
that were in
the icebox

and I was pissed

perhaps even
murderously so
since i had been
saving them
for breakfast

the rage I felt
was exquisite

but know this
about poets:

we don't
actually
kill people

it is so much finer
to let your words
stew in the rage;
it gives them
a poisonous flavor
that the reader
can taste
and recognize

if I'd killed
herman mildew
for eating my plums
I would have
only been able
to kill him
once

but the poet
has the advantage
over the murderer;
the poet can kill
a thousand times
in a thousand
different ways
in a thousand
different poems
without any weapon
beyond a pen

blood
is not nearly
as satisfying
so why
bother
with blood
when you
can use
ink?

Sarah Darer Littman

Did I have motive? Sure. I'll admit I wanted nothing more than to see Herman Mildew pop his clogs. He deserved it, the cantankerous old carbuncle. Why, you might ask? Herman Mildew deserved to die because of his uncommon cruelty to cheese. It sickened me to see the hunks of the stuff he left lying around everywhere to mold and desiccate, all because he was too heartless and slothful to perform the proper rituals of cheese care.

Cheese is something I take extremely seriously, having lived on a dairy farm in Dorset, England for ten years, where I was involved in the production of some of the UK's finest farmhouse cheddar.

Herman Mildew read an interview in which I'd joked that I was probably the only woman in Greenwich, Connecticut who could hold an intelligent conversation about the lactation yield curve of a dairy cow. Within the hour, he somehow managed to get hold of my unlisted phone number. So imagine this: a well-known editor calls and the first thing he says after "Hello, are you Sarah Darer Littman?" is,

"Talk dairy products to me." Can you spell C-R-E-E-P-Y?

But hey, we authors do what we have to do to sell books, right? So despite my qualms, I launched into a discussion of pasteurization temperatures, microbial rennet, and the cheddaring process, while the dude was heavy breathing on the other end of the line. After half an hour, when I'd got to the "aging in temperature-controlled stores for up to eighteen months" part, and was wondering where this conversation was going next, he interrupted me with a brusque, "Who's your agent?"

I told him and suddenly there's a dial tone in my ear. I figured that was the end of it. It's the story of my life—another day, another wacko. But next thing I know, I've got a book contract and Mildew is my editor.

Except I never actually get to meet him in person. He calls me once in a while; supposedly to talk about the book, but after about five minutes of editorial discussion he inevitably starts interrogating me about red Leicester, double Gloucester, and Wensleydale.

It's weird. So strange that I talk to my agent, but she tells me to go with the flow, that Mildew, like all editors, is wildly eccentric.

So the other day I was in the City and I stopped in at the Herman Q. Mildew and Co. Publishers' office, curious to meet the guy. But I didn't get to see him. Apparently no one does. I *did* get to hear Mildew firing some poor intern over the PA system in language that would make milk curdle. Seriously, if it had been TV, most of it would have been bleeped out.

And then I saw it: fine farmhouse cheddar lying abused and mistreated on a desk. Nearby, on the floor near the obligatory Ficus tree, lay some similarly maltreated Stilton.

In fact, once I started looking around the office carefully, I realized there was moldy, mistreated cheese everywhere. It made me sick to my stomach. But more than that, it filled me with a rage more powerful than the smell of Pont L'Eveque.

See, if it were one of the French varietals, I could understand, because those cheeses smell like a teenage boy's athletic supporter. But treating fine English farmhouse cheeses that way . . . well, chaps, it's just not cricket.*

"Who did this?" I demanded of the nearest hapless employee of Herman Q. Mildew and Co. Publishers.

"T-t-t-that would be M-m-m-mr. M-m-m-m-ildew," the Hapless One stuttered. "D-d-d-does it all the t-t-t-time."

That's when I knew that Herman Q. Mildew deserved to die.

Motive. Yeah, I had it.

But how to do it? I knew, from a well-placed bribe to Hapless—and as it turns out, underpaid—Employee, that Mildew drank a large glass of pickle juice every morning at precisely 11:07 on the dot. No doubt this contributed to his less-than-charming disposition.

What I lacked was opportunity. I couldn't figure out how to get the poisoned pickle juice to the guy. Plotting has never been my strong point. Just read any of my books.

Which brings me to the final point of my defense. Herman Q. Mildew was *publishing my book*. I'm an author, trying to make a living. Let's face it, if it comes down to a moral choice between justice for cheese and selling books, what do you think I'm gonna do?

---

*By cricket, I refer to the bizarre game played with bats and wickets that one must be a native of the United Kingdom or one of its former colonies to comprehend, rather than the insect known as Gryllus assimilus.

Barry Lyga

What's that? You'll have to speak up. I'm partially deaf in one ear and my hearing aid is on the blink.

Oh. Mildew. Right, right, yes, of course. Herman Mildew. Herman *Q*. Mildew, if we're being accurate, and God knows we want to be accurate, right? If you wrote a book with something—*anything*—off-kilter for that son-of-a—

Ahem. You were saying?

Oh. Oh, no, I didn't kill him. Of course not. Don't be ridiculous. Those books on my shelves, the ones about police forensics, body disposal, and crime scene analysis—they're *research*. I'm a writer, for God's sake. I *need* to read these things. And I've never even touched that samurai sword hanging over my mantle. It's research, too.

What's that? Speak up. Oh, yes, right, I see. How could it be research if I've never touched it? Quite simple: my character doesn't *use* a samurai sword; he just *owns* one. So I need to own one, too. To see what that's like. That's also why I own those guns. And that big ax. And that bottle with the skull and crossbones on it. (Whatever you do, do *not* add that to your drink!)

I take my research very seriously.

Pardon me a moment. I need to take some pills. I suffer from a number of maladies, in addition to my deafness. There is no pill for deafness, of course. The only cure for that is inserting a small bit of plastic and electronics into my aural canal. If someone would make a pill for deafness, I would take it.

Fortunately, my other defects are treatable with a glass of water and a collection of tiny pills, gel caps, tablets, capsules, caplets, and two different liquid suspensions. These are for such ailments as my upside-down heart, my off-center middle toe (right foot), too-centered middle toe (left foot, natch), my inverted gallbladder, my suspiciously too-normal blood pressure, my debilitating ESS (Empty Sinus Syndrome), the chalky discharge from my fingernails, and what doctors refer to as a "diffident frontal lobe."

As you can see, I am a weak, infirm man, ancient at forty and could not possibly have—

Oh, all right! All right, damn you! I can't abide your penetrating, accusatory glare! And that light you're shining in my eyes is wreaking havoc on my near-terminal case of dry eye.

(Pardon me while I apply some medicated eyedrops. . . .)

Look, I'm not saying that I killed Mildew. God knows he deserved it—the man made me rewrite a sentence once, which took a *whole six minutes* **and** caused my carpal tunnel syndrome to flare up—but that doesn't mean I did it.

I just can't say for sure that I *didn't* do it.

You see, as I may have mentioned, I take a number of medications. And medications have *side effects*. One side effect common to all my medications is this one: "May cause or increase thoughts of suicide."

Follow me on this: at around the time Mildew was . . . disposed of, I was, in fact, feeling quite suicidal. I actually had dinner with Mildew that night, if you want to know the truth. (I didn't particularly like him, but, like most editors, he was usually good for a free meal.) I was heavily medicated, per usual, and feeling quite suicidal. And here's the thing: another side effect of multiples of my medications is, "May induce hallucinations."

I think you see where I'm going with this.

Is it possible that, addled as I was, I *hallucinated* that Mildew was, in fact, me? That, in the throes of suicidal despondence, I attempted to kill myself, killing—instead—Mildew? Is it possible that I then dragged the body into a filthy alley, hacked it to pieces with a hatchet, and fed the remains to the cats and rats and occasional stray dog?

Um, or, some other series of events, of course. Not that it has to be that specific. . . .

Is it possible that Mildew's death resulted from a misfiring suicidal impulse? I'll tell you this: the night is a blur to me (other than Mildew's constant belching of cheese-smelling gas in my direction in the cab after dinner). The only certainty remaining in my mind is a desire to kill myself. And in the morning, I woke up just as certain that I *had*, in fact, killed myself! (I was so certain that I was dead, in fact, that I did not venture near the Internet all day, since, as Shakespeare wrote, "The dead do not tweet.")

As the day wore on, though, I eventually came to realize that I was not, in fact, dead, that I had not killed myself.

But what if. . . ?

No, no, you're right. It's ridiculous. It's absurd. I couldn't have killed Mildew, even under the misapprehension that he was me. I'm innocent.

Totally innocent.

Pretty sure I *did* kill Libba Bray, Dan Ehrenhaft, and Jon Scieszka, but they don't count, right?

Adam Mansbach and Ricardo Cortés

No way you can pin this on Cortés and Mansbach
We got ten thousand fans that will tell you a jam-packed
crowd watched us ransack the track and make hands clap.
After that? Canopies. Stoags the size of manatees.
The one-armed man? He stole the show single-handedly.
But candidly? We were sleeping by ten—how dull is that?
You better turn the hell around like a cul-de-sac
And find the right dude—I had a whole entourage with me!
And Rico? Lost in the trees. Camouflage frisbee.
Next morning, woke up on a yacht. Did the breaststroke.
Water was warm, anchor tied to Glenn Beck's throat.
But I digress—go find the killer, be that man's jailer
take some drastic measures like a fat man's tailor.
You're wasting your time here, and ours. I oughta laugh.
Keep it moving, Huckleberry. We got books to autograph.

Leslie Margolis

This is not an ice pick in my pocket. It's a pointer. Yes, it needs to be that sharp. I often point to miniscule things wedged in tiny places or stuck next to other miniscule things.

No, this is not a knife. Okay, fine I lied. It's a knife. But it's meant to cut cheese. I always bring my own cheese knife when Mr. Mildew throws a party. The ones he offers are usually covered in cat hair and I am rarely in the mood for Brie or sharp cheddar and the hair of a cat. Separately they are fine, or cat hair bundled on the side of a cheese plate like a sprig of parsley is lovely. It's the combination of cat hair and cheese that I find unsavory. Call me crazy. You wouldn't be the first.

Please strike that last sentence from the record. No one calls me crazy because I am not crazy.

Why are you looking at me like that?

No, I did not plan on using this knife or this ice pick on Mr. Mildew or, as I call him, Hermando, Herm, the Hermerator, Hermattack, Herm and cheese sandwich, or Hermorrhoid.

Please strike that last word. I have never called Herman Hermorrhoid, at least not to his face.

Know what? While you're at it why don't you strike that entire last paragraph?

What rope? Oh, this is the rope I use to tie knots, a wonderfully rewarding hobby. I can do the bow's hitch and the butterfly and a clove hitch and a cow hitch and a sheep shank. Yes, those knots are all real—look 'em up! And here's a new one I invented. I call it the, "Not Tight Enough for Herman."

Oh wait. Never mind. That I did make up. Just now. Did I say Herman? I meant Hermione.

No, not the *Harry Potter* half-breed Hermione; I mean the other Hermione. The one who gave me a "negative five star" review on Amazon. You didn't know it was possible to give negative stars? It's usually not but Hermione got special permission. She also trashed my latest book on Goodreads and wrote nasty comments on my very own blog on my very own website.

But I didn't try and kill her. Or Herman. Not even when I found out that Hermione is Herman's doppelganger. Especially when I found that out because it's bad enough having one evil editor out to get me. Two I cannot deal with.

You can quote me on that.

On second thought, don't quote me on that or on any of this. I need to go. In fact, I'm not even here.

Julia Mayer

I'll admit it, the gun in my purse does seem like damning evidence. I had considered killing him of course. But I doubt you'll find anyone here who hasn't. The man gave me my big break and then, poof! Like that! He took it away. No call, no note, not even the courtesy of "This is not what we expected when we signed you." As though *he* hadn't been the one to approach *me*. As though all I were . . . as though I were filler, and they had found something better to take up the space I was allotted.

I had spent *years* working on that haiku. Decades reworking just the right word arrangement. Two years before I noticed that the first line had six syllables and then months to figure out how to fix it. I lived and breathed five-seven-five. And I finally run into him in a restaurant and confront him and do you know what he says? "Sometimes, all the work is for naught. Just goes to show our plans mean nothing." Don't you see? He killed my haiku with a haiku of his own:

Sometimes all the work
Is for naught. Just goes to show:
Our plans mean nothing.

A bad haiku of his own at that! Believe me, I know a good haiku. That was not it. And do you know what they did with the space I was allotted? They printed a photo of a panda. Cute, cuddly, and adorable? Yes! Artistically equivalent to what I had created? Absolutely not!

So yes, I thought about it. I planned it. I was going to walk up to him, gun in hand and say:

You believed you could
Replace me with a panda?
YOUR plans mean nothing.

But I was only going to scare him; it was a tactical move. I was never going to shoot him, then my haiku would never have been printed. Well, honestly, maybe, who knows, maybe I would have done it if I had the chance. Only after he signed an agreement stating that no matter what, my haiku would appear in the next printing of course. But I haven't seen him. All I did was eat appetizers and chat with other authors who have been jilted in the same way. Let me tell you, there are an awful lot of talented folks in the same position I'm in.

But all that is neither here nor there. You asked for my alibi, didn't you? Well fine, all I have to say is this:

Could not have been me
I was eating mushroom puffs
The whole entire time.

Barnabas Miller

Dear Accusers of Captain Barnabas Miller,

In circles of undercover intelligence, I am called "Oswaldo," but you cannot know me by face. I do not think I said this correctly, but my language buttress is the least of our concerns right now. El Gato has smelled my scent, so I must be brief and to the target if I am to save Captain Miller's life and clear his name.

I have stolen the attached document from sub-level 23 of a military bunker deep beneath one of the CIA's many American Apparel cover locations in downtown Manhattan. It was there, in the cold bowels of the city, that I witnessed this cruel interrogation of Captain Miller by Agents Samuel L. Jaxton and Alan Rixtman. It was there that I first learned of Project Kill-Dew.

Unfortunately, this transcript has already been redacted by a crack team of crate-trained rhesus monkeys, but I still believe this document will prove once and for all that Captain Barnabas Miller, aka "Asset 7" could not possibly have carried out his hypnotically implanted assassination mission. You see, his psyche has already been reduced to rubble. I only hope you can taste the grisly truth of the matter before the fat lady hums and Captain Miller is "decommissioned." Miller is innocent, I tell you. It is *we,* the brainwashing, assassin-training divisions of rogue intelligence operations, who are guilty. Please read on while I run away. . . .

CIA File #JXX-Q7677D [Incident Report]
RATING: *CLASSIFIED*
RECORDED - ███████   20:15:43 hours
ADMINISTRATING: Agents Samuel L. Jaxton and Alan Rixtman
SUBJECT: Capt. Barnabas Miller aka "Asset 7" aka "Tommy Tilex"

AGENT SAMUEL JAXTON: All right, is SOMEBODY gonna tell me what the ██████ just happened? 'Cause I'm about to crush some██████ skulls right now if I don't get some ██████ answers. Captain Miller, why weren't you at the██████at 1938 hours and forty-three seconds, terminating El Gato with *extreme prejudice*? You were supposed to zip line from the██████ building, jump across the two roofs on ██████and ██████ use Parkour to jump from the third floor to the second floor and back to the third floor, crash through four windows, snap the necks of those two dudes with the soul patches, slip on an argyle sweater and hipster glasses, and switch out Mildew's runny Camembert with our cyanide-infused, undetectable

Government Kill Cheese! So, do you wanna tell me what the ▇▇▇▇ went *wrong*?

CAPTAIN MILLER: Rory, can you chill, please?

JAXTON: For the last ▇▇▇ *time*, my name is not Rory! It's *Jaxton*. Agent Samuel L. Jaxton! And *you* are "Asset 7" aka "Tommy Tilex!"

MILLER: Rory, please. It's me. Katie.

JAXTON: No. You are not Katie. You're the most ruthless killing machine north of Sao Paulo. We *trained* your scrawny nebbish ▇▇▇ for *years*, waiting for this *one* opportunity.

AGENT ALAN RIXTMAN: Oh, for God's sake, Jaxton, will you please release Captain Miller . . . from . . . that . . . headlock.

MILLER: You guys, I don't know what this whole "Captain Miller" routine is about, but—oh my God, wait. *SHHHHH*. It's happening. It's happening right now.

JAXTON: What's happening?

MILLER: She has cramps. I feel her pain.

JAXTON: What the—?

MILLER: Her name is . . . J-something. It definitely

starts with a "J." Jenny or Jessica. NO, it's *Jody*. Jody. It's that time *right now*, you guys. This is Day One.

JAXTON: *Excuse* me?

MILLER: We can still help her if we hurry!

RIXTMAN: My God. I know what this is, Jaxton. (*Taps chin in rhythm.*) I . . . think . . . I . . . may know . . . exactly . . . what—

JAXTON: Stop pausing for emphasis and finish a ▇▇▇▇ sentence.

RIXTMAN: Don't you *see*, Jaxton? Mildew's people have gotten to him. They've been on to us this entire time. They've erased all the memories we implanted in Captain Miller and replaced them with Katie McGrady's memories! Miller's been twice brainwashed, like a bag of Dole salad mix. He actually believes that he . . . is . . . Katie . . . Mc—

JAXTON: WHO THE ▇▇▇▇ IS KATIE MCGRADY?

RIXTMAN: Have you even *read* his file, Jaxton? Don't you remember how Miller came to us in the first place?

JAXTON: I only read cover copy.

RIXTMAN: The boy was only twenty-two years old. He'd just written the next *Catcher in the Rye* and his manuscript had gotten Mildew's attention. We knew he was our best chance to infiltrate Mildew's organization and finally put to an end to his illegal hamster trafficking ring, so we initiated Project Kill-Dew. But it took forever for Miller to get close enough. Mildew had promised to edit Miller's first novel, but instead, he insisted that Miller ghostwrite a series called *Katie McGrady: Time-of-the-Month Psychic* under the pseudonym "Solange Estranger." It was supposed to be a six-book series, but Mildew somehow managed to sneak a clause into Miller's contract that committed him to fifty-four more Katie McGrady books. Miller was just in the middle of revising episode 45, "I Know Why the Caged Teen Wears Sweatpants"—in which Katie and her best friend Rory Tobias try to rescue a girl from irrationally breaking up with her boyfriend—when we gave him the kill order. The poor bastard is but a pale pubescent shadow of his former self. We spent five additional years training him to write in a teenage girl's voice, and now he is a teenage girl. And for *what*, Jaxton? For some illegally trafficked hamsters? To rescue the world from the smell of Herman Q. Mildew? Miller gave his *brain* for America, and all he ever asked of us was that we call him "The Captain," despite the fact that he had no military rank or experience whatsoever.

JAXTON: Damn. He's not even a captain?

MILLER: Um, you *guys*, we can't just *sit* here anymore. We need to get to Jody. We need to find her NOW!

RIXTMAN: Mildew's going to pay for this.

JAXTON: So what do we do with Katie?

RIXTMAN: The only thing we can do. We help her find Jody.

JAXTON: Whatever. Even if this Jody doesn't exist, she has a better shot at capping Mildew than this sorry ████.

Jacquelyn Mitchard

Who was Herman Mildew to me? Or me to Mildew? You may as well ask, What's Hecuba to him, or him to Hecuba? That's Hamlet.

Hamlet.

HAM-let?

No, it's not about a little pig.

Whatever.

Herman Mildew was my editor, my muse, my lover, my prince, my nemesis, a knight with rapier red pencil, a maker of queens, the gentlest and most perfect editor, a beast with a blunt hammer of cruelty in his pen, an executioner of reputations. He could be gallant. He could be cruel. He could be a bright and shining leader. He could be a slobbering fat moron.

As for his death, he had it coming.

Don't we all?

I mean, if we're living, our death is coming. That's all I meant.

I slept through it. To be utterly honest, I didn't hear a thing.

They had to positively haul me out in my velvet Snuggie, like the ones seen on TV? I have ten, specially made, that I take everywhere. I cannot bear to have anyone else's sheets next to my body. You know that 80 percent of house dust is composed of human skin, don't you?

I slept through it. And I am not a sleeper.

If Mildew's little pudding hadn't given me a pill during the party, when I collapsed with a severe migraine, I would have at least *heard* the details.

She gave me a pill, and she gave me the room right next to theirs.

I heard plenty of giggling going on when I was unpacking.

Just like Mildew and me, when I was his little pudding!

Oh yes, they all said that was how I got my first big contract, but the truth is, plenty of great publishers wanted *The Wind Screamed Rosa!* Yes, that was mine. I did write that.

Of course I'll sign one. For your *grandmother*?

Well.

Back then, Herman was in his prime. I was a mere child. I thought that together, we would build a great cathedral of novels. But when I dropped to number ten, he dropped me.

That was when the sleep problems began.

Insomnia? Please. It's sleep drought. That's what my psychiatrist says.

It's bad on the Upper West Side.

Even with soundproofed walks, quadruple thick windows, my Soothy Snoozymaker turned to ocean (I cannot tolerate the not-at-all soothing sound of the real ocean) and the masks that Ramona sews for me every week with the softest Peruvian cotton, I'm lucky to get . . . three hours.

In the country, of course, it's worse.

All those sinister sounds: deer positively *clomping* about

outside, leaves bashing against the branches of trees, raccoons with those terrifying little hands, fish splashing, bugs scuttling, owls hooting . . . you may as well be on safari!

It's the brain, of course. Leonardo. Thomas Jefferson. Charlotte Brontë. The mind simply will not stop. The price of genius is, well, it's exhaustion.

I should never have come. But when Herman wrote to me, saying his fête would be flattened without my presence, that others were coming only to meet *me*, well, I agreed. After all, before we parted, he did sell *The River Sobbed Violet!* to the Doo-Wop Music Channel for an original movie.

Well, yes, they do make their own movies.

So I had the driver come to darkest Connecticut. I'd have one sip for old times and be gone by dawn. Little did I know that the "party" was really a "wedding."

And little did Little Miss Twenty-Seven Weeks at Number One know what she would wake up next to after her wedding night.

A is for Ampersand: A Keyboard Mystery.

This is what they take for literature today.

The swollen, marbled red face.

The protruding tongue and bulging eyes.

The clutching of the throat, the gargled cries.

That muffin paunch shaking and the obvious toupee askew, the pathetic little man he had become—doddering drooler, closet alcoholic, blurry little ferret-faced follower of fads.

"Nothing lasts forever, darling!" he said.

Indeed.

How do I know about the mottled face? My dear, I invented the mansion mystery genre. Poison always leaves a cherry-red complexion.

How do I know it was poison?
I'm a good guesser, I guess. I have no idea at all.
I slept through the *whole thing*.

Sarah Mlynowski
and
Courtney Sheinmel

INT. PICKLE FACTORY. NEW YORK - MORNING

Enter SARAH MLYNOWSKI and COURTNEY SHEIN-MEL. Remarkably short writers. They're in their mid-thirties, but neither looks a day over twenty-one. Fine, twenty-five. Okay, twenty-nine. All right, all right: thirty-four. But really, that's the ceiling.

SARAH
Excuse me! Excuse me! I'm ready to give my alibi! Who do I talk to?

COURTNEY
(pulling on Sarah's arm)

Calm down. You're not speaking to ANYONE. We're here for information gathering purposes ONLY.

SARAH

No, I want to talk to someone. I HAVE to talk to someone—to explain what happened. I know about this—I watch a lot of *Law & Order*. A LOT. The regular episodes, *Law & Order: SVU*, *Law & Order: Criminal Intent*. I even watched *Law & Order: Trial By Jury* and *Law & Order: LA* and no one watched those. The only one I haven't watched is *Law & Order: UK*. I don't know why, the wigs just really freak—

COURTNEY
(clapping a hand over Sarah's mouth)

Sarah, you've got to stop talking about *Law & Order*. In fact, you've got to stop talking about *everything*. I'm sure you watch a lot of courtroom TV, but I'm the one who went to law school and practiced law for SIX YEARS. I've been in actual courtrooms, and I've prepped dozens of clients. You know the first thing I always told them? Remain silent. Don't say anything without an attorney present.

SARAH
(pulling Courtney's hand away)

But you're an attorney, and you're present.

COURTNEY
You know what they say—the attorney who represents himself has a fool for a client.

SARAH

Ooh, I once heard that on *Law & Order*! Okay, I get what you're saying. Except the other thing on the show is the perps who don't talk always look guilty. And then they go to jail. We could be sent to JAIL.

COURTNEY

Technically we'd be sent to prison. Jail is a short-term facility.

SARAH

So you think we'll be going away for a long time?

COURTNEY

We won't be sent anywhere if we keep our mouths shut.

SARAH

I just want to tell the truth, that we were writing in my apartment together.

Enter ALYSSA SHEINMEL. She's younger than the other two. And taller.

ALYSSA

I did my interview! Don't you think this is the perfect "I'm innocent" outfit?

(twirls)

Don't you think it makes me look so trustworthy? I told them I was with you, Shortney.

COURTNEY

Don't call me that.

SARAH

Whoa, whoa whoa!!! You were not with Courtney! I was with Courtney! Omigod. I can't breathe. Need air. Need air!

COURTNEY

Alyssa, now is not the time to make up stories. You were not with me.

(Sarah is audibly hyperventilating)

I was in Sarah's living room, writing.

(Sarah puts her head between her knees)

She had *Law & Order* on in the background like always. You could have come over too. You were invited. You know it upsets me when I invite you to things and you don't show up!

ALYSSA

I had a doggy emergency.

COURTNEY

You always pick Donald over me!

ALYSSA

I'm sorry, Shortney. I saw something that looked like a nail and thought he ate it. He was acting out of sorts—but since the vet didn't see a nail on the X-ray, he probably just missed you.

COURTNEY

Oh, that's so cute. Really?

ALYSSA

Really. You should've seen him. He was all—

(mimes dog with paws up looking sad)

—and sitting by the front door, like he was waiting for you.

SARAH

The Sheinmel sisters are throwing me under the bus! I'm going to pass out. I'm going to pass out and when I wake up I'll be handcuffed to my hospital bed. It happened on *Law & Order*! And it was the polygamous husband who did it. It's always the polygamous husband. And I don't even have a polygamous husband. At least I think I don't.

(turns to Sheinmel sisters)

Are either of you married to my husband? Are BOTH of you married to my husband?

COURTNEY

No, but if you're in prison, maybe I would marry your husband. He's a great guy, and I'd totally move into your apartment. It's bigger than mine, and close to my sister.

ALYSSA

Omigod! We can double date!

SARAH

Yup, under the bus I go.

ALYSSA

No, no, I'll just edit mine and say the three of us were together. Not a big deal. No need to freak out.

SARAH
(deep breath)

Perfect.

COURTNEY

But that's not true either, and that's not even your biggest problem. They already have you on tape. This isn't like a manuscript you hand in, and then get back to make changes once, twice, three times—

SARAH

Or four. If you want to really piss your editor off. Sorry Herman.

COURTNEY
(clamping hand over Sarah's mouth again and glancing frantically around room)

No apologizing to Herman. As I was saying, the problem is that your confession is already done.

SARAH

What about Miranda's rights? I don't totally understand who she is or why she has rights but on *Law & Order* she gets a lot of people out of jail.

COURTNEY

Miranda is a he, not a she.

ALYSSA

I don't know why people do that to their children, naming a boy a name clearly meant for a girl.

COURTNEY

No, it was his last name. He was arrested and questioned for hours. Finally, he confessed to the crime. But that whole time, he'd never been advised of his right to an attorney or his right to remain silent. That's why his conviction was overturned. Now it's the law that when you're arrested, you're read the Miranda warnings.

SARAH

So it's like his confession never happened. Great! Let's do that!

COURTNEY

But we can't. Alyssa wasn't arrested. She showed up here completely of her own volition, just like us.

ALYSSA

So we have to steal back my confession. Okay, here's how we'll do it. Sarah, you go back there and steal it. Then we'll destroy it and we're in the clear.

SARAH

How do I steal back a confession?

ALYSSA

Easy. Grab the videotape with my name on it. I saw the video guy writing up a label: Sheinmel, A.

SARAH

But why me?

COURTNEY

Someone has to do it. And it's too obvious if it's me. She's my sister.

ALYSSA

Exactly.

SARAH

Fine. I'll go. I'll be back in five.

(zips up sweater and ties hood around her face)

COURTNEY

(waits for Sarah to leave the room, then takes out her phone and dials 911)

I have a crime to report. Author Sarah Mlynowski is about to steal a videotape from the interviews in the Herman Mildew murder. Obviously the only reason she is stealing a videotape is because she's trying to hide her own involvement in the murder. I'm an attorney and I've seen this kind of thing before. What? Where was I? I was with my sister. If you don't believe me, just ask her. She'll tell you. Thanks.

(Sheinmel sisters high five and cackle)

216

ALYSSA

So Sarah's going to jail?

COURTNEY

Not jail. She's going to prison. The difference is—

ALYSSA

I know, I know.

(her voice grows wistful)

It's a shame no one will ever see my interview though because this is the perfect alibi outfit. But anyway. Well played.

COURTNEY

(links arms with sister)

I know. I saw it on an episode of *Law & Order*.

Lauren Myracle

You silly ol' silly, I would be delighted to talk to you about poor Hermie's ghastly demise. It simply wouldn't look right if you didn't approach *all* of sweet Hermie's party guests, now would it? So—wink, wink—of course I'll provide a statement. Anything to help you nail the onion-eyed slop-wallower who ripped out poor Hermie's heart and shook it till it was goo, the way a mongrel would shake a child's beloved doll. I can see it now—poor Hermie, flung hither and yon until his eyes popped out and his limbs flew off! Until his innards were scattered everywhere, like pig intestines flung willy-nilly across a concrete floor!

Mr. Investigator, I ask you: Have you witnessed the mess a pig makes when it reaches the slaughterhouse? The frightful sleight of hand accomplished by the teams of maggots, swarming so relentlessly that one might swear the carcass had resurrected its foul self? The stench of bone soup, yellow as bile and so greasy that once touched, the slick of it stays on a person forever? The ubiquitous boar hair, too coarse to be pulverized by even the most relentless of hammer mills?

Oh my. Please excuse me. I get . . . overwrought at times. It's my delicate constitution, you understand. I absolutely cannot abide ugliness, and to that end, I fill my mind solely with images of angels and butterflies. No doubt it's because I'm southern, where ugliness is tucked neatly away into the dark place, and where appearances still matter. *You* know what I mean. Where a lady is a lady and a man is a man, and . . . oh, *my*! Have you been working out, Mr. Investigator? Those biceps! You don't mind if I give those fine, strong muscles just the teensiest little squeeze, now do you?

Pardon me? Why . . . why, I *never*! You, sir, are two sandwiches shy of a picnic, and that is my *sleeve* brushing up against you, for heaven's sake. I suppose I could forgive your confusion, since my skin *is* as soft as silk (and don't bother inquiring about my moisturizing regime, as that's a secret I'll take with me to the grave!). I refuse, however, to dignify your crass allegation regarding my "attempt" to flirt with an investigator of crimes because sweetheart? I don't "attempt" anything. What Mama wants, Mama gets.

And since you insisted on going there—write this down, now—your biceps are hardly swoon-worthy, unless one happens to fancy pigeon eggs, which believe me, I do not. I'm sorry for licking the red from your candy, Mr. Investigator, but I was merely boosting your ego. Isn't that what men want, affirmation from a blushing beauty such as myself? It's certainly what Hermie wanted, and so yes, I played his little game again and again. I, the cooing ingénue; Hermie, the wizened editor. Oh! The *wise* editor, I mean! Gracious, the heat must be getting to me. Is it hot in here? Do you suppose I could have a glass of iced tea? Sweet tea, obviously. I don't drink it any other—

No? Not even a glass of water? Not even a shot of

Southern Comfort? Kidding! I'm kidding, Mr. Investigator, but you're right. It's neither the time nor the place, just as it was neither the time nor the place for dear Hermie to tease *me* the way he did. At his party, I mean. After all, I performed my role perfectly. I admired his suit, although, *shhh*, a man as short as a fire hydrant shouldn't wear horizontal striping, now should he? And frankly, pleats are not an ideal choice for anyone with a pear-shaped bottom. But no matter. I am a writer! An artiste! Creating fiction from fact is my job, and I do it well. I even complimented Hermie's thickly gelled pompadour, and I told him with whole-hearted conviction that women are indeed drawn to men with full heads of hair.

Did I clarify that follicular transplants don't count? No, but why would I? That would be like shooting my own foot, which I would never, because Mr. Investigator, I wear a size seven triple A. Shoot all the wide-soled size tens you want, but remember, it is a sin to kill a foot as slender and delicate as mine.

At last, after lathering Hermie with flattery, I asked him what he thought of my latest work: a novel-told-in-origami of which I'm exceedingly—and justifiably!—proud. Do you know how many paper cuts I suffered during my grueling week of drafting?! How weary my eyes grew as I slaved away in front of the TV? And my tongue, afflicted even now with dozens of small but painful sores, the result of consuming what may have been, in retrospect, too many bon-bons! How could an *artiste* consume too many bon-bons, you ask? I have no answer. I can only agree that it is the greatest tragedy imaginable: a genius such as myself, dependent on high-grade chocolate for creative sustenance, yet doomed for all eternity to suffer for my art.

I'm sorry . . . what? *Ohhh*. Yes, I suppose one could argue that death, too, is tragic, but—

Well, aren't we putting on the dog? I *do* have a point, and yes, I will *get* to that point. I'd be there already if you hadn't interrupted, don't you know?

Back to the party. I had praised Hermie, and so it was his turn to praise me. This is the agreement all authors and editors live by. The ones who stick around for the long haul, that is. But Hermie—may his soul rest in peace—chose instead to toy with me, telling me that . . . that. . . .

Do you have any tissues? It's my delicate constitution, acting up again. Quite a trial. *Quite* a trial, and *I'm getting to it, all right?!* I know you want to hear what Hermie told me. I understand that. But do you understand that before I can share the details of Hermie's feedback, I must at the very least tell you the title, price, and pub date of the work in question, sure to be an instant classic? It's called *Dances with Paper Cranes*, soon to be e-pubbed exclusively on paper tablets called iSpirals, copyrighted by yours truly. So take that, Hermie! I'll be dancing with dollar bills . . . thousands of them! Thousands on thousands, all folded into dollar bill cranes! *I'll* be dancing with the origami equivalent of *The Period of Evening Between Daylight and Dusk*, while *you*—my "friend," my "editor"—will dance only with coffin bugs and worms!

Oh dear. Did I, ah. . . ?

Gracious. That was disturbing, wasn't it? That voice, saying those deeply *deeply* disturbing things? Not *my* voice, and I'd be much obliged if you struck those remarks from the record, since clearly we were, ah, visited by a poltergeist just now. Either a poltergeist or—not to tell tales, a lady never tells tales—but . . . come a little closer, please . . . *it could have been Sarah Mlynowski, projecting that pure-as-berries voice of hers through a hole in the wall.* Have you checked these walls for holes, Mr. Investigator? I ask because I did *not* intend to disclose the sordid details I'm about to share. But that voice . . . those horrible dreadful things. . . .

Well, it brings me back, sure enough. Back to the night of the party, back to that golden time when dear Hermie still graced us with his presence. Are you writing this down? Because I know for a fact that Sarah Mlynowski saw Hermie only moments before I did. She will spin a different version of her nocturnal activities, of that I am sure. How do I know? Because she is a caution, bless her heart. Also because she— like me, like all great *artistes*—writes her little stories in front of the television, only unlike me, she doesn't watch *Glee* or *Suburgatory* or *How to Hide a Body: A Discovery Channel Original.* Sarah watches one show and one show only: *Law & Order.* And do you know *why* she watches nothing but that *one crime show?* No? Well, then you're as useless as teats on a boar hog, aren't you?

All right, Mr. Investigator. Perhaps this will help you put the pieces together. May I point out how terribly convenient it is that Sarah rustled up not one but two "character witnesses" to defend her innocence? And did I mention that the two witnesses are *sisters?* As if sisters can be trusted, especially with one of them so tall and the other so short. (Are we sure they're really even sisters? I, myself, would think long and hard before trusting the testimony of such a Jekyll-and-Hyde pair, Mr. Investigator.)

And consider this, if you would be so kind. Right as I was approaching Hermie to discuss *my* magnum opus, I heard Hermie invite that Sarah into the janitor's closet for "an editorial meeting." And what did she do? She followed him in willingly, Little Miss Peaches and Cream! Even knowing his temper! Even knowing the foulness of his breath! And afterward, did she emerge red-eyed and sniffling? If only!

But no, she did not, which is why I would keep an eye on that one if I were you. She's a wild one, a she-devil in Bruno Maglis, and don't let those pouting lips of hers fool you. And that Ziploc baggie of fingernail clippings you found tucked into my brassiere? *She* put it there. She stuffed that baggie right down my blouse, that's right. Sarah Mlynowski, M-l-y-n-o—

Pardon? Oh. *That.* He wasn't in his right mind, clearly, but I will admit that Hermie wasn't as taken with *Dances with Paper Cranes* as I expected him to be. What, exactly, did he say about it? He called it . . . well, he called it snore-igami, if you must know.

So I stuffed him into a pickle barrel, nailed shut the lid, and shipped him off to my uncle's pig rendering plant in Tennessee. It's called We Render While You Wander. Clever, don't you think? Same day service, and free pig chuckles to anyone with red hair.

Oh, for heaven's sake, now I've gone and gotten your feathers all ruffled again! *I was kidding*, you silly ol' silly! Such gullible creatures you men are. If I put on my sweetest voice and asked you to climb on into this here pickle barrel, would you say yes? Really? Well, shut my mouth. Even a blind hog finds an acorn now and then, I suppose. Climb on in, then. That's right. One leg and now the other . . . scrunch on down, you cutie . . . just a *weensy* bit farther so I can get this lid on tight. . . .

Good Lord, you big baby. Quit hollering like a stuck pig! Of course I'll let you out . . . just as long as you swear on your mama's grave to have a nice long talk with Sarah Mlynowski. Do you? Do you swear, now? That's right, Sarah Mlynowski.

M-l-y . . . n-o-w . . . s-k-i.

Greg Neri

Yes, I killed Herman Q. Mildew.

- I ran over him with my car after we'd left a sales conference where he proceeded to tell everyone I couldn't turn a phrase if it had power steering.

- I dropped a safe on his puny head when he refused to pay me for a manuscript I delivered one day late—my daughter's birth being "no excuse."

- I strangled him in his office where he belittled me in front of Philip Roth, making me fetch coffee so they could insult my "writing" behind my back (but not out of earshot).

- I poisoned his glass of Château Mouton Rothschild after we went to the most expensive restaurant in New York and when the bill came, he claimed to have forgotten his wallet.

- I pushed him down 102 flights of stairs after he

refused to hold the last elevator for me at the top of the Empire State Building, saying "Maybe a bit more suffering would improve your verse."

- I suffocated him with my birthday cake after he tweeted my fans that I was now too old and out of touch to write YA because I didn't own an iPhone or know why birds were angry.

- I stabbed him with my special pen after he failed to point out that my contract gave him final say on my novel—and yes, instead of black cowboys from the inner city, could I make my heroes white girl scouts from Poughkeepsie?

I killed him a thousand times in a thousand different ways. An arrow through the heart (alas, he didn't have one). A bullet in the brain (ditto). I drowned him in a vat of melted cheese. I threw a toaster in his bath and watched him fry. I told the Mossad he was a former Nazi hair stylist. I strapped him to a chair and blasted endless reruns of *The Suite Life of Zack & Cody* till his head exploded. I refused the Heimlich maneuver when he choked on a pickle. I told a busload of teenage girls he was Justin Bieber's dad (the one who grounded him). I slathered him with honey and dropped him into the bear exhibit at the Bronx Zoo.

All these, and hundreds of other fantasy nightmares—wasted! Because the final insult by this loathsome liar of literature was his *real* death. This human abomination of an editor, this manipulator of mayhem, this odorous ogre of destruction left this earth *not of my doing!*

Such is the life of a writer. All that work, then someone beats you to the punch!

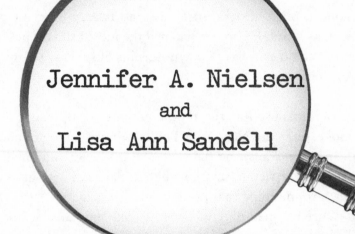

Jennifer A. Nielsen
and
Lisa Ann Sandell

For me, Jennifer A. Nielsen, and my partner in crime—er, writing—Lisa Sandell, the question is whether we are guilty in the death of our editor, that evil twerp, Herman Mildew? The answer, of course, depends on what your definition of "cold-blooded murder" is. If you mean it in the bad way, then no, we are almost entirely innocent.

Now, did we try to kill him? Well sure (except for some key parts of the plan, it was all Lisa's idea), but anyone could understand our reasons.

Typical. Jennifer would try to pin it all on me. I mean, I *am* responsible for the most brilliant plot the world may ever have seen. Plot as in storyline, that is—certainly not a plot to murder a foul-breathed, mealy-mouthed editor who claimed said plot was implausible and then refused to publish our masterpiece. An implausible plot. Hah, as if such a master of the pen as I could even dream up an implausible plot. Editors . . . such squidgy, unimaginative know-nothings.

We slaved away at our crime novel for seven years, three

months, thirteen days, six hours and twenty-four minutes. And, as I said, I, erm, *we* hatched the most brilliant plot the world could ever have known—genius, if I do say so myself. And very, very lethal.

In our manuscript, the murderer kills by tipping over a bookcase at the New York Public Library. Like dominoes, the next one falls, and the next, and the next. Until finally it lands on the victim, smashing him as flat as . . . as flat as . . . um, a round thing that just got smashed flat.

Once Herman rejected our so-called "implausible" draft, we had no choice. Lisa said, "What should we do now?" I said, "Go for pizza?" She said, "The only way to get published is to prove that our plot works. Let's give Herman Mildew death by bookcase." I said, "Okay fine. But let's do it after we eat." Because by then, I was hungry.

He didn't reject us. We rejected him! We rejected his whiny-editor-crybaby-complaining about "logic" and "sense." Herman was not fit to edit our novel! He was not fit to occupy the same city, state, *universe* as our glorious manuscript. So, I—I mean, *we*—vowed to flatten him, right then and there. Quite literally. Except Jennifer wouldn't stop complaining about her pathetic empty stomach—I mean, who can think about hunger at a time like this? Honestly! And greasy pizza to boot. At the very least, the situation called for indulging in a wickedly sinful chocolate mousse cake or pineapple upside down cake or . . . Ahem, sorry, lost my train of . . . or even a terribly rich hot fudge sundae! Well, we postponed our plan for a few hours while we ate some pizza and cake. And ice cream.

Then we wrote Herman a letter. A most devious letter

that drew him out and lured him to the library for the flat-tening. "Fancy yourself an editor, eh?" we asked. "Well, Mr. Know-It-All, why don't you show us some books that are more 'plausible' than ours? Why don't you meet us in the stacks at the New York Public Library? We'll be waiting. . . ."

Only, when we arrived at the library, which was exactly as described in our manuscript, with its soaring columns and grand, wooden bookcases, we found the bookshelves were bolted to the floor. Oops.

Herman—that conniving editor with his cheesy toenails and bony fingers that have drawn the very spirit and life-blood out of who knows how many hapless authors—was right. Alas, our plot was . . . implausible.

AND IT'S ALL JENNIFER'S FAULT! She didn't research the library!

It's true, it's true—Lisa gave me only one job ("Don't mess up"), and I ruined it!

In the end, we learned three very important rules. First, research is more important than eating hot fudge sundaes. Second, listen to your editor, even if he makes Voldemort look like a kitty cat. And third, capital murder is probably not the best way to get published.

Michael Northrop

Sure, it looks bad, what with the blood and all. It's all over me. I think you even have a little on you, from when we shook hands just now. And yes, I look guilty: sweating profusely, wringing the blood from my cuffs, and not once looking you in the eyes.

Look, I've seen the cop shows. I know what you're thinking:

I had the means, the most obvious of which is this pistol here—nice, right? Careful, it's loaded—but don't sleep on this switchblade. It's too choked with congealing blood to flip open right now, but I can assure you that wasn't the case a few hours ago.

I had the motive. It was no secret how much I hated that man. My death metal song "Scrub You, Mildew" was a minor hit in Turkey. That album, *Mildeath*, contained eleven songs, all about his gruesome and untimely demise.

And, of course, I had the opportunity. As I'm sure you know, my name is written prominently in his calendar. He has an entire hour blocked off for me: the hour when he died.

But I didn't kill him. I couldn't possibly have. I was killing someone else at the time, you see. And Mildew? Well, he was supposed to be *my* alibi!

The first part is easy enough to prove. The blood on my knife, my clothing, my, well, everything, should be enough. Here, I will give you some for the boys in the lab. You think I'm wearing red underpants, but they were white this morning. I'll just . . . take these off . . . and . . . here you are. They're a bloody mess now, but they were the fruit of someone's loom once. If you have a plastic bag, that would be ideal. Gives a whole new meaning to the term legal briefs, doesn't it? Chilly in here.

You will find that this blood is an exact match for that of one Babcock T. Spooneybarger, whose mortal remains can be found under a bridge in the next town over. He should be pretty easy to find. I thought there was water under there when I pushed him over, but it turned out to be an old railroad bridge.

Not that there's much blood left in him, mind you, but there should be enough for the tests required to clear my name. Which is spelled N-O-R-T-H-R-O-P, by the way. Some people put "U-P" at the end there. That was Spooneybarger's mistake.

As for the part about Mildew being my alibi, allow me to point out two things:

1. That rat never set aside an hour for anyone. I heard he scheduled fifteen minutes for his own mother's funeral—and it was out of state! A full hour for me, a mere writer? Ha! He was obviously up to something.

2. I know what that something was. He had big plans for that hour, big and very, very bad plans. Let's just say that, for Mildew, the words "puppy" and "smuggling" were nearly synonymous. I know because I was supposed to be his alibi, too. I, his; he, mine—the perfect crime!

Or so we thought.

Lauren Oliver

Do you have to keep saying that word—*murder*? You must have used it at least seventeen times since I sat down. What happened to all those colorful, vivid euphemisms you used in the introduction?

Let's see . . . what were your words then? *Herman Mildew took a long walk off a short pier, he kicked the bucket, he shuffled off the mortal coil!* Glorious. Variety is so important when it comes to language; otherwise, you're in danger of losing your audience.

Murder. There you go again! Even the word gives me the chills. It has such an ugly ring to it, don't you think? Do you know what word I prefer?

Karma.

I'm not saying that Mildew deserved to die, exactly. I just think that almost anyone who has ever come into contact with that despicable insect of a man would—

I'm not getting upset. I'm being descriptive. Please remember, I'm a writer. Writers describe, and we strive to describe accurately. And Herman Mildew had all the kindness of a hollow bone. He was a roach dressed up as a human being. He wasn't even a roach. Cockroaches have families—large ones, in fact. I should know; I live in Brooklyn.

Think about it: even a cockroach can find another cockroach to love! But not Herman Mildew. Isn't that interesting? I'd even say it was *significant*.

I have another question for you. Did you ever wonder just how *long* it must have taken him to draw in mustaches on all my author photos? Did you ever stop and consider *that*? Do you know how many thousands of photographs that represents?

I do. 10,457 to be exact. I had to find and destroy them all, so that my readers wouldn't think I was in desperate need of a wax.

This is a vicious business, my friend. Appearances are everything.

But just because I hated him doesn't mean I killed him. I have another favorite term: *probable cause*. It's a beautiful thing—especially when, as in my case, the police don't have any, and detain a completely innocent young woman on her way to a dinner date with her friends—who I'm sure will be absolutely furious by now—and all in order to bark up a tree that isn't going to yield a single, solitary bloom.

That's a metaphor, by the way. I'm supposed to be the tree, and what I mean is I didn't do it. How could I have? At the moment of Mildew's death, I was happily ensconced on my couch at home, sipping red wine and watching a movie with my fiancé. He'll vouch for me—call him.

Of course no one else saw us together that night! It was a date. We don't exactly live stream our romantic episodes. I'm an author, not a reality TV show actress! Look, we ordered *Bridesmaids* from On Demand. That *proves* I was at home. What thirty-something-year-old male do you know who would choose to watch *Bridesmaids* on his own? Be reasonable.

I don't mean to sound condescending. I don't pretend to know more about this than you—after all, this is your job! I'm just a writer. And it's obvious that the literary view of the justice system has very little in common with police proceedings in the real world. For example, in books, detectives are always so sharp, so absolutely clever. They can solve the most complicated murders based on only the thinnest shreds of evidence—an abandoned cigarette and a misplaced lampshade, for example! Clearly, the detectives of fiction are quite different from their real-life counterparts.

No, no. I'm not calling you stupid. I'm just engaging in *literary criticism.*

Trust me. I'm a writer; it's just part of my job.

David Ostow

Micol Ostow

I, _____, being of sound mind and
(name of person in the room)

body, do hereby _____ attest to a plea of not guilty in
(adverb)

the murder of the most _____ editor in the world,
(adjective)

Herman Mildew.

   In the interest of offering the truth, the _____
(adjective)

truth, and nothing but the truth, I will say: Mr. Mildew was

not my favorite _____. Though I have yet to glimpse
(noun)

him with my own two _____, most everyone
(part of body [plural])

knows of his legendary temper, his paranoia, and his more

_____ habits: namely, collecting _____
(adjective)   (adjective)

cheeses, and toenails from _____. Surely
(type of animal [plural])

you can understand why I tried to avoid _____
(verb ending in 'ing')

with Mildew too often.

But kill him? Certainly not! You can ask any _____
(noun)

that knows me: I am a kind, caring, _____ , not capable
(noun)

of violence against any person, no matter how _____
(adjective)

he or she may be!

However, if you need specific proof as to my where-

abouts on the evening in question, I can provide it. In fact, I

could offer _____ alibis to you, but these are the five
(a number)

most persuasive:

1) I was walking my _____.
(type of animal)

2) I was washing my _____.
(body part)

3) I was in bed, reading a very _____ book and
(adjective)

having a glass of _____ milk.
(adjective)

4) I was at the latest _____ movie, by myself.
(name of celebrity)

(I prefer to see movies alone so no one bothers me with

their _____ or their _____.)
    (verb ending in 'ing')   (verb ending in 'ing')

    5) I was organizing my _____ collection.
                    (noun)

    So, there you have it. There's no way I could have killed Mr.

Mildew! My defense is as airtight as the day is _____.
                                    (adjective)

What's that you say? You find it _____—and mighty
                         (adjective)

suspicious—that none of my claims can be corroborated

by other _____? Well, now that you mention it, I can
    (plural noun)

see how that may not look good. Alas, this statement is all

I have to offer, and I will swear to it _____.
                              (adverb)

    Indeed, all of the above is true and _____, or my
                                  (adjective)

name isn't _____.
            (name of another person in the room)

    Whoops.

Alison Pace

I didn't do it. I couldn't have done it. And while I don't have an alibi per se, I can tell you that I was writing. I can assure you that I was working hard at being a worthy author. Worthy. Just the kind of author that Herman, that horrible, horrible editor, wanted me to be.

This is how it happened. I sat down at my desk with my revisions. The revisions that Herman had given to me. I opened up my laptop and my document and I got ready to revise, even though, really, I had a hard time wrapping my head around any of the improvements, if you could really call them that, that Herman had suggested. Like when he writes in the margin in red pen, "We got it!" what does that mean? But still, I soldiered on.

But then my contact felt funny. And so I had to go have a looksee. I resolved my contact issue but no sooner than I had, I became aware of an eyebrow situation. I got out my tweezers. In life, I believe it's important to know when your eyebrows need attention vs. say when you just don't want to write. Sometimes it's hard to know the difference. I returned to my desk. I entered the creative phase I like to think of as bargaining. I told myself that if I finished chapter sixteen and started on chapter seventeen, I could leave my desk and go for a run, or I could do my yoga DVD. It was my choice.

I spied my dog, there in her bed, across the room.

"Hi, Carlie," I said.

"Who's my gorgeous, gorgeous girl?" I asked. Perhaps because the question was so obviously rhetorical, Carlie did not answer.

I felt a bit peckish. A look in the kitchen confirmed my suspicions: there was nothing interesting there. I decided to venture out for a snack.

I walked several blocks to get a snack. I may or may not have passed Herman's apartment en route. I returned home, a while later, with my snack. I sat at my desk and ate it there. I thought about the penthouse apartment that is available in my building. It has a terrace as big as the apartment. I'd like to move there. I chewed a piece of gum and returned to my revisions, determined, as ever, that I was going to finish strong. I observed that an almost empty yogurt container can entertain my dog for the better part of an afternoon.

I then had a slight sense of malaise. I moved, with my laptop, from my desk to my couch. I wondered aloud if my book was very boring, and then, if the changes Herman had suggested would make it even more so. Because at that point, I was a little bored. I wondered how Lady Gaga had wound up on my Pandora station. I didn't get a lot of work done that day. But I consoled myself as I sometimes do, with one of my favorite quotes: "The work goes on, the cause endures, the hope still lives, and the dream shall never die." Ted Kennedy.

And also: my dog can vouch for me.

Joy Preble

I did not kill Herman Q. Mildew. That's what you want me to say. That's what you expect me to say.

It is also the truth. (Let me interject here that truth is a squirmy bastard with a tendency to get stuck in life's drain like a clump of soapy hair. Look in your own tub if you don't believe me.)

You wouldn't even be questioning me if it weren't for the cheese. Yes, *that* cheese. Doesn't everyone carry a black Prada microfiber tote of cheese just in case? You're investigators. Detectives. Private eyes. Gumshoes. You've seen it all. You and your trench coats and fedoras and shoes that never squeak. Your tiny storefront offices and your secretary named Millie or Effie or Gertie or Roz. She's a tall broad with seams down her stockings and a swell hat she wears at a rakish angle and sensible thick-heeled black shoes. Secretly she loves you, but you're married to your job. She'll drink her cup of joe at the corner diner and curse the day she fell for a wise-cracking palooka like you.

But I digress. I did not bump off Herman Q. Mildew.

But I wanted to. And the reason is in that Prada tote of cheese.

Go ahead, take inventory. That's right, one at a time. Careful now, coppers. You may want to grill it after you've grilled me. Take those shocked looks off your mugs. A girl has a right to save cheese memories. Herman Q. Mildew wouldn't understand this. But I know you do.

I snatched the wedge of Stilton the night he made me stay late to organize his toenail collection. I knew I'd be in Dutch with him, but I couldn't help it. It sat oozing on his desk, clots of blue mold like diamonds. I shoved a hunk in my mouth while I sorted. Mildew wanted them organized by toe. I argued that time of clipping was a better arrangement. I should have kept my mouth shut. The Stilton was lingering on my tongue.

The next night, it was the Limburger. I caught him using it to wax his head. He threatened to sock me in the kisser if I said anything. "I'm no stoolie," I told him. But when he took off his shoes and thrust his dirty feet out the window trying to make the squirrels go nuts, I swiped the cheese.

Good cheese should not be wasted on someone like Herman Q. Mildew.

"They're gonna send you over for this," Mildew told me. We were taking turns spitting into the pickle juice and then tightening the lids. I swear it wasn't my idea. He promised if I helped him, he'd stop leaving footprints in the mascarpone. He lied.

Brie. Munster. Roquefort. Camembert. I admit it. I took them all.

Ask yourself this before you throw me in the hoosegow: What would you do?

You'd save the cheese, that's what you'd do. No dairy product deserves to be manhandled by the likes of Herman Q. Mildew.

But plug him full of lead? No way. Ask some other tomato. I'm not your girl.

Margo Rabb

I would never kill Herman "The Mouth" Muttonhog Mildew—how could I want to rid the universe of the International Lord of the Lamb Champion, who held the world record for consuming twelve legs of lamb in ten minutes (even if I did see him illegally toss slimy wads of gristle into his secret pocket)?

We were a team for years. Serious athletes. Nobody trained harder than us. The practice, the endurance, the psychology—most people don't know what it takes to excel in the sport of Professional Competitive Eating. The Mouth captained our team of five: Fred "Frydaddy" Horsencrantz; Peter "Ritz Bits" Goulstein; my little brother, Igor "Sweet Cheeks" Smith; The Mouth; and me.

We each had our own specialty. The Mouth's was meats. Lamb, hamburgers, pot roast, hot dogs, sirloin, cold cuts, meatballs, honey baked ham, sausage, bacon, T-bones, cow tongue, pig's ears, bison, goat belly, chicken feet, bone marrow—he held the title for all of them.

Winners in each division got a crown and some cash.

Frydaddy got five hundred bucks when he won the Cheese Fries Championship. Ritz Bits won a thousand in the Uncrustables Eat-Off. Sweet Cheeks wowed us with five grand from the Boston Cream Pie Smackdown.

I was the pickle girl. I did pretty well too, if I say so myself. I won ten thousand kroner in the Norwegian Pickle Playoffs, five years in a row.

All was fine and dandy for a while. Our team was the best in the world.

Then The Mouth changed. Meats weren't enough for him, he decided. He encroached on our territories. He beat Frydaddy at the Fried Okra Festival. He clobbered Ritz Bits at the Cheez Whiz Bowl. He poisoned Sweet Cheeks at Chocolate International, putting guinea pig poop on Sweet Cheeks's plate where the chocolate chips were supposed to be.

Then he set on the pickles.

Now, let me tell you a thing or two about pickles. You say "pickle," most people think pickled cucumbers. Not true. For the Pittsburgh Picklefest I achieved top ranking in pickled carrots, green beans, olives, lemons, cauliflower, eggs, and my coup de grâce: herring.

The Mouth decided he wanted to hold the world record for herring, too.

We faced off.

Herman The Mouth Muttonhog Herringphony did his usual trick of sticking half the herring in his secret pocket. In his underwear. Pickled fish in his underwear. "His tush smells like a swamp," my mother said when she sat next to him at the World Crown Ceremony.

We complained to the authorities, but they didn't believe us. I even told them about his secret pocket. Just once, I said, I'd like to see The Mouth eat a leg of lamb or a pound of herring in forty seconds with someone else's pocket-less underwear on.

I'd like to see him eat lamb and herring until he could no longer breathe.

After ousting us from our titles, The Mouth told us he was quitting the professional eating circuit to become an editor. A *food editor*, he said. And he said he was going to write.

The portrayal of Picklepuss in his memoir *The Magic of Mutton, the Magic of Mildew* is not loosely based on me. There's no relation to me whatsoever. It's not true that my greatest wish in the world was to beat him. My greatest wish was to expose him for what he was: a fraud, a poor excuse for an athlete, and a pox upon the great Professional Competitive Eaters of the world, Major League Division.

But, I digress. This is the truth: I was *not* the one who sent him the sixty-pound barrel of rotten herring that he almost drowned in. And I have no idea how this leg of lamb got in my purse.

Lisa
and
Laura Roecker

Lisa: Check Yahoo mail.

Laura: Can't. On a run.

Lisa: Eeew. Stop being so athletic and check our email. Immediately.

Laura: Fine, fine. I'm checking.

Lisa: Do you see it? Do you? Freaking Mildew hated our manuscript. He called us hacks!

Laura: But at the end he says he's just going to send it to print, so that's good news at least.

Lisa: Oh you haven't read the P.S. yet. Read the P.S.

Laura: Wait, he can't do that right? He can't put an adverb warning on the cover of our book. That's absolutely, completely, entirely, *ridiculously* nasty.

Lisa: He can. He *will*. The adverbs are your fault, you know. You love a good adverb.

Laura: You're not pinning all those adverbs on me. Remember when I tried to delete all of them and you claimed it was cramping your stylistic voice?

Lisa: Everyone knows "firmly believes" sounds better than plain old "believes." It just *does*.

Laura: Yeah, everyone except Stephen King.

Lisa: Well, we've got to do something. No one will ever take us seriously with an adverb warning on our book.

Laura: Seriously.

Lisa: Well, you're just going to have to kill him. Come over when you're done with your run, and I'll let you borrow some of my rat poison. You can bake him a cake or something.

Laura: Why do I have to be the one to kill him? Why can't you kill him? You're the oldest.

Lisa: God, you love reminding me of that, don't you? It's only two years! It's not like you're 23. We're both in our mid-thirties.

Laura: I'm still in my early thirties.

Lisa: I hate you. Also, you're baking that cake. He'll never believe that one of my notoriously amazing cakes tastes like rat poison. Luckily your baked goods almost always taste poison-y.

Laura: Fine, fine. I'll immediately bake the dastardly cake.

Lisa: Right. Bake the cake quickly. And put a few adverbs in icing. Make him think we're having a good laugh about this whole thing.

Laura: Ooh, new mail from John Scieszka. Shiny!

Lisa: Well, that's kind of random. . . . Oh, whoa. Not shiny. NOT shiny.

Laura: Someone already killed Mildew. Yay! I really didn't feel like baking that cake.

Lisa: Betcha it was Stephen King.

Laura: You really haven't read *On Writing* yet, have you?

Lisa: Yeah . . . no. Sure haven't.

Laura: Unbelievable. By the way, do you often have email access when you run. . . ?

Marie Rutkoski

I can smell decay.

Don't believe me? All the coffee on your breath, and the Wrigley's gum you chew to mask it, can't hide the two cavities in your lower molars, blackening their way into your dental plan. I smell them, just like I smell your patience dying as you interrogate yet one more person with motive to kill Herman Mildew.

Oh yes, I had motive. He made me inspect his cheeses: the stinky ones, the runny ones, the mottled blues, the patties coated with a light fur, which, he claimed, "gave texture." You can imagine what happened with a nose as sensitive as mine. Nosebleeds. Blood running over my lips and chin. Dripping onto the cheese in an abstract pattern that made Mr. Mildew laugh. He would laugh and I would know that this was why he had cajoled me into his office: for the joke of taking my gift and turning it into a curse.

You may well ask why I let him.

Was he not my boss?

Was he not the sort of person people loathe so much they

loathe themselves, and thus go to great lengths to disprove their hatred? To agree to favors, however unreasonable? I gave him a card on every birthday. When I signed my name I signed away that squirm of shame for wishing he had never been born.

But that is different from murder. And trust me, murder would have been redundant. Mr. Mildew reeked of decay. He had a waterlogged wood odor to him, the sort of rot that swells before the end. He already smelled like a grave. I didn't need to push him into one.

And I have an alibi. You see, I met a man in the grocery store. I took him home with me. He was in my bed when Mr. Mildew was killed.

Don't blink like that. I may be the beak-nosed secretary of a hated waste of a person, always at his beck and call, but I stole moments for myself. I am not so unattractive as you think.

I saw someone in the produce section. I was at the store to buy cheese for Mr. Mildew, but I am always drawn to the fruits and vegetables. To the heaped-up colors and shapes. The way everything resembles a still life painting, hovering somewhere on the spectrum of hard or ripe or speckled with liver spots. Does that mango dimple under your thumb? Will that green bean snap, so crisp? Is there one berry in the pint that oozes, laced with mold? Examine it all, Mr. Investigator, under the magic spray of those automatic produce misters, and you will see why I did not immediately do as ordered by Mr. Mildew, and head straight to the cheesemonger for the latest shipment of Époisses.

There was a thin man standing by the tomatoes. Mr. Mildew would have sneered at him, called him a pickle of a person, so slender he was, shoulders curved, spine stooped.

I did not care. I saw him reach for six perfect tomatoes still on the vine. I could see, I could tell, that there were no better tomatoes in the store, and that this man knew the peak and prime of things. What more could you ask of a lover? Nothing, I thought, as he threaded his fingers through the vine, tomatoes dangling like blown glass baubles.

Of course I will tell you his name. As soon as I remember it.

You know, even your doubt has a smell. It is the decay of trust.

Decay is the resin at the bottom of a wine glass, blended with spit. A used toothbrush. The yellow smear of nicotine in a glass ashtray where someone's left a filterless cigarette burning. It is black paper from an old photograph album, crumbling onto the table, as black and blank as all the forgotten names that no one can place to the album's blurry sepia faces.

Decay smells like worry. Desperation. Futility.

And I can smell it, sir, on you.

Casey Scieszka
and
Steven Weinberg

Steven and I definitely did not kill the world's worst editor. I mean, *our* editor. Sure we might have had a few reasons we would have liked to. (Finger painting set for Steven's Christmas gift because his illustrations are "childish and amateur"? Not cool, Mildew. Sack of tears for me because "this is the extent to which I was bored reading your latest manuscript?" Totally not cool, Mildew!) But that doesn't mean we'd *kill* the good-for-nothing, imagination-less troll.

And besides, we've totally got the alibi to prove it: we were out of town when the deed went down.

See, we travel all the time. Mostly it's to research whatever new book we're working on. And so, at the time of Monstrous Mildew's death we were . . . let's see here . . . oh yes! We were in Germany taking an amateur alchemy class.

Yes, we were planning on writing a historical thriller about a serial killer who poisons all her victims with handmade brews, but then Mildew pulled the plug on it. Hm.

Oh wait! No, no, sorry about that. We weren't in Germany when Mildew bit the dust. We were in Brazil learning how to street fight from the fiercest of all *favela* slum lords.

This book was going to be a tormented love story between a rough and tumble street fighter who falls for his mentor's daughter only to—oh wait. Mildew vetoed that one too.

Sorry, I must be getting my dates confused. When did you say this all went down again? Oh! OK, now I remember. It wasn't poison camp in Germany or hand-to-hand combat training in Brazil. We were in *Kenya* doing research for a murder mystery we were working on, set during a hunting safari. We hooked up with this company called Death Safari. They loaded us up with weapons and ammo after a brief training and just let us loose. Their company promise is that the five-day trip will provide you with the ability "to track and hunt down *anything* or *anyone* in the world or your money back guaranteed!"

Our guide was really impressed by Steven's and my natural ability to wield a weapon. He said people with revenge on the mind often make—

Oh no wait a second. I'm so sorry. Mildew canned that one as well. "Too touchy-feely. Not enough vampires," he said.

Let me get out my calendar. See? We travel *so* much it's easy to get our schedule confused.

Right! I'm sorry. Steven and I were on *vacation* when Mildew ate it. We had treated ourselves to an artist's retreat and spa in Tahiti. We spent the whole time writing, painting, meditating, eating healthily—it was just wonderful. Totally rejuvenating and inspiring. I think Mildew really could have benefited from a trip like that. It's a good thing he's dead. Oops! I mean, it's too bad he's dead.

Kieran Scott (occasionally Kate Brian)

Iknow *I* didn't kill him. I mean, I couldn't. It's not in my nature. You don't even understand. I'm a total goody-goody. Ask anyone. Ask my mother. Ask my sister. She'll gladly give you an earful about how perfect little Kieran has never made a mistake in her whole entire life. Ask my high school boyfriend, even. He got so frustrated by my absolute purity that after we broke up he went on a three-year-long bad-boy bender that was like *True Blood* meets *Jersey Shore* only with less physical restraint and more booze. I couldn't hurt a cockroach, let alone a human being. Although Mr. Mildew did have some cockroach-y qualities, didn't he? Like saving his boogers in plastic wrap? I mean, ew! I could imagine someone offing him over that lovely little habit, but it wasn't me.

Of course that doesn't mean it wasn't *her*.

You know who I mean by "her," don't you? I'm talking about my other half. Not *better*, mind you, just other. That girl is definitely capable of murder. Just look at the stuff she writes. Kidnappings, stalkings, faked suicides? A teenage serial killer with a bigger body count than Tom Ripley? She definitely has a dark side, that one. Sometimes? When I wake up from a prolonged blackout? I find the most disturbing things in my room. Like a box full of carefully detached squirrel heads and a series of close-up photos of pussy goiters and hairy brown moles.

And you should see the pages she bookmarks on my browser. Things like "Deadly Drug Interactions" and "One Hundred Ways to Kill Your Roommate" and "World's Grizzliest Animal Attacks." I mean, what does she do with this knowledge? I hate to imagine that my hands, *these* hands, the hands that have typed up so many stories about happy-go-lucky cheerleaders and first loves and best friendships, may have closed their skinny fingers around that awful man's sinewy, papery, age-spotted throat and squeezed and squeezed and squeezed until that bulbous purple tongue lolled out the corner of his frog-like mouth and he feebly sucked in his last raspy, rancid, garlicky breath. . . .

Really. I hate to even imagine it.

But it's possible. Because she? She is obviously disturbed. So maybe you should be talking to her. Yeah. Ask her where *she* was the night of the murder. Because I was in blackout. I know because I still have that night's episode of *Cupcake Wars* saved on my DVR, and if I hadn't been in blackout, you know I would've watched that puppy live. So that means she was out there somewhere doing God knows what to heaven knows who. She's the one you should be interviewing here. Trust me.

If you want to talk to her all you have to do is show me something really disturbing and she'll come out. Like some juicy road kill or one of those *Star* magazine pictures of real celebrity cellulite. I don't usually let her out by choice, but if it'll clear my name, sure. Anything to put this behind us so I can get on with my life. I'm sick of that rhymes-with-witch and all her bestselling books anyway. Good riddance. So go ahead. Bring her out. Do it! I'm just dying to know what she has to say for herself.

Wait. If she goes to jail does that mean I have to go, too?

Alyssa B. Sheinmel

For the record, this is not a confession. I have nothing to confess. And it's not a denial either, because the word "denial" implies that I have something to deny, and I don't. I had nothing to do with the death of Herman Mildew. In fact, I have an alibi. I was with my sister.

And just so you know, she's the one who knew Herman Mildew. I never met the guy. Well, not in the traditional sense. But no one met him in the traditional sense. I may have shaken a hand I presumed to be his, once. Maybe twice. Maybe we'd reached the level of a kiss-on-the-cheek hello, but I never let his lips actually touch my cheek, because, well, ew.

But she's the one who introduced us. She was much friendlier to him than I was. She's the friendlier sister. Ask anyone. She'll even be friendly to someone like Herman Mildew.

But like I said, I barely knew the guy. Okay, yes, fine, I did sort of meet him, once, twice, maybe three times. But it was only sort of meeting him. My sister is the one who said it was him. She may have been lying, but that doesn't mean she had anything to do with his death. People lie all the time, but that doesn't mean they've got something to hide. I mean, often it does. But it doesn't always.

I'm not a fan of mildew. The mold, I mean, not the man. It's always disgusted me. The stench of it. The way it thrives in the cold and the damp, the way it clings to wet laundry left to dry in a pile on the floor. The only thing that smells worse was Mildew himself—the man, that is, not the mold.

The first time I met him—or the man that my sister said was him—and shook his hand (a slimy and weak handshake, of course), I thought he smelled like pickles gone bad—no mean feat, since I'd always been under the impression that pickles didn't really go bad, being, inherently, you know, pickled. But he smelled like rancid pickles, old pickles, mildewed pickles, if such a thing is possible. And the worst part? His smell leaked onto me when he shook my hand. For days afterwards, I washed my hands with anti-bacterial soap, hot water, even detergent like the kind you use to rid your towels of mildew, but the smell lasted for two solid weeks.

The second time I saw him, I managed to turn our handshake into something shorter—more of a hand slap, really. Still, I ran to the bathroom immediately afterwards to wash my hands before the stench of him could settle into my skin. But the third time was when he tried to kiss my cheek, and if I'd thought the smell of him an arm's length away was bad, it was nothing compared with the stench of that face hovering next to mine. I ran to the bathroom again; this time because I thought I was going to vomit.

But did I want to kill the man? Of course not. Sure, I may have remarked to my sister that if he got that stench on me one more time, I would murder him myself—but that was just some sisterly hyperbole. And yes, I may have told her that I thought he smelled half-dead already, but come on—that doesn't mean I wanted him completely dead. Half-dead was just fine with me.

I mean, that is, fully alive, but smelling half-dead, of course. I would never actually want anyone dead. Or even half-dead. I'm a very peaceful person.

If you don't believe me, just ask my sister. She'll tell you.

Sara Shepard

Okay. I'll admit it. We hooked up once. Though it could have been one of his doppelgangers. You know he has doppelgangers, right? He says they're his henchmen. They spread bad tidings when he's busy. They dress in grey and do a lot of grunting.

I met him at a knitting class. I had decided to take it because my parents had been bugging me to get out of the house more and write less, and I thought a knitting class would piss them off. They probably hoped I'd join a cult or hang out with the miscreants by the river who set fire to things. They thought it was weird that I wasn't into people my own age, that I'd applied for an AARP card despite the fact that I wasn't eligible. "Stop hanging out with your seventy-year-old Chinese dentist!" they said. "Go volunteer! Go to a cocktail party!"

He had been the only man there. He was very good at knitting socks. His fingers could *fly*. He made me a pair in the first hour. They were more like Chinese finger cuffs than socks, per se, but I was still touched. When our instructor,

Gladys—who'd brought her three Bedlington terriers to the class and whose said Bedlingtons menacingly positioned themselves around her chair—announced a ten-minute break, he and I made eyes at each other over the coffee tureen and the Krispy Kremes. I told him I was planning on making a fisherman's sweater. He told me he was going to knit a giant spider web that could capture human prey. I asked him about his intriguing cologne. He told me it was pickle juice. He also said he liked my peg.

We made out in the back alley. The lamb-like Bedlingtons watched us through the window.

I'd wondered if he'd ever kissed a girl before, because he devoured me like he was slurping up a pot of Greek yogurt. But when we pulled away from each other, I was in love.

"Can I call you sometime?" I asked him.

"I don't really do the phone," he said.

I gave him my number. I floated through my front door when the class was over. I tasted that kiss again and again, the pickles and the donut glaze and a slight tinge of shoe polish, which he'd told me he sometimes used to blacken his teeth. In the course of four days, I knitted him seven pairs of argyle knee socks. I opened jars of pickles just to sniff the vinegar. I made the stupid mistake of sitting by the phone and waiting for him to call. Which, of course, he didn't.

I don't really do the phone, he'd told me. I'd thought it was some kind of line.

I saw him once more after that, at the abandoned pickle factory. He pretended not to know me. He said that it was one of his doppelgangers who'd gone to the knitting class, not him. But I knew. I saw an errant strand of yarn sticking to his wool pant leg. I saw the double-pointed needles sticking out of his pocket. Funny how getting your heart broken feels rotten no matter who does the breaking, whether it's a camp counselor who only danced with you because he was temporarily blinded, or a convenience store clerk who kissed you because he thought you were that *other* one-legged girl, or a grouchy old editor named Herman Mildew who should've known a good thing when he saw it.

Admittedly, I did think about killing him for a while. Hanging him by looped-together threads of Suri alpaca. Strangling him with a skein of cashmere. Suffocating him with one of the socks I'd made for him. My parents got in touch, worried again because I was locking myself away again. "You've got to get over this," they urged. "You can still live a productive life." But they were talking about something different. They didn't think I had the capacity for love.

I would never kill him, though. I loved him too much to hurt him. I wasn't the one who did this. I was in my bedroom that night. *Every* night. I can guarantee you I was sitting on my bed when it happened, thinking that if I just smiled more, it would make everyone's lives so much easier. Or I was lying on my floor, thinking about pickle juice and what the drivers through the alley must have thought when they noticed a peg-legged girl and rotund man kissing.

I was hysterical and broken and never sure I'd be whole again, but I wasn't and am not a murderer. Ask my parents. Ask anyone. It's true.

Jennifer E. Smith

The first thing you should know is this: I've known Herman Mildew since I was a kid. He was my cousin's best friend's sister's uncle. So, in some ways, it feels like he's been around forever.

I'm not saying that's how I got this gig or anything.

I'm only saying that we go way back.

When I was six, I sent him my very first short story. It was about a rabbit who learns his mother is a duck, and after being an outcast for a while, is eventually accepted by both the ducks and the rabbits. At our family's annual Christmas gathering—which Herman attended as a guest of his niece's brother's best friend's cousin—he handed me back the pages, which were so covered in red ink, it looked like someone had been murdered quite nearby.

At the very bottom, he'd written five simple words: "Ducks don't have bunnies, dummy."

Of course, I thought. I have to write what's real.

So the next time I saw him, at my cousin's best friend's sister's uncle's annual Easter brunch, I tapped him on the shoulder. He was, as usual, hovering near the food table, munching on pickles smothered with stinky cheese. He tipped his warty nose at me and narrowed his eyes.

"Here," I said, turning over my pages with the hopeful heart of a newly minted writer. This time, the story was real. No silly tales of ducks and rabbits. Instead, I'd written about the time I got lost in a grocery store and managed to knock over an entire display of baked beans.

A few weeks later, I found an envelope in the mail. Inside were the pages, once again covered in red ink. At the very bottom, Herman had written only this: "Avoid baked beans, idiot."

I took his words to heart, and by the next year, when I was eight-years-old, I was finally prepared to present him with my best story yet. This one was about a young writer who meets a famous editor at a Christmas party, and I'd painted Herman in the best possible light you could ever paint someone like Herman, leaving out the parts about how his sweaters were always too small and his feet smelled like moldy bananas. I didn't even mention how he always spit pickle seeds at me across the buffet table whenever I tried to talk to him at these events.

Usually, it took a few tries to get him to actually take my stories. First, he would make little paper airplanes out of each page and send them sailing all over the room. Then, when I'd run around collecting them—pulling them out of people's eggnog glasses or the bowl of cranberry sauce—I would tuck them in his coat, and he would proceed to roll them up and pelt them at other kids as if they were snow-balls. It would always go on like this for quite a while, until, eventually, he'd get bored and stuff them in his pocket. When they finally came back to me in the mail, they'd always be covered in food stains and torn at the edges, but smoothed out just enough to appease the U.S. Postal Service.

But this one Christmas, as I wandered around the party looking for Herman—stopping politely to say hello to people like his niece's brother's best friend—I couldn't find him anywhere. It wasn't until I rounded the corner near the front hallway that I saw something that still haunts me to this day.

There, in our living room, was Herman Mildew. He was sitting cross-legged on the blue carpet beside our Christmas tree. And where before there had been piles and piles of beautifully packaged gifts, now there was nothing but a sea of wrapping paper.

Herman looked up when I walked in, but there wasn't an ounce of guilt in his beady eyes. I guess I shouldn't have been surprised. He was wearing a tie meant for my dad, and the pair of mittens I'd saved up to buy for my mom. His coat pockets were bulging with other things: a small radio and a model car, golf balls and tubes of lipstick, and even a row of chocolate snowmen, who peeked out over the top with their wide, unblinking gazes.

My eyes met Herman's across the room, and a smirk appeared on his face. He glanced around at the debris, noticing one last unwrapped present. Even from the doorway, I could see that it was meant for me.

"My favorite," Herman said as he tore it open, before he even knew what it was. As it turned out, it was the jump rope I'd been hoping for; it had purple handles and a sparkly rope and was tied neatly in a bow.

"That's mine," I said, and Herman grinned a Grinchy grin.

"Consider it payment," he said, "for suffering through your stories."

And with that, he stood up—pockets clinking—and swept by me, moving straight past the other guests as if nothing had happened, and right to the buffet table, where he positioned himself beside the sour pickles, looking quite pleased with himself.

Right then, right there, as I watched him make off with my Christmas loot, I made two promises to myself.

First, that I'd one day write the best short story the world has ever seen about a duck-raised rabbit who comes into uncomfortably close contact with a can of baked beans (see my award-winning, highly acclaimed, gigantic bestseller, "Rabbit Stew").

And second, that I'd one day get back at Herman Q. Mildew.

But I swear to you, tonight was not that night.

Yes, it's true, I did have a piece of rope with me. But no, it was not a noose.

It was just a gift.

After all, I know how much Herman Mildew loves jump ropes.

Lemony Snicket

There is a small, musty postcard shop, just off Horacio Moya Square, in the Correspondence District of a certain city known for its unexpected violence and meatballs. If you enter the shop while Señora Pushkin is at the counter, and ask to see the collection of porcelain postcards in the locked glass case, you will instead be slipped an envelope and ushered out the door. The envelope contains a bus token.

I was lucky that the bus was not too noisy, so I heard the signal to disembark, which was the bus driver's radio playing "I Don't Want to Set the World on Fire" by the Ink Spots. I've always liked that song.

The weather was cold and clear. The trees had white bark and low-hanging leaves, and here and there were bits of green thread leading the way. Green thread is difficult to spot in trees. As a method of marking a pathway, it's not quite as lousy as sprinkling breadcrumbs through a forest, but it's close. The door of the building was brick and mossy.

There were six guests in all, plus ten regular members of the Society. The party, obviously, was by invitation only.

Fried eggs were served, resting on slices of rye toast and sprinkled with tiny bits of morel mushrooms. A few guests did card tricks to kill time. The six of clubs had just been produced from the handkerchief in my pocket when the co-chair of the Society called the meeting to order by hitting a thick, rusty bell.

Obviously, the identities of all those present, and the exact nature of our discussions, must remain undisclosed until Arbor Day. Nevertheless, I offer to the authorities, as verification of my alibi, a copy of the agenda of the meeting, as well as these *easily confirmable facts:*

1. The Ink Spots have indeed recorded a song entitled "I Don't Want to Set the World on Fire."

2. Morel mushrooms are delicious.

3. You can't un-ring a bell.

5:00 P.M.	Arrival, Eggs
6:00 P.M.	Call To Order
6:15 P.M.	Introductory Dances and Slide Show
7:30 P.M.	Assessment of Present Situation
8:30 P.M.	Treasurer's Report
8:45 P.M.	Establishment Of Alibi In Case Anybody Is Murdered Today
9:00 P.M.	Looking Towards The Future: The Society's Plans For Revolt, Revolution, Tea Shop, etc.
9:45 P.M.	Adjournment

10:00 P.M.   Please Leave

10:30 P.M.   Seriously, It's Late, Get Out

If you've ever seen a container with an airtight lid, then you know how my alibi could best be described.

Jordan Sonnenblick

This is more than an alibi. It's the Humble Suggestion for the Freeing Up of Much-Needed Prime Rent-Controlled Real Estate, the Restoration of Upward Mobility in the Publishing Industry, and the Bolstering of the Local Supply of Freshly Rendered Meats.

A depressing sight to anyone who spends any time at all in the more exclusive areas of Manhattan: the endless droves of fur- and diamond-encrusted dotards crowding the sidewalks, stumbling along behind their canes and walkers, their bifocals fogged with the fetid breath that gasps forth in great torrents past their yellowed dentures. They fill the restaurants from 4 P.M. on, chattering away at the top volume demanded by their failing ears. They claw and elbow their way past any unlucky soul who might attempt to purchase a baked good on a weekend morning wearing anything short of full body armor. And have you ever tried to catch a cab on the Upper East Side on Friday evening? Forget about it.

These people need to go. But they are not going anywhere, because of two small words: RENT CONTROL.

What each of these loathsomely entitled codgers is paying in monthly rent to live in the most coveted neighborhoods in the universe is roughly equal to the price that normal humans might pay for, say, a mediocre twenty-seven-inch television. This is because the rent on their apartments has been frozen since roughly 1946.

As a young New Yorker attempting to make my way in the world, what chance do I have? For that matter, what chance does any of us have? I mean, is there any justice in a world that has a kind, talented artist like me paying FIVE TIMES as much for a horrendous dump in the wilderness of Staten Island as the amount my talentless, soulless, cheese-guzzling hack of an editor Herman Mildew was paying for the seven-bedroom Park Avenue palace or wherever he lives?

At the same time, as anyone who has ever worked in publishing knows, there are roughly seventeen twenty-three-year-old publicists busting their butts for pathetically low salaries to every highly-paid editor. Each of those publicists is living from hand to mouth in a state of virtual starvation, in the hope that that editor will retire or die, thus rendering a one-in-seventeen chance that the beleaguered publicist might slip into the vacated position.

Herman "Scent-O" Mildew, for example, has held his editorial position for forty-six years—or so I've heard—since the day he was hired, with no experience, straight out of high school.

Anyway, every December I cook up a bunch of fresh and delicious meaty snacks to help feed the hungry people at our local soup kitchen. This got me thinking, there are too many annoying, entitled old people in this city. They are occupying all the best apartments, paying unfairly low rents. In my particular field, they are also taking up all the most coveted jobs so that younger, more talented, more pleasant people who don't spit little flecks of feta whenever they are shouting down their noses at the authors with whom they are privileged to work, are stuck working publicity. Why not ask these elders, who have skimmed the cream off our city's life for decades too long, to give something back? Why not, to be quite blunt, sacrifice them for the common good?

And hey, why not start with Herman "Bleu-Stache" Mildew?

Hey, is this meeting going to take a long time? I've left a whole bunch of crockpots going back in my apartment. The smell is absolutely heavenly, but if you let the meat cook down too long, the cleanup is murder.

Would you like a piece of fresh jerky? It's a little tough, but what do you expect? I wasn't exactly working with veal.

Natalie
Standiford

From the Investigator's Report:

- Ms. Standiford came to the pickle factory wearing a "necklace" (Ms. Standiford's term) made of a very long, very heavy, industrial-strength steel chain and "decorated" with a high-security steel-laminated closed-shackle brass padlock (or "charm," according to the suspect);

- Furthermore: the chain is exactly long enough to wrap twice around Mr. Mildew's large, coffin-like meat freezer and the padlock is the perfect size to lock the chain around said freezer so securely that, should someone be shut inside, they couldn't break their way out with a sledgehammer (and thus would freeze to death, obviously);

- Also, said lock and chain are steel-colored, clashing with Ms. Standiford's gold sequined dress, which would seem to suggest that they are actually hardware and not rapper jewelry as she claims;

- Plus, a diary was found among her belongings, containing this sentence: "Today I felt an irresistible urge to kill my editor, Herman Mildew;"

- Ms. Standiford has a motive, as demonstrated below.

Ms. Standiford's Statement:

I could not possibly have killed Herman Mildew and here is why: I have crippling writer's block. Look, here's a note from my doctor:

To Whom It May Concern:

Please excuse Natalie from gym for the rest of the year. She has been diagnosed with a crippling case of writer's block and cannot possibly be expected to wield a hockey stick or dodge a ball.

Sincerely,
Rita N. Wiepe, M.D.

This writer's block is so severe that I am incapable of even *conceiving* a plan—a *plot*, if you will—that comes to a satisfying conclusion. And I think we all agree that Herman's death is a satisfying conclusion. Not that I *wanted* him to die or anything. Um . . . can I take back what I just said?

The fact is, Herman himself would have told you that I can't plot my way out of a paper bag and I have proof—here, his last editorial letter to me.

Dear Natalie,

I just finished reading the latest draft of your magnum opus, "Thrones: A History of the Litterbox." I'll start with the good news: cat books are popular, and this is, ostensibly, a book about cats. So there's that in its favor.

The story, however, still needs a lot of work. Your prose style is, as always, execrable, but I was expecting that. What I failed to realize before I gave you a book contract is that you are incapable of constructing a plot. The book begins with a description of the imperial cats of ancient Egypt pawing the sands of the desert and ends with modern American felines triumphantly using the toilet on YouTube. You have failed to provide the reader with a conflict, someone to root for. Where, my dear, is the heart?

I'll give you one more chance to revise, Natalie, but if the next draft doesn't scream "Movie Adaptation Starring Jennifer Aniston" I'm afraid we'll have to cancel the contract.

Yours in mustache-twirling evil,

Herman Q. Mildew

P.S. You couldn't plot your way out of a paper bag. There, I said it.

I rest my case. He said it himself: I can't plot. Therefore, I must be innocent. Yes, Mr. Mildew's insensitivity caused my incapacitating writer's block, which may sound like a motive for killing him. As I've already pointed out, however, I'm incapable of planning anything so plot-driven as a murder. It honestly never occurred to me that this giant reinforced-steel chain I'm wearing could be used as anything other than a very, very heavy necklace. And the industrial strength pad-lock dangling from the end is, of course, a charm. What's its significance? Why, it's the lock from my diary! My giant, giant diary. Which I can no longer write in, because of the aforementioned crippling block.

Oh—I see you found the diary. Thank you, I was look-ing all over for it! Yes, this is my handwriting . . . Did I write this line about having an irresistible urge to kill Her-man? Um . . . Well, you can't use my *diary* as evidence. This isn't really a diary at all—it's an idea notebook, that's right, it's full of ideas for future stories and novels, novels that, sadly, will never get written now, thanks to Herman's edi-torial cruelty. You do know that I wrote *fiction*, don't you? Do they teach you cops what the word "fiction" means in cop school? It means "made up." "Not true." It means, "can't be used against someone as evidence in a court of law." Just ask any judge.

Oh, and all this meat and ice cream defrosting on the pantry floor? How should I know how it got there?

Rebecca Stead

Here's the thing: I liked him.

He taught me so much. Yes, he could be rude, cheap, and maybe occasionally malicious, but I believe that some of life's most important teachers are "difficult people," or so-called "enormous jerks." I think it must be the burden of knowing *so much more* than others, and trying to share that knowledge (with other, less-knowing people) in the sometimes-rather-short time they are granted on Earth, that makes them so testy.

I don't mind unpleasant teachers. All I ask is to learn.

For instance: my AP pre-calculus teacher, Mr. Huffish, was not a nice man in the opinion of most people. He freely and imaginatively insulted the intelligence of his students, and always handed back our tests in grade order, from the highest grade in the class to the lowest. When I took the polynomial functions quiz with a fever of 104 (no complaints; I am not a complainer), I was the very last person to be handed my paper the following Monday—along with a few words about how girls should not attempt higher math.

I happen to remember that Douglas Fine, a known cheat who had a perfect score on that quiz, laughed. But did I hold any of this against Mr. Huffish? Never. Why? Because he was a gifted teacher. No one was more saddened than I when he died just before graduation, apparently after eating something bad.

Another example: my boss Ellen at the Ice Cream Depot, where several of us worked for the summer after high school graduation. She was a model of morality, the number-one most ethical person I've ever encountered, to this day probably. Ice cream shops don't pay particularly well, of course, but it was wrong of me to think that a free cone might be an occasional perk of the job. She was right to charge me double when she found me in the utility closet, eating a single scoop of Koffee Krunch™, no sprinkles. (I had picked out a broken cone on purpose, knowing it would otherwise be thrown out, but that was no excuse.) She was a true credit to the company until she was found in the walk-in freezer on Labor Day, apparently locked in overnight, which wasn't even supposed to be possible.

I was quite shaken, because I had learned such a lot from Ellen. I shuddered to think that it could have been any of us stuck in there, slowly freezing to death. It could have even been Douglas Fine.

And now we come to my truest mentor, my longtime editor, poor Mr. Mildew, who just last week so *effectively* managed to convey his feelings about my new manuscript: "Boring and unoriginal." Three words! How many people are capable of saying so much with so little? I still had much to learn from him. (And I was more than happy to treat for lunch.)

I realize that all this makes me unusual. Most people have

no idea how to accept criticism. They complain endlessly, without any idea of how to move forward. I, on the other hand, am a "doer." Unlike the whiners of the world, I'm *grateful* for what each of these genuinely superior people was willing to share—if anything, I was *extra*-fond of those generous enough to correct me. And since I had no motive (whatsoever) to kill Mr. Mildew, there is obviously no need for an alibi.

Even a fool like me knows that.

Todd Strasser

Oh, no.

Don't tell me you're still reading this.

What am I, the fifty-fifth author in a row who's supposed to spew out the same nonsense about the death of some pompous jerk named Herman Mildew? (At least, that's what they've been telling you, right?) Okay, here's the deal. You may as well read this because I'm the only one who's going to tell you the truth . . . which is, you've just been scammed.

But don't feel bad. Not only has every person who's read all this been fooled, but so have the authors who wrote for it. Hard to believe that all these people who are supposed to be so smart would fall for something so obvious.

I mean, some of these writers are famous. Some have won major literary awards. And even the ones who haven't surely didn't have time to waste on junk like this.

But they did.

And for what?

Listen, I went to the 826NYC website. You take the

letters from the name Herman Mildew and from 826NYC and rearrange them, and you know what you get?

"W8, he can read my mind, 2."

Maybe you didn't have to use all the letters and numbers, and you had to use a few letters twice, but you get the picture, right? Here's what's really going on: someone's taken control of all these authors' minds, including mine. Someone got us to waste an immense amount of time trying to outdo each other. The result? We spent hours, days, weeks(!) trying to be cleverer than the next author, each of us trying to write the one piece in this book that you'll want to tell your friends about.

Meanwhile, deadlines were missed and contracts went unsigned. Proposals weren't delivered. Authors forgot to show up at conferences, and at those dumb school visits your teachers make you attend so you can learn how important it is to read and write, and what unattractive and unpopular dorks the authors were when they were your age. . . .

And here's something else you should know. The "someone" behind this murder isn't one person, it's two.

That's right. There are two guys who never stopped making their deadlines and signing contracts and showing up at appearances. They filled the void left by all the rest of us while we toiled over our entries for this book. Those two will probably get rich and famous and win all sorts of awards the rest of us would have won had we not been messing around on this book.

Don't you hate being made a fool of?

I sure do. I hate, hate, HATE it!

But listen, there's good news.

I know who those two guys are.

One of them is that stinky cheese guy. The other guy is a

bestseller in France, where they love stinky cheese. (See the relationship?) I bet those two have been laughing like crazy.

Well, I have news for you. They're not going to get away with it.

Because I won't let them.

Believe me, nobody makes a fool of me and gets away with it.

So look out, Scieszka and Ehrenhaft, because some foggy, drizzly, chilly night on a dark street in Brooklyn, when no one else is around, I'll be waiting for you.

Heather Terrell

It's my turn to tell you my alibi? Ummm, did you know that the word "alibi" was first used in the seventeenth century, and that it actually means "elsewhere?" Like, if you're under suspicion for a crime, you have to prove you were "alibi?"

Oh, you don't want to hear the historical origins of the word alibi. You have a long line of suspects who need to give their alibis too. I'm sorry. I sometimes slip into historical-writer-babble when I'm really, really nervous.

No, no, you misunderstand me. I don't have any reason to be anxious. I mean, it's not like I killed or hurt or did anything harmful to Herman Mildew. It's just that my alibi—my "elsewhere"—is kind of unbelievable.

What is my alibi? You want me to get to the point, I can tell by the way you're tapping your pencil. I'm not trying to stall, I swear, it's just that I'm a little scared. You promise that you won't haul me off to a loony bin like Herman threatened?

Well . . . I couldn't possibly have killed Herman Mildew, and here's why. The last time I saw him was outside the entryway to the ancient Egyptian Temple of Dendur at the Metropolitan Museum of Art, minutes before the museum closed. Herman was very much alive. In fact, he was ranting and raving—promising that he'd lie and tell the world that my historical research was one big fraud if I left him to go to another publishing house for my new book, *Hatshepsut, The Pharaoh Herself.* Or worse.

I couldn't listen to his threats a second longer. After all, Herman knew better than anyone that my research was insanely accurate; he understood the huge risks that I take to capture every detail and nuance of the past. Stupidly, I had trusted him with my secret when he first became my editor. So, I left Herman and the Temple of Dendur behind, and walked into a connecting room that housed ancient Egyptian artifacts. And I've been "elsewhere" from that very moment until I entered this ridiculous pickle factory party. You see, I couldn't have possibly killed him.

Where did I go in the meantime? Where is my "elsewhere"? Ummmm . . . ancient Egypt.

You're laughing. I know it sounds crazy. But it's absolutely 100 percent true. I don't know how I do it, but I simply touch an artifact, close my eyes, and shift into another time. Today at the museum, I touched this colossal statue of Hatshepsut and stepped back into 1500 BC. You should have seen the scene! I walked right into a ceremony at the Djeser-Djeseru temple at Deir el-Bahri overseen by Hatshepsut herself. The temple was astonishing—the hieroglyphics so colorful, not that drab sandy shade you see today—but even better was the fight I witnessed between Hatshepsut and her nephew Thutmose III. Some historians have theorized that it was Thutmose who tried to destroy all evidence of Hatshepsut after her death.

Today, Thutmose was screaming, "A woman should not rule as Pharaoh!"

Hatshepsut didn't dignify his outburst with a response, of course. She was way too regal for that. But she did shoot Thutmose a look, like she wanted to slip a little poisonous belladonna in his wine.

Such juicy material for my book! And what a coup! Do you understand that it solves the long-standing mystery of who tried to wipe out all mention of Hatshepsut and why? Historians will be abuzz when they read my new book.

You don't believe me? I can see by the way you are rolling your eyes that you don't. Truly, I've gone back in time before; it's how I do my research. Have you heard of my first book, *Elizabeth I, The Virgin Queen*? Well, I touched that famous fifteenth century portrait of her that hangs in London's National Gallery, and waltzed right into Westminster Abbey on Elizabeth's coronation day. How else do you think I got all those amazing details about the coronation, including all that gossip about her affairs?

What did you just say? You think that I can get the really juicy stuff in the library? No way. The real primary source is to go there yourself. That's what I do, and Herman knew it. That's why he wanted to keep me all to himself. But he should have been more careful about calling me crazy; it brought about my leaving him for another publisher. Still, that doesn't mean I'd kill Herman. I've seen a lot of royal beheadings and hangings in my research, and it's made me a pacifist.

Can I prove my alibi? Is there some way that I may demonstrate beyond a shadow of a doubt that I was in ancient Egypt at the time Herman Mildew was killed? Why, yes. Right here in my pocket, I have a thirteen-inch, marble statue of Hatshepsut that I brought back with me when I left the Djeser-Djeseru temple and re-entered modern times. One of Hatshepsut's handmaids gave it to me as a gift—kind of like a party favor—as I left the ceremony. Here, take a look, but be careful. It's from 1500 BC, and Herman almost dropped it when I let him hold it at the museum.

What's that you say? Did I get this at the museum store? Of course not. Don't be ridiculous. A price tag on the bottom? Hand that back to me, please.

That monster! Herman switched out my original statue for a cheap reproduction to undermine my evidence. That vindictive, inhuman creature planned this whole thing (even his own demise) just to destroy me. He knew that I'd have to tell you my secret to absolve myself, and that would be the end of me. What reader—or new publisher—would buy "historically accurate" books from a crazy lady?

Herman Mildew, I didn't kill you, but I wish I had.

Ned Vizzini

I'm a very lucky writer. All you have to do is read my bio, which that old buzzard Herman never bothered to do, to learn how I started out young and found great success, like Dickens but with fewer words. I even have a family! It's sickening!

But before you hate me too much, you should know that I have bad luck too; and sometimes, such as on the night of Herman's murder, it can be tough to tell which is which.

It began with my trip to the Pickle Factory. I wasn't keen on going but you have to attend parties as a writer; that's where the stories are—and the food. So I put on my second-finest shoes and slipped into my 1982 BMW 633CSi, which my wife calls "The Shark."

The Shark is a two-door coupe with a hood that tapers to a point like a jet-black predator. I feel great when I drive it, but I pay for this feeling in cash, as the car currently has 157,000 miles and I've spent four times the money on repairs as I did buying the thing.

I was making good time on the highway when the engine

died. The change was sudden and refractory. No matter how I pushed on the accelerator, the needle dipped from 85—I mean, 55—to 45, 40, 35 . . . all while other cars humiliatingly and dangerously whizzed past me. One of the quirks of The Shark is that it has no hazard lights, so I could only put on my right turn signal as I pulled into the shoulder of an off ramp, hoping desperately that the engine would hold out long enough to get me to a gas station . . . and then I stopped. *Well,* I thought, *it's lucky that this off ramp has a shoulder!*

Although the car would start, it absolutely refused to move. If I brought it out of park, it began rolling backward toward the highway, which wasn't good for anyone.

I got out and walked to the bottom of the ramp, leaving the turn signal blinking, and there I met a homeless guy.

"Engine trouble?" the homeless guy asked. He was standing with a sign that said "Hungry, Please Help," so I assumed he was homeless, but really he could've just been exploring alternative income streams. "I can help," he said.

"I'm okay; I'm trying to find a gas station," I said.

"I heard you up there. That engine won't take you anywhere. I'll give you a push."

I hesitated. I didn't have cash on me but I had my second-finest shoes, and could feel a pocket of bad luck opening up.

"You don't have to trust me if you don't want to," the guy said, "but you're not going anywhere without help."

I assented. He told me his name, Ron, as we went back up the off ramp. He had clean sneakers and a new-ish leather jacket; he was lucid and polite and had none of the attitude of the tow truck driver I'd assumed I would have to call. He dropped down on the asphalt as we reached the car, shining a flashlight underneath.

"Your transmission fluid line snapped!" Ron said. "That's why you can't switch gears. You don't even need a push. I can fix this easy."

He pulled out a huge knife. The blade flashed in the glare of approaching headlights. "You should really have hazards," Ron said before clenching the knife between his teeth. "Thith ithn't safe."

In five minutes, he had squiggled under the car, cut the ruptured portion of the fluid line, and reattached it to the transmission. "Try it now," he said, and I got in The Shark and found that it worked beautifully.

"You're a lifesaver!" I told Ron. "How can I repay you?"

"Honestly, I need a job. Warehousing."

"I don't do any warehousing. But let me get to an ATM and I'll give you some cash."

"Sounds good!"

We both got in. I knew a mechanic would charge hundreds of dollars to fix a line like that, so I got Ron one hundred dollars and considered it a bargain. He thanked me and gave me his cell phone number (never judge a person by their handmade sign) before going back to his spot by the off ramp.

I marveled at my good fortune all the way to the party—until the cops spotted the knife that was kicking around in The Shark's back seat! As they pulled me away for questioning, I tried to explain that it wasn't mine, but they told me they'd heard that before (which they had, from me, but that's a different story) and asked me, "What right do you have carrying around a twelve-inch Bowie knife? Who are you, Crocodile Dundee? Don't you know these things are illegal?"

"It's Ron's!" I said frantically. "Ron's!"

"And where were you when Herman Q. Mildew was killed?" the cops pressed.

"With Ron!" I promised. "The Shark was broken but now it works!"

Well, those cops weren't buying any of it. They took me to central booking and had me write a statement . . . and I hope they're satisfied.

Adrienne Maria Vrettos

I was not here, killing Mr. Mildew.

In fact, it's been years since I've even seen him. He no longer publishes my work. I did recently reach out to him about a new project, but received a grammatically disastrous rejection letter in response. I am guessing it was written by his horse-faced assistant and that Mr. Mildew did not take the time to read it himself.

If you must know where I was at the time of the murder, pass over that pen and paper, and I will draw you a map. You will need to retrace my steps to find evidence of my whereabouts, as I am guessing my word will not do.

This, right here, is the highway. You will follow it deep into the nothing until the exits are few and far between. You will take the exit that looks most like it leads into a haunted wood. You'll know which one I mean when you get there. The off ramp will end in a T. Turn right and follow that road until you start to wonder if perhaps you've gone the wrong way.

There will be a turnoff. It will look at first like a road, but it is a driveway. Follow it up, into the trees. Roll down your windows if you like. The air smells of pine and vindication. The forest will seem to open up after a long while, and the driveway will end in front of a house.

The house is empty, and has been for some time.

When you get out of the car and scan the area you will realize you are alone, except for the forest and its secrets. The feeling of emptiness all around you may be alarming. Not alarming in a pressing-in way, not like you're a child stuck under a couch cushion while an older, stronger sibling sits on your head until your body voids from fear. It's not like that at all. It's a feeling that if you could stretch your arms so far into the darkness they thinned and sagged like pulled taffy, you would still never touch another person. Your fingers will tingle with the absence of other flesh.

Unless you've brought someone with you. I did. You should let them out of the car at this point. If they've been lying down, give them a moment to find their balance, to stand. Watch as they feel the same emptiness you do. Watch for a flicker of hope. Of bravery. Assure them there is nothing for miles around. Make note of the low temperature. And their lack of footwear.

Did I say something shocking? You've paled. I can see your pulse bumping against the skin of your neck. Yes, please, take a sip of water. I don't mind if we share a cup. Let me know when you would like me to continue.

Now then.

It will be time to go inside. Be careful on the front steps, the wood is soft, especially if you are struggling with an uncooperative "plus one."

The door should be unlocked, as it was when I found it.

You will not find proof of my visit downstairs. You will

need to go upstairs. You can take a moment to explore the three bedrooms and small bathroom on the second floor. It will feel a bit like you are in one of those "living museums" after hours—the kind you visited as a child to see women churning butter. There is a nursery, but I don't suggest you linger there. It is a sad room. I could feel it right off. Leave the room to its memories and move on.

You will be going to the attic.

In the hallway in front of the bathroom there is a rope hanging from the ceiling. Pull on it. The fold-down apparatus is rusty, and if you are trying to unfold the attic stairs with one hand while holding something wiggly with the other, be forewarned that it will take some strength.

Also, being a pull-down, the staircase is steeper than most, and if you are dragging behind you a heavy bundle as you climb, it may take you a few tries to get up the stairs.

The bundle may take a tumble.

I suggest you hurry down the attic stairs after it. You will be amazed at how quickly a tied-up thing can move. If you end up giving chase, please remember that you are in charge here. I urge you to not panic and finish things in a flash of rage the moment you make contact. You will be left with a let-down feeling. Like you've had your first kiss but it was so fast that you are left with nothing to reflect on, no echo of feeling on your lips. You will feel empty.

Back to the attic with you and your bundle.

You'll find the attic to be full of *things*. Boxes, sheet-covered furniture, trunks. Remember that you are not there for antiquing. It doesn't matter how much Brooklynites at a flea market will pay for the ephemera of the aged. You have other business to attend to.

Turn around and look behind you. There will be a narrow

space under the eve, filled with small boxes. You may wonder how to get back there, since the space around the staircase is also filled with boxes, leaving no path.

You have some work ahead of you. I made sure of that. Move the boxes to clear a path, and then move the boxes that are under the eve. See now that between the studs of the slanted roof, pink blankets of insulation have been pressed in. And see now how in the area from which you moved the boxes there is one panel of insulation that seems to be lying less than flat.

Go to that panel. You seem to be about my height. Poke your finger into the insulation a bit below eye-level. You will have to wiggle it a bit. Press your finger in until it touches a rubbery something that is firm at first and then gives way. Use your fingertip to feel around until you detect a horizontal seam. Press your finger into the seam until it is forced to part. You will feel two rows of polished stone. Use your finger to pry between them and push farther in. Ignore the thing that feels like a slab of bumpy ham. Instead, hook your finger to grab the dry-feeling thing, the hunk of something that feels as if it doesn't belong. That's what you've come for.

Pull it out.

What you have found will need to be separated into pieces and dried before it can be reconstructed. You will see it is a letter. You will see it is grammatically disastrous.

I was not here, killing Mr. Mildew.

I was elsewhere, doing other things.

Melissa Walker

Okay, I know it doesn't look good that my cache shows several visits to alibinetwork.com, but my membership on that site has nothing to do with the night in question. The Alibi Network Excuse Specialists are under my employ strictly for personal matters—nothing *professional*, meaning nothing related to my very formal relationship with Herman Mildew.

It's no secret that Mr. Mildew and I did not see eye to eye on very many things. He frowned upon violence; I adore Liam Neeson in the best action movie of all time, *Taken*. He liked full-sized pickles; I am strictly a cornichons girl. He always wanted a happy ending; I prefer the open-ended fade-away. He grows fungus on his body; I won't let a mushroom touch my plate. But all that is neither here nor there.

Am I suspicious because I don't look *sad* enough upon hearing of his passing? Well, I'd only been working with him for a few years, after all. I never even got to the point where I felt comfortable calling him Herman.

The truth is this: he didn't *know* me. He was like one of

those people you hang out with five times and yet they still greet you with, "Nice to meet you." It's vaguely offensive, how *wrong* he was about me. When my last book came out, he sent me a bouquet of those neon-dyed daisies to celebrate. Who likes a neon-dyed daisy?!

I guess maybe people have heard me gossiping about him. It's no secret that my high school yearbook senior quote was, "If you can't say anything nice, come sit by me . . . " but that in itself is evidence that my gossiping was a nasty habit long before Mr. Mildew and I were acquainted. Yes, my rumor-mongering is widespread and far-flung, undiscerning and willy-nilly. It targets everyone and no one in particular. Not even this man with whom I had a professional relationship where I poured my heart out for him while he barely noticed he'd met me. (And why would he? He thought I was a neon-daisy type.)

But is that a reason to commit murder? Certainly not! Besides, anyone who knows me at all (and it's good that Mr. Mildew is not here to misjudge me again!) knows that on the night in question there was both a new reality show debuting on Bravo and a Carolina Tar Heels basketball game. I like to live tweet both of those things, so I'm obviously quite innocent.

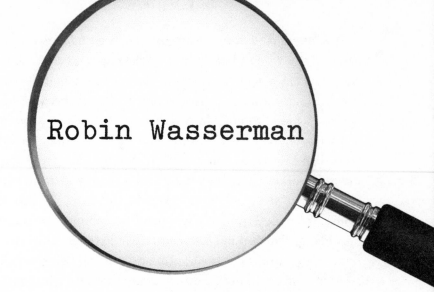

Robin Wasserman

I'm sorry, you must have me mistaken me for a moron. I am no moron.

You think I don't watch TV? Oh, trust me, I watch TV. Though not an unhealthy amount, as a certain Mr. Herman Q. Mildew had been known to suggest every time he barged into my house and planted himself *directly* in front of the biggest of my six screens, his hideous mountain of flesh inevitably blocking my view of the final, crucial key moment of whatever episode he'd elected to interrupt. But even Mildew's monstrous torso and foghorn voice couldn't prevent me from deriving a few fundamental facts of life from the school of television, first and foremost of which is, *never speak to the cops without a lawyer.*

Now, I know what you're going to say, because it's what they always say on TV. You're going to say that asking for a lawyer makes me look guilty. And then I'm going to say what I always promised myself I'd say when the cops came calling—

What's that?

No, of course I don't mean that I've been *rehearsing* what I would say when I had to talk to the cops. It's not like I've stationed myself in front of my mirror on a nightly basis preparing my story until it sounded authentic, because first, if I had wanted to kill Mr. Mildew for, oh, let's say, spoiling the series finale of my all-time favorite show that I had to record and watch later because Mr. Mildew just *had* to meet me in his office that night right away—except that he never showed up, and you know when he *did* show up? At my house, the next day, precisely when I was about to watch the episode, at which point he proceeded to step in front of the television, flap his flabby mouth, and tell me, before I could stick my fingers in my ears and scream, exactly whodunit—

No, I am *not* saying I would have killed him for that. Fortunately for Mr. Mildew, I happen to possess inhuman restraint. Did I kill him when he accidentally on-purpose deleted my entire collection (341 VCR tapes collected over a period of sixteen years) of Saturday morning cartoons? Or when he ("Oopsie!") reprogrammed my DVR to record only educational shows about sewage treatment plants, quilting, and cheese?

No I did not.

Mind you, that wasn't even the worst of it. You know what really stuck in my craw? Not just that he kept inter-rupting, not just that mountain of flesh blocking my view, but that this supposedly great cultural arbiter, this man in whom I'd entrusted my entire creative future, this . . . this *editor* had no appreciation for Art. I'm going to tell you something now, something that's going to make you want to pack up this entire operation and leave the corpse to stew in its own foul juices as a monster like this deserves.

Herman Q. Mildew didn't even own a television.

I didn't kill him for that, either. Tempting as it may have been.

All I'm saying is that if I *had* killed him, I wouldn't have bothered to prepare a statement for the cops, because I've seen enough TV to know how to kill someone without the cops ever getting a whiff of a clue. For one thing, I wouldn't strike him down in an abandoned pickle factory filled with his nearest and dearest. More likely I'd contrive to bump into him outside his office on his way to his weekly knitting class. When I passed him I would be wearing a wig and a bright pink skirt suit that I happen to know from a distance would make me resemble (and thus cast suspicion on) one of his other authors who shall remain nameless but who once made the mistake of turning off my favorite show to watch a *basketball* game. I'd inject him with an untraceable chemical agent that acted on a time-delay. Then I would make sure I had an alibi for the rest of the day, so that when he dropped dead I could tell anyone who asked that I was snug at home on the couch, watching TV.

Well, yes, of course I realize that sitting home alone watching TV is a classically poor alibi for *most* people, but anyone who knows me would tell you that I would never, under any circumstances, miss my shows. (Why do you think I became a writer? Do you know how hard it is to spend all day watching TV when you have a *real* job?)

As you can see, I know exactly what to do if I want someone dead, and I know how to do it without getting caught. So I'm by no means afraid of getting tripped up by any of your sophomoric interrogation techniques. But even so, and even though I'm innocent, I'm going to tell you what I long ago promised myself I'd tell anyone who asked, what I've learned to say from watching one TV criminal after another fall prey to constabulary and legal minds far brighter than yours: I want a lawyer.

And until I get one, I'm not saying a word.

Lynn Weingarten

Well if you must know, on the night in question I was having a quiet evening alone. I did not speak to or see anyone. I did not answer my phone. I was in a meditative mood, you know, gathering my thoughts and all. So I sharpened my knife collection, which really I find very soothing, and then I went out for a little stroll. Then I spent some time dissolving some old steaks in my bathtub, which I had filled with lye. After that I burnt a pile of clothes in the backyard, buried the ashes, and cooked myself a dinner of quinoa and roasted root vegetables. I had been experimenting with a new recipe. And I must say it was quite a success.

But I, of all people here tonight in this pickle factory, should not be considered as a suspect in connection with this tragedy. In lieu of a "provable alibi," I would like to present you with this heart. No, not literally a bloody heart. HA HA! A figurative heart. Mine. Heavy with sadness over the loss of this man who was so terribly, terribly misunderstood. But aren't so many of us?

So yes, perhaps you too have heard the stories:

1. That Mr. Mildew liked to make writers sit in his office and watch him mark their manuscripts, which he would often do with the help of a giant, novelty Welcome to Wisconsin pen just to make it more humiliating;

2. That Mr. Mildew kept a gun inside his desk drawer and sometimes when writers were late delivering manuscripts he'd take the gun out and point it at them while saying something like, "Well I'll show you a *real* DEADline;"

3. That he only ate very smelly ripe cheeses and especially enjoyed bringing them to long meetings on hot days in rooms where the windows wouldn't open;

4. That sometimes while he ate the cheese he'd take his dentures out because his favorites were soft enough to gum;

5. That while his dentures were out, *he'd make his editorial assistant brush them;*

6. That his dentures, by the way, were made of sharks' teeth, or endangered panda bones, or implanted with tiny webcams and the only reason he ever smiled was to give them an unobstructed view;

7. That his teeth were bought from a tribe of cannibals and so, no, he'd never eaten a person himself, but he did like knowing that his teeth had;

8. That he spread all those rumors himself just to mess with people;

9. That he'd sometimes set up incredibly earnest Internet dating profiles for his authors, filled with the authors' desires for "a partner in crime" who "loves to laugh as much as I do!" and then would leave these profiles open on computers all around the office;

10. That he had many fake accounts on Goodreads which he would use to give one-star reviews to books *he had not even read*;

11. That—remember Mr. Mildew's gun that you heard about? It wasn't actually a gun at all, just a very realistically gun-y-looking camera with a lens in the barrel, and while he was threatening to shoot his writers, he was also taking photos of them looking terrified, which he would sell prints of through the Etsy shop he had set up solely for this purpose.

Contrary to all of these rumors—entirely baseless unless you count the notarized photographs, certified videos, DNA evidence, a couple of lawsuits, a signed confession, and a small FBI file—here is truth: Mr. Mildew was a good and decent man who was horribly and unfairly judged. The only thing he ever did wrong was not dispelling these rumors when he had the chance, so that more people could have known and loved him like I did.

Kiersten White

A hem. I'm here to offer my alibi.
No, HERE. In front of the line. Quit motioning the people standing behind me forward! I'm next. I don't care if my nose barely comes to the top of the counter. I'm still standing here. Please don't make me jump up and down to get your attention. It's humiliating. No! Person-so-tall-I-can't-quite-see-your-face, don't you *dare* cut in front of me! He was—I am—oh, for the love. Fine. Just a second.

NOW I AM A STANDING ON A FOOTSTOOL. YOU CANNOT IGNORE ME. IT IS MY TURN.

What do you mean an alibi isn't necessary? Don't you wave dismissively! You demanded *everyone* give an alibi, and I'm here to give mine. It is airtight; if it were a color it would be sparkling white and it would smell like jasmine tea. I'm fully prepared to give you a minute-by-minute account of my whereabouts during the murder.

I—excuse me? I must be hearing you wrong. Did you say I'm too short to be a suspect? No, no, your exact quote was, "Someone as adorably wee as you couldn't possibly have committed such a heinous crime." You're not even going to interview me just because I'm the size of an average (okay, maybe smaller than average) eleven-year-old? Do you have any idea what eleven-year-olds can do?? Clearly you have forgotten sixth grade entirely.

No, I will not step out of the way so the woman behind me can explain the surgical gloves she has been wearing all evening! Since you're not interviewing me, you probably also don't want to know about what's in my purse. Allow me to dump it out on the counter for you. Well, on second thought, allow me to ask the person behind me who can actually reach the counter to dump the purse out on my behalf.

See that? It's the hot pink Taser that I did not knock him out with. Oh, and underneath it, the pepper spray that I did not use to stun him before knocking him out. And next to those, the iron knuckles that I use merely as a paperweight, and not to deliver a few key blows to the abdomen in retaliation for one-too-many times being patted on the head by his big, sausage, pickle fingers. And to your right, those are not the keys to his car (which reeks of despair, past-due checks, and cat pee, and has a conveniently body-sized trunk). No, those are merely clever replicas.

Yes, that is a clothing receipt from a Gap Kids store. Shut up. It's completely irrelevant. Moving on.

Shouldn't you be writing this down? And shouldn't you also be wondering why no one can account for my whereabouts from the time I arrived until twenty minutes ago? (Though I will inform you I was merely placed in the coat closet by mistake because my coat was too large so they thought no one was in it.) And shouldn't you—wait a minute. Are you humming "Short People Got No Reason to Live" under your breath?

THAT'S IT, MISTER. YOU DON'T BELIEVE ME THAT VERY SMALL PEOPLE CAN BE CAPABLE OF VERY BIG VIOLENCE? You'll never doubt I'm the murderer again! Even though I'm not! But you should at least do me the dignity of suspecting me! YOU. ME. NOW. I'm going to leap over this counter and show you exactly how murderous I can be!

Well, just as soon as someone brings me a stepladder so I can actually climb over the top to strangle you.

Yes, you can interview the next person while I wait.

You're welcome.

Mo Willems

M Y ALIBI KILLS
by Mo Willems

I couldn't have done it, because at that exact same time
I was busy murdering someone else.

Oh.
(I probably shouldn't have said that.)

Rita Williams-Garcia

Yes, I know I'm not helping my case by laughing but I can't help it. Just give me a moment and I'll pull it togeth—

Sorry. Sorry. There! It's out of my system.

Okay, Okay. I know how it looks, with a witness seeing my Subaru parked outside Mildew's townhouse earlier and me banging on the door. And yelling. Cursing. Threatening? Mr. Lonelyhearts Busybody caught that too?

Mildew wouldn't take my calls. Why lie about that when you can easily check the phone records? Yes. I called him seventeen times the night before. Another thirty, give or take, in the morning. But the wormy soul crusher owed me a face-to-face. He owed me!

No. I won't calm down. You don't know what he did to me. You can't possibly understand the incalculable loss. You can't—

You know about that? Didn't think it was public, but it was a matter of time. And digging.

The bastard bought my book proposal on the spot. No

waiting, no editorial suggestions. Just a big fat check and a contract within weeks. Unheard of. My critique group said they'd heard things about Mildew. "Be careful. Get an agent." I chalked their caution up to veiled envy. I should have known better.

He didn't just buy one book. He offered a three-book series contract with an "exclusive clause," but with one caveat. I was to deliver all three manuscripts at once. Lo and behold, I write, deliver, and then receive the balance of the advance. All's ducky, right? Well, instead of a book launch, I get my twenty author's copies of each book, along with a notice from the remainder department saying I'm invited to purchase the stock of 10,000 copies each at a dollar and a quarter a piece. I have until Friday to courier my check because thereafter, the stock will be grounded into a pulp and donated to Urban Outfitters to make journals for aspiring writers.

It gets better. Herman's house then releases a killer wombat series—not similar to mine, but a killer wombat series nonetheless—yes! *That* killer wombat series. Your child already has the Killer Wombat lunchbox?

As much as I'd gladly take credit for the demise of Herman Mildew, I can't claim that honor. What Mr. Lonelyhearts Busybody didn't tell you is, since I couldn't get in through the front, I ran around to the back. I was about to climb over the iron gate when I saw, blooming in the garden, rows of hyacinth.

Do you know what happens to me when I come into contact with hyacinth? I can't breathe. Mildew might as well have his hands gripped around my throat. And my eyes swell to pillows.

The minute I saw the hyacinths in bloom, I raced to my

Subaru and sped to the nearest pharmacy. The pharmacist can attest to filling the emergency prescription from my allergist.

And do you know what the pharmacist said as he handed me the prescription? Do you? He said, "With your eyes puffy like that, you slightly resemble that popular killer wombat."

Maryrose Wood

Wait: Herman Mildew is dead?

Herman? Sweet, stern, misunderstood Herman?

Look, I know it's fashionable to trash your editor. And Herman was, admittedly, a nut job. Did I ever tell you about the time that he circled my every use of the lowercase letter *m* in a manuscript and told me to revise the whole book to get rid of them? "Hideous letter," he explained. "Reminds me of a bad experience I once had with an ill-tempered dromedary." Of course I knew he meant camel. Dromedaries have one hump, not two. But that's exactly the sort of factual boo-boo I'd expect Herman to make. He was that kind of editor: a stickler for error.

Still, I loved the guy. How could you not love someone who called you hourly, every night starting at 2 A.M., wanting to know how the book was coming along? I had my number changed, twice, but somehow he found me. Then there were the royalty statements full of suspicious deductions. "Tahitian expenses," one read. I asked him what that was about; he said he had to take my first draft to Tahiti so he could concentrate properly on his line edits. "The light was better there," he explained.

I didn't argue. How could I? Herman Mildew made me what I am today: an insomniac cab driver with a box of unpaid bills and unfinished manuscripts riding shotgun in my taxi, and a prescription for industrial strength Xanax stashed in the glove compartment. "Yeah, I used to have a publishing contract," I tell the rearview mirror, as I check my eye twitch (it's getting worse, thanks for asking). "Herman Mildew was my editor. 'Sign here,' he said. 'I'll make you the next J. K. Rowling! I'll get you on *Oprah*!' But things didn't quite work out that way, did they, Hermie old bean?" That's when people start honking at me from behind.

Anyway, forget all that. Water under the bridge. I liked him. I liked his "every day is casual Friday" sweat suits, and that comb-over that swirled around his scalp like the Milky Way. I liked how he took me out to lunch and then pretended to have forgotten his wallet, so I'd have to pay. What a joker! I wouldn't have killed him even if I'd had a chance, which, to be honest, I did.

Yeah, I could have killed him. I could have circled his office in Midtown, day after day, until at last I got lucky and picked him up as a fare. Then I could have waited patiently for him to recognize me as I drove him to the river. He wouldn't notice where we were going until it was too late. Herman and his Blackberry, right? Then, finally, I could have reintroduced myself as one of his former literary stars-to-be. Imagine it: the shock of recognition, the thud of the trunk slamming shut, the horrible sucking, slurping sound as the car tipped forward and sank to the bottom of the Hudson. . . .

But I can prove it didn't happen, and here's how: see this

receipt from Costco? I just put new tires on that car a week ago. So tell me: What kind of lunatic would kill his editor by knocking him out with a blow to the head (staplers make good weapons, by the way, but only the heavy-duty kind), putting the body in the trunk of a 1988 Chrysler LeBaron, and then pushing it in the river, a mere week after paying for new tires for that very same car? Not me, buddy. I may be creative, but I'm not stupid.

Glad that's settled. Say, are there any pickles left in this joint? I haven't eaten for a while, starving artist and all that, and I sure could go for a gherkin. You're not an editor, are you? Mind if I pitch you a few books? I have the manuscripts right here. I know the pages are a little wet—long story—but trust me: the plots are airtight!

Jennifer Ziegler

How could I kill Mr. Mildew? He was my dad!

Not my *actual* dad, of course. Mr. Mildew doesn't have any blood-related offspring that I know of. The women he managed to wrangle, bribe, or trick into a relationship never stuck around long enough to give him children. Most of them now live in a special ward at the hospital. They shuffle around in their nightgowns and make lanyards. One just keeps saying "nougat" over and over.

No, I was his *adopted* daughter. I know what you're thinking. You're wondering why super editor Herman Mildew would adopt a grown woman who still hasn't mastered the rules for comma usage. At first I assumed it was because he was fond of me. "I think of you as a daughter," he'd say, and it made me feel all glow-y inside. Because mainly he shouted at people until they wet their pants. When he proposed making it official and having me live with him, I figured he thought I'd be a worthy heir.

And I said yes because . . . um. . . .

Have you seen his penthouse? It's awesome. It's got a

pickle-shaped pool on the roof and a balcony that overlooks Central Park with a giant, mounted slingshot.

It's true that our arrangement didn't exactly turn out the way I'd hoped. Mr. Mildew made me study grammar all the time and never let me chat with friends. He also had to approve my outfits before I left the house. That's why my wardrobe became nothing but dirndls and high-collared blouses. I didn't get many dates, and when I did he would scare them off with his passionate discourse on pickling and preserving body parts.

But I knew Mr. Mildew only wanted what was best for me. Was I hurt when he said he only adopted me because he missed having someone to verbally abuse after work? No. Did I mind when he threatened to leave me nothing in his will but his thirty-seven-year collection of toenail clippings? No.

In fact, I decided to give him a present—a sweet, fluffy kitten.

How could I have known he was allergic? OK, I guess I did live in his house and may have had access to his medical information. But I never went snooping! Honest! All I wanted to do was give him a gift.

Why did I give him *five hundred* kittens? Um . . . to spread even more love!

I put them all in that room where he stores manuscript submissions (he only goes in there to blow his nose on the pages) and told him I'd gotten him a rare jar of Transylvanian gherkins. I don't know how the door slammed and locked behind him.

Hey, did you know that five hundred freaked-out kittens can claw through a wooden door in seconds? They can. It's kind of awesome, actually, like a screechy tornado. Only it's not so awesome if you happen to be standing in their path.

You have to believe it wasn't me. Look at my face. OK, so it's kind of striped red right now from all the cuts and greasy from Neosporin, but still, can't you see that I'm telling the truth?

I swear I haven't seen Mr. M—I mean, Dad—since that night. I have a new place to live now. It's not as fancy, but it's nice. There are lots of smiling people in white coats.

Here, have a lanyard.

Michelle Zink

"*Thorough research is the font of all literary genius.*" Ernest Hemingway said that.

Okay, it may not have been him. It could have been Jane Austen. Or Charles Dickens.

It may even have been my esteemed—and currently missing—editor, Herman Q. Mildew himself.

But I digress.

The *point* is, it is a well-known fact that one can't embark on a project of superior literary craftsmanship without proper research. In fact, it is only through such research that one may realize—as Mr. Mildew himself pointed out when referring to the subsequently unfinished manuscripts stacked in the halls and against the walls of my apartment—that an idea is boring, defunct, used-up, tired, lacking, migraine-inducing, or generally not worthy of human consumption.

Far better to have such an epiphany after two months of research and fifty finished pages than after a year of research and four hundred pages.

And if such attention to detail results in 163 unfinished

manuscripts (or somewhere thereabouts, because it's not like I *count* mine), so be it. It's all in the name of literary immortality.

And if some—okay, *all*—of my many incomplete projects coincidentally feature the death of a victim with the given name "Herman" and/or the surname "Mildew," it still doesn't mean I killed Herman Q. Mildew. I am, after all, a writer of mysteries, and what is a mystery without an unsolved murder? What is an unsolved murder without a name as a placeholder until one finds a more suitable, permanent moniker?

And if the authorities turn up a knife in my apartment with a blood-like residue, one need only refer to my unfinished manuscript from 2007 titled MILDEW MEETS HIS END to see why it was necessary to conduct research on various kitchen implements and their possible uses as a murder weapon.

Similarly, if one were to find in my apartment a freshly bleached baseball bat with a large dent near the top, one should not assume it was used to bash Mr. Mildew over his (horrifyingly) large head. Instead one need only consult my unfinished manuscript from 2009, THE UNTIMELY EXPIRATION OF HERMAN in which a needlessly cruel, glacially slow editor is bludgeoned to death with such an object. In my effort to create literary masterpieces that stand the test of time—and the well-informed forensic expert—it only makes sense that I would thoroughly research all possible bludgeoning instruments.

Furthermore, if you're going to bring up the rat poison under my kitchen sink, just . . . don't.

Poison was the most commonly used killing method in medieval times, you know (oh, all right! I can't cite my sources due to a recent hard drive crash, but I'm sure I can find the statistic again given a few hours' time and access to a certain well-known search engine). This is a fact that was required to continue work on my ultimately abandoned manuscript titled, TREACHERY IN KING MILDEW'S COURT (okay, I didn't actually finish that one! But I was going to until my esteemed editor suggested it would be put to better use lining the litter box of Princess Mittens).

In fact, all this points to only one thing: I am nothing if not thorough.

And I have done my research.

VERDICT
BY JON SCIESZKA

Very interesting.

Over eighty suspects. Over eighty questionable tales.

What a lazy bunch of fabulators and fabricators, hoodwinkers and hornswogglers, leg-pullers and flimflam artists, bamboozlers and tricksters, humbugs and four flushers!

Based on careful reading of all the evidence and close examination of all your alibis, it has been decided:

You are all guilty.

Each and every one of you came here tonight with the expressed intention of doing in the dear old terrible editor, Mr. Herman Mildew.

You are also all innocent.

Because I have just been informed by this letter that Mr. Mildew is not deceased, demised, defunct, or in fact dead.

And now that you have all signed your sworn statements, I am at liberty to read this, Mr. Mildew's Not-Last Will and Testament.

Ahem:

Dear Authors / Illustrators / Ne'er Do-Wells,

Thank you so much for spending your evening here at the Pickle Factory. Oh, and thanks for once actually meeting a deadline, producing both stories and artwork, and so forth.

You look shocked. You shouldn't be.

I knew the only way to get anything out of you layabouts would be to invite you to someplace fabulous . . . and then make you write for your lives.

So that is what I have just done.

And you all, as usual, have forgotten to read the fine print.

In signing your alibis, you have directed that your works be collected in a book called Who Done It?, and that any monies earned will go to 826 NYC.

So you have been properly hornswoggled. But at least it was for a good cause. Thank you.

Your Not-Dead Editor,

Herman Q. Mildew

M any times when kids visit 826NYC on a class field
trip—no, make that *every* time kids visit 826NYC on
a class field trip—a booming voice over the intercom startles
them. It is almost inevitably Mr. Mildew (sometimes Mrs.
Mildew, on his behalf) demanding fresh books for his publishing company RIGHT NOW!

Mr. Mildew always happens to need the exact same number of new books as there are kids on the field trip.

The staff scrambles to action, suggesting that their visi-
tors help them out by working together to write those books.
The kids brainstorm and collaborate on the beginning and
middle of a story. Different passing illustrators (who fortunately always happen to be in the room) help by illustrating
the beginning and middle.

At the very climactic moment, every visitor is then asked
to write and illustrate his or her own ending—to finish indi-
vidually the books they have all created together.

The unseen Mr. Mildew reads each and every completed
version of the work. And he approves or disapproves of each

one to the relieved cheers of the entire class. (So far he has always approved.)

So what could be more fitting in composing an anthology to benefit 826NYC than to use the very model of writing-for-a-real-purpose used by 826NYC itself?

Exactly. Nothing.

Mr. Mildew has demanded the goods from over eighty writers and illustrators. Does the Herman Mildew method work? You hold the answer to that question in your hands.

ABOUT 826NYC

826NYC is a nonprofit organization and superhero supply company dedicated to supporting students ages six to eighteen with their creative and expository writing skills, and helping teachers inspire their students to write. Over the course of a typical week, 826NYC and its volunteers will help students complete over 300 homework assignments, work with three classrooms (and H. Mildew) to publish original books, collaborate with twelve students to create an anthology of stories (or comics, or songs, or poems, or screenplays), and edit and revise personal statements written by a class of high school seniors.

www.826nyc.org

www.superherosupplies.com

ABOUT THE SUSPECTS

KATE ANGELELLA (www.kateangelella.com), a former editor at Simon & Schuster, is currently a full-time freelance writer and editor. She is also co-owner of Violet & Ruby—a blog dedicated to books and other sparkly, pretty things.

J.R. ANGELELLA (www.jrangelella.com) is the author of the novel *Zombie*. He holds an MFA in Creative Writing and Literature from Bennington College and teaches creative writing in New York City. He also happens to be married to Kate. Visit their website: www.kateandjrangelella.com.

Born to non-farmers in a California farming community, MAC BARNETT now lives near San Francisco. He's on the board of directors of 826LA, a nonprofit writing center for students. He is also the author of two children's books and the founder of the Echo Park Time Travel Mart, a convenience store for time travelers.

JENNIFER BELLE burst onto the literary scene with her critically-acclaimed debut novel *Going Down*. Her essays and stories have appeared in many publications, including *The New York Times*

Magazine, *Cosmopolitan*, *Ms.*, and *Harper's*. She leads writing workshops in her home in Greenwich Village, where she lives with her husband, two sons, and dog.

JUDY BLUNDELL is now in the witness protection program. Her code name is "Sparky."

LIZ BRASWELL was born in Birmingham, England, but grew up in a small New England town. Her major at Brown was Egyptology, and yes, she can write your name in hieroglyphs. Before becoming a full time writer she produced video games, which really was exactly as cool as it sounds. Liz likes skiing, single person RPGs, sitting third row center at the movies, and plants that make food. She has two kids, one frog, a husband, eight Sea-Monkeys, and a large stash of yarn and robot parts. Her books include *Rx* and *Snow* (under the name Tracy Lynn), *The Nine Lives of Chloe King*, and the story "One of Us" in *Geektastic*. You can email her at me@lizbraswell.com, and visit her online at www.lizbraswell.com.

LIBBA BRAY is the *New York Times* bestselling author of The Gemma Doyle trilogy, the Michael L. Printz Award-winning *Going Bovine*, the *LA Times* Book Prize Finalist *Beauty Queens*, and *The Diviners* series. She is originally from Texas but makes her home in Brooklyn with her husband, son, and two sociopathic cats. You can find her online at www.libbabray.com.

STEVE BREZENOFF is the author of young adult novels *The Absolute Value of -1* and *Brooklyn, Burning*, as well as dozens of chapter books for younger readers. He grew up on Long Island, spent his twenties in Brooklyn, and now lives in Minneapolis with his wife, Beth, who is also a writer for children, and their son, Sam.

ELISE BROACH is the author of many books for children and teens, including *Masterpiece*, a *New York Times* bestseller.

Notwithstanding her complicated relationship with Herman Q. Mildew, she adores all of her editors. She has never been convicted of a crime.

LISA BROWN writes and draws books and comics. Some of her favorites include: *How to Be, Vampire Boy's Good Night, Baby Mix Me a Drink*, and, with author Adele Griffin, *Picture the Dead*, an illustrated ghost story for young folks. As long as she stays out of jail, she will continue to draw *The Three Panel Book Review* comic strip for the *San Francisco Chronicle*.

PETER BROWN is an author and illustrator of children's books. His award-winning titles include *New York Times* bestsellers *The Curious Garden, Children Make Terrible Pets*, and *You Will Be My Friend!*

When JEN CALONITA isn't plotting *Revenge*-style takedowns of Mr. Mildew, she can be found dreaming of Disney World, cupcakes, and movie trailers. (She's a total cheeseball, if you haven't noticed.) She also writes books like the *Belles* series and *Secrets of my Hollywood Life*. Jen welcomes you to yell, praise, or send her cupcakes through her website: www.jencalonitaonline.com.

PATRICK CARMAN is the award-winning author of many books for young adults and children, including *The Land of Elyon* and *Atherton*. He grew up in Salem, Oregon, and graduated from Willamette University. He spends his free time fly fishing, playing basketball and tennis, doing crosswords, watching movies, dabbling in video games, reading (lots), and (more than anything else) spending time with his wife and two daughters.

SUSANE COLASANTI is the author of *When It Happens, Take Me There, Waiting for You, Something Like Fate, So Much Closer*, and *Keep Holding On*. As a teenage Jersey girl, Susane felt like her true home was across the water in New York City. The knowing began when she saw *Late Night with David Letterman* for the first time in junior high. She now lives in the West Village.

RICARDO CORTÉS has written and illustrated books about grass, Chinese food, and the Jamaican bobsled team. He also illustrated the hugely popular *Go the F**k to Sleep*. But it all started with his oceanographic studies of dolphins and electric eels, through his research laboratory, the Magic Propaganda Mill. Visit him at www.rmcortes.com

ELIZABETH CRAFT keeps company with vampires, werewolves, and ghosts—and that's just her day job. She resides in Encino, CA.

MELISSA DE LA CRUZ is the author of many books and series for teens and teens-at-heart. She is best known for her *Blue Bloods* vampire series which has sold three million copies—not to be confused with the cop show on CBS starring Tom Selleck, although she does get a lot of fan and foe mail and cheerfully responds as its creator. (Hey, why not?) Her newest novels, *Witches of East End* and *Serpent's Kiss*, are racy paranormal books for grown-ups, but she will happily accept royalties from the underage and their clueless parents. She lives in Los Angeles, Palm Springs, New York, Dubai, Helsinki, and Cairo. She has never committed murder, but she is a fashion victim.

JULIA DEVILLERS always has the perfect alibi for any mischief she gets into—an identical twin sister. Her twin is also her co-author of the Trading Faces series about identical twins who switch places (Simon & Schuster). Julia's book *How My Private, Personal Journal Became a Bestseller* (Dutton) became the Disney Channel movie *Read It and Weep*. Her next book series will be *Emma Emmets, Playground Matchmaker*. Her website is www.juliaauthor.com.

She won't tell you any other incriminating information here, so you'll have to follow her on Facebook or Twitter, and visit her website: www.claudiagabel.com.

MICHELLE GAGNON is a former modern dancer, dog walker, bartender, freelance journalist, personal trainer, model, and Russian supper club performer. To the delight of her parents, she gave up all these occupations for an infinitely more stable and lucrative career as a crime fiction writer. She is also the author of the YA trilogy *Don't Turn Around* and *Stragelets*.

ADAM GIDWITZ didn't not write the award-winning *A Tale Dark and Grimm*, nor did he not write *In a Glass Grimmly*.

ANNA GODBERSEN was born guilty. Perhaps for this reason she went on to become the author of the young adult series *The Luxe* and *Bright Young Things*.

JOHN GREEN is the *New York Times* bestselling author of *Looking for Alaska, An Abundance of Katherines, Paper Towns*, and *The Fault in Our Stars*. In 2007, Green and his brother, Hank, ceased textual communication and began to talk primarily through videoblogs posted to YouTube. The videos spawned a community of people called nerdfighters who fight for intellectualism and to decrease the overall worldwide level of suck.

When ADELE GRIFFIN is not ordering hot fudge sundaes, she is writing novels such as *All You Never Wanted, Tighter*, the *Vampire Island* series, and, with Lisa Brown, *Picture the Dead*. Find her online at www.adelegriffin.com, at your local bookstore, or off somewhere pleading her case.

LEV GROSSMAN has written for *The New York Times, Salon*, the *Village Voice, The Believer*, and many others. He has also written four books, including *The Magicians*, which became a *New York Times* bestseller. He lives in a creaky old house in Brooklyn with his wife and two daughters.

JANET GURTLER is hiding out in her home in Canada, talking out loud to her laptop.

F. BOWMAN HASTIE III works for Ms. Cheddar as her studio assistant, valet, spokesperson, and biographer. His biography *Portrait of the Dog as a Young Artist* was published by Sasquatch Books in 2006. Tillamook Cheddar, a 14-year-old Jack Russell terrier, is widely regarded as the world's preeminent canine artist.

GEOFF HERBACH is the author of the award-winning *Stupid Fast* YA series. In the past, he wrote the literary novel, *The Miracle Letters of T. Rimberg*, produced radio comedy shows, and toured rock clubs telling weird stories. Geoff teaches creative writing at Minnesota State, Mankato. He shares a log cabin in dark woods with a tall wife, hordes of mice, and terrifying wolf spiders that crawl into his shoes.

JOANNA HERSHON is the author of the novels: *Swimming*, *The Outside of August*, *The German Bride*, and *A Dual Inheritance*. She's taught in the undergraduate creative writing department at Columbia University, guest taught at the phenomenal 826NYC, and lives in Brooklyn with her husband (painter Derek Buckner) and their twin sons (who are both keen on superhero supplies).

MANDY HUBBARD is a literary agent at D4EO Literary as well as the author of several YA novels, including those written under the pen name Amanda Grace. Her titles include *Prada & Prejudice*, *You Wish*, *Dangerous Boy*, *But I Love Him*, and others. She's currently living happily ever after with her husband, daughter, and cow. Learn more at www.mandyhubbard.com.

EMILY JENKINS is the author of the Toys trilogy (*Toys Go Out*, etc.) and the *Invisible Inkling* series, plus a number of picture books. There is no truth to the rumor that she writes under a pseudonym, so don't go asking her publishers about it. Still, it may interest you to know that E. Lockhart's latest book is *Real Live Boyfriends*.

MAUREEN JOHNSON is the *New York Times* bestselling author of ten YA books. Her work is published in twenty-two languages and has been featured six times on YALSA's Best Books for Young Adults lists, as well as the Teen's Top Ten in 2006 for *13 Little Blue Envelopes*. She was a 2006 Andre Norton Award nominee for *Devilish*, and *The Name of the Star* was nominated for the 2012 Edgar Award for Young Adult Literature. Maureen spends a great deal of time online, earning her some dubious and some not-as-dubious commendations, such as being named one of *Time Magazine*'s top 140 people to follow on Twitter. She splits her time between New York City and a mysterious dwelling outside of London.

LINDSEY KELK is a writer, columnist, karaoke enthusiast, and WWE obsessive. No, really. When she isn't writing books or studying choke slams, she's watching more TV than is healthy or volunteering at the Brooklyn Superhero Supply Store. Lindsey is a bit of a nerd. Please don't hold it against her.

JO KNOWLES is the author of *See You at Harry's*, *Pearl*, *Jumping Off Swings*, and *Lessons from a Dead Girl*. Some of her awards include the PEN New England Children's Book Discovery Award; YALSA's Best Books for Young Adults; Bank Street College's Best Children's Books; and the SCBWI Crystal Kite Award. Jo lives in Vermont with her husband and son, where they often enjoy cheese—as long as it's not too stinky.

GORDON KORMAN is the author of 77 books, most recently

Ungifted and *Showoff*. He categorically denies knowing any of these people. Come to think of it, this bio never happened.

DAVID LEVITHAN's first mystery novel, an attempt at being P. D. James when he was a Jewish eighth grader in New Jersey, was never completed or published. Instead, he's written books that include *Boy Meets Boy*, *Every Day*, *Nick and Norah's Infinite Playlist* (with Rachel Cohn), and *Will Grayson, Will Grayson* (with John Green).

SARAH DARER LITTMAN spent ten years living in Dorset, England, where she acquired firsthand knowledge of lactation yield curves and rennet. After the first of her now regularly scheduled midlife crises, she finally gave herself permission to pursue her teenage dream of being a writer. You can learn more about her books at www.sarahdarerlittman.com and follow her exploits on Twitter @sarahdarerlitt. In addition to writing for teens, Sarah is an award-winning political columnist for www.ctnewsjunkie.com.

Along with other novels, BARRY LYGA also writes the *I Hunt Killers* series. But you shouldn't read anything into that. Really.

ADAM MANSBACH's books include the #1 *New York Times* bestseller *Go the F**k to Sleep*, the California Book Award-winning novel *The End of the Jews*, and the cult classic *Angry Black White Boy*. His work has appeared in *The New Yorker*, *The New York Times Book Review*, *Esquire*, and on National Public Radio's *All Things Considered*. He will publish two novels in 2013, *Rage is Back* and *The Dead Run*.

LESLIE MARGOLIS is the author of *Fix*, *Price of Admission*, *Boys Are Dogs*, and *Girls Acting Catty*. She grew up in Los Angeles, California, and now lives in Brooklyn.

Born and raised in Brooklyn, JULIA MAYER originally wrote her first novel, *Eyes in the Mirror* in the back of the Superhero Supply Store also known as 826NYC. She knows firsthand the difference even one summer at 826NYC can make in a teenager's life and is thrilled to be a part of their continued success.

BARNABAS MILLER has written many books for children and young adults. He is the co-author of *7 Souls*, a 2011 Edgar nominee. His latest book, *Rock God: The Legend of B.J. Levine,* asks the eternal question: might a thirteen-year-old Jewish boy be the second coming of Jon Bon Jovi? He also composes music for film and television. He lives in New York City with his wife, Heidi; their cat, Ted; and their dog, Zooey.

JACQUELYN MITCHARD is a *New York Times* bestselling author whose first novel, *The Deep End of the Ocean,* was the inaugural selection of the Oprah Winfrey Book Club. She is the editor in chief of the young adult imprint, Merit Press. She lives in Massachusetts with her family.

SARAH MLYNOWSKI is the author of *Ten Things We Did (and Probably Shouldn't Have)*, *Gimme a Call*, and both the *Magic in Manhattan* and *Whatever After* series. Sarah also ghostwrites all books attributed to Lauren Myracle. Yes, all of them. Including the one that was dedicated to Sarah.

LAUREN MYRACLE is the kind and gentle *New York Times* bestselling author of squillions of books, including *Shine*, the Internet Girls series, and the Winnie Years series. Unfortunately, she is currently locked in a cage in E. Lockhart's moldy basement, which smells of cheese. Please join the Free Lauren Myracle movement by tweeting the nefarious @elockhart and begging "E" to let poor Lauren go.

GREG NERI is a storyteller, filmmaker, artist, and digital media producer. He has written three books for teens and has a long list of projects in the works. He currently lives off the Gulf Coast of Florida with his wife, Maggie, and their daughter, Zola.

JENNIFER A. NIELSEN is the author of *The False Prince* (Ascendance series), *Elliot and the Goblin War*, and a forthcoming book of Scholastic's Infinity Ring series. She battles the daily challenges of being left-handed, and in fact, has considered starting a movement for other left-handers. But somehow the phrase, "Even lefties have rights" doesn't work. Jennifer remains hard at work for her picky, er, patient editor, Lisa Sandell. She can be found online at www.jennielsen.com.

MICHAEL NORTHROP is the author of three of the following four novels: *Gentlemen* (2009), an ALA/YALSA Best Book for Young Adults; *Trapped* (2011), an ALA/YALSA Readers' Choice List selection; *Plunked* (2012), a middle grade baseball novel; and *Moby-Dick* (1851), a timeless work of American literature. His new YA novel, *Rotten* (2013), is the tale of a rescue Rottweiler.

LAUREN OLIVER is the author of *Before I Fall, Delirium, Pandemonium, Liesl and Po*, and many other manufactured fictions, such as why-she-was-too-sick-to-do-the-laundry and what-happened-to-the-last-brownie-in-the-pan. In her spare time, she enjoys fantasizing about—but definitely not enacting!—violence against people who have betrayed her, belittled her, or bought any of the things she owns for a better price on Ebay.

DAVID OSTOW was born in New Jersey, which explains his fascination with tollbooths, smokestacks and industrial decay. In 2009 he published the award-winning illustrated novel *So Punk Rock (And Other Ways to Disappoint Your Mother)* with his sister, the novelist Micol Ostow. David currently works at an architectural design firm in New York City and maintains his passion for illustration, cartooning, and storytelling. He lives in Brooklyn with his wife, the music publicist, Lily Golightly, and their dog, Elephant. Please visit David on the web at www.davidostow.com and feel free to say hello.

MICOL OSTOW has published dozens of books for children, tweens, and teens, including (along with her brother, David Ostow) the critically acclaimed illustrated novel *So Punk Rock (and Other Ways to Disappoint Your Mother)*. Before becoming a full-time author, she worked as a children's book editor, at one point overseeing the Mad Libs program for Price Stern Sloan. Micol received her MFA in Creative Writing from Vermont College of Fine Arts, and teaches a popular teen fiction course through mediabistro.com. Her next book, a horror novel called *Amity*, drops in the fall of 2013. In the meantime, you can visit Micol at www.micolostow.com. She would be very <u>ADJECTIVE</u> to hear from you!

ALISON PACE is the author of five novels including *If Andy Warhol Had a Girlfriend* and *Pug Hill* and of the essay collection *You Tell Your Dog First*. She lives in New York City where she may or may not harbor ill will toward editors. You can visit her online at www.alisonpace.com

PAIGE POOLER is a freelance illustrator living in Los Angeles, California. She likes hiking with her Boston terrier, Gracie, eating tacos, sipping on green juice, laughing with friends, and the smell of gardenias.

JOY PREBLE was born somewhere and lives somewhere else but without a signed NDA, she won't admit to either. She went to school, although honestly, what good did that do? Her musical tastes are questionable, at least according to one Daniel Ehrenhaft, a man who questions too much and too often and who is thus as unreliable as that NDA. Rumor has it that she's written some books that people have actually read.

When she is not training to be a professional competitive eater, MARGO RABB writes novels, essays, and short stories, including a top secret novel which will be published by Delacorte next year.

LISA AND LAURA ROECKER are sisters-turned-writing partners with a passion for good books, pop culture, and Bravo programming. Not necessarily in that order. Lisa has always been a phenomenal liar and Laura loves to write angsty poetry, so writing for young adults seemed like a natural fit. The sisters live in Cleveland, Ohio, in separate residences. Their husbands wouldn't agree to a duplex.

MARIE RUTKOSKI is a professor of English literature at Brooklyn College and is the author of several books for children and young adults. Her most recent novel is *The Shadow Society*.

LISA ANN SANDELL is the author of the young adult novels *A Map of the Known World*, *Song of the Sparrow*, and *The Weight of the Sky*. When she isn't writing, Lisa's evil alter ego, executive editor at Scholastic, remains holed up in her cave of an office, hard at work repairing—er, editing—the writing of her pesky author, Jennifer A. Nielsen. Lisa lives in New York City. You can visit her online at www.lisaannsandell.com.

CASEY SCIESZKA grew up in Brooklyn but has lived in the likes of Beijing and Timbuktu. She's a writer and graphic designer and works frequently on projects with her boyfriend Steven Weinberg. Their first book, *To Timbuktu: Nine Countries, Two People, One True Story*, is an illustrated account of their two-year post-college adventure around the world. Visit her online at www.caseyscieszka.com.

JON SCIESZKA was born in Flint, Michigan, on a Wednesday around lunchtime. Jon thought about being a doctor, but he decided to move to New York, where he earned his MFA in Fiction Writing from Columbia. Fast-forward a few years, and Jon's books have won a whole mess of awards and sold over eleven million copies around the world. Jon lives in Brooklyn with his wife, Jeri, and their two kids, Casey and Jake. He also has a number of pets, including two zebra finches, two owl finches, two cordon bleu finches, and the last time he counted, seventy-five Western Harvester ants.

KIERAN SCOTT is the author of the popular He's So/She's So trilogy, and her new series of True Romances will be hitting stores in February 2014. She also penned the Non-Blonde Cheerleader trilogy and the novel *Geek Magnet*. In her spare time, Kieran writes for *Alloy Entertainment* under the pseudonym Kate Brian. She has written the new series *Shadowlands* and the *New York Times* bestselling *Private* and *Privilege* series. Kieran has lived in New Jersey all her life (but looks nothing like Snooki), and graduated from Rutgers University with honors. Kieran loves to bake, read YA, watch football (Go Giants!), take classes at the gym, and hit the shore with her husband and sons. She's also kind of obsessed with TV. You can find out more at www.kieranscott.net, or follow her on Twitter at @KieranScott.

ALYSSA SHEINMEL is the author of *The Stone Girl*, *The Lucky Kind*, and *The Beautiful Between*. She grew up in Northern California and New York, and attended Barnard College. She worked in book publishing for nearly a decade, and now lives and writes in New York City. You can visit her on the web at www.alyssasheinmel.com and follow her on Twitter @AlyssaSheinmel. She really doesn't like mildew of any kind.

COURTNEY SHEINMEL graduated from Barnard College and Fordham School of Law, and worked as a litigator for several years. But these days, she doesn't practice law; she just writes about it … sort of: the parents in her books are sometimes lawyers, or sometimes need to hire lawyers. Courtney is the author of several books for kids and teens, including *All the Things You Are*, *Sincerely*, and the Stella Batts series. Visit her online at www.courtneysheinmel.com.

SARA SHEPARD is the author of the *Pretty Little Liars* and *The Lying Game* series, both of which are shows on ABC Family. She also wrote two novels for adults, *The Visibles* and *Everything We Ever Wanted*. She lives in Philadelphia. She might be a liar, but she hasn't been questioned for any other murders.

JENNIFER E. SMITH is the author of five novels for young readers, including *The Statistical Probability of Love at First Sight* and *This Is What Happy Looks Like*. She earned her Master's in Creative Writing from the University of St. Andrews in Scotland, and her work has been translated into twenty-seven languages. Also, she most definitely did not kill Herman Q. Mildew.

LEMONY SNICKET is currently at large.

JORDAN SONNENBLICK writes novels for children and young adults. He swears the editors of his nine books are completely healthy, and have not been broiled, fried, braised, fricasseed, or even lightly toasted—although one of them may have retired suddenly last year under rather mysterious circumstances. Anyway, you can learn more about Jordan's work at www.jordansonnenblick.com.

NATALIE STANDIFORD is the author of *How to Say Goodbye in Robot*, *Confessions of the Sullivan Sisters*, and *The Secret Tree*, among other books for young readers. She lives in New York City and plays bass in the all-YA-author band Tiger Beat, with fellow-contributors Libba Bray, Daniel Ehrenhaft, and Barnabas Miller. She doesn't really have crippling writer's block (*shhh. . .* don't tell her gym teacher).

REBECCA STEAD is a lifelong New Yorker and, more recently, a writer. She's written three novels for youngish people: *When You Reach Me*, *First Light*, and *Liar & Spy*.

TODD STRASSER is the author of more than 120 books for teens and middle graders, including the best selling *Help! I'm Trapped* series. His books have been translated into more than a dozen languages, and he has also written for TV and a number of publications, including *The New York Times*, *Esquire*, and *The New Yorker*. When he's at home, he likes to spend time with his kids, fish, and surf.

HEATHER TERRELL worked as a commercial litigator in New York City for over ten years before trying her hand at writing. After publishing three historical novels—*The Chrysalis*, *The Map Thief*, and *Brigid of Kildare*—she turned her attention to the realm of young adults. She is the author of the *Fallen Angel* series, as well as the young adult series *The Books of Eva*, which will debut in the fall of 2013. She lives in Pittsburgh with her family.

NED VIZZINI is the author of *The Other Normals*, *It's Kind of a Funny Story*, *Be More Chill*, and *Teen Angst? Naaah...* He has written for *The New York Times*, *Salon*, and Season 2 of MTV's *Teen Wolf*. His work has been translated into seven languages. He co-wrote the forthcoming fantasy-adventure series *House of Secrets* with Chris Columbus. He lives in Los Angeles.

ADRIENNE MARIA VRETTOS is an alias found on the spines of young adult novels *Burnout*, *The Exile of Gigi Lane*, *Sight*, and *Skin*. Her official residence is listed as www.adriennemariavrettos.com.

MELISSA WALKER is the author of six young adult novels, including *Small Town Sinners* and *Unbreak My Heart*. She is the co-founder of www.iheartdaily.com.

ROBIN WASSERMAN is the author of *The Book of Blood and Shadow*, the Cold Awakening trilogy, *Hacking Harvard*, and several other books for children and teens. She has committed only one crime, but she won't tell you what it is. (Although you can find some clues at www.robinwasserman.com.)

STEVEN WEINBERG is an illustrator based in Brooklyn, though he has dragged his art supplies as far as Timbuktu. He frequently collaborates with his girlfriend, Casey Scieszka. Their first book, *To Timbuktu: Nine Countries, Two People, One True Story*, is an illustrated account of their two-year post-college adventure around the world. Visit him online at www.stevenweinbergstudio.com.

LYNN WEINGARTEN is a writer, editor, content developer, eater of snacks, and friend of dogs. Her first young adult novel, *Wherever Nina Lies*, was a YALSA Teens' Top Ten nominee and an ALA Top Ten Popular Paperback for Young Adults. Lynn grew up in New York state, spent nine years in New York City, and is currently living in Scotland with her physicist husband.

KIERSTEN WHITE is the rather diminutive author of the bestselling *Paranormalcy* series. At eighteen, she volunteered in an elementary school and was told to go outside for recess. It's all been downhill from there. When not not-murdering people, she spends time with her husband and two children and avoids the beach—a harder task than you'd assume when one lives in San Diego.

MO WILLEMS is nothing but trouble. His three Caldecott Honors, two Geisel Medals, six Emmy Awards, and "Most Likely to Improve Ribbon" (3rd grade division) were acquired by suspicious means. Personally, I would not trust him farther than I could throw him (results may vary). It's best to avoid his work by refusing to type www.mowillems.com into your browser.

RITA WILLIAMS-GARCIA author of *One Crazy Summer* and *Jumped*, is allergic to Brazilian cockroaches, mice epithelials, soy, a condiment whose name she dares not type, and tree nuts. She first came across a wombat pressed into a page in her beloved family dictionary. Although not impressed, she knew she would one day include this creature in a story. She encourages her MFA students at VCFA to dig deep into the folds of childhood to uncover those long forgotten aardvarks, emus, and wombats.

When not driving a cab or on a killing spree, MARYROSE WOOD keeps herself occupied by writing *The Incorrigible Children of Ashton Place* series for middle-grade readers. She's currently working on book four of the planned six-book series, and sometimes wonders how many people will have to meet a gruesome end before it's all over. She lives in the Bronx with her kids and pets, all of whom are just to die for.

JENNIFER ZIEGLER is the author of *How Not to Be Popular*, *Sass & Serendipity*, and other suspicious-sounding works. She is probably in the middle of a madcap adventure, asking herself how she got into such a mess and wishing she were wearing more sensible shoes.

MICHELLE ZINK is the author of the *Prophecy of the Sisters* series and *A Temptation of Angels*. She lives in New York with her four teenagers and many objects of doom, er, research.